AMULET BOOKS
NEW YORK

THE MOVIE VERSION

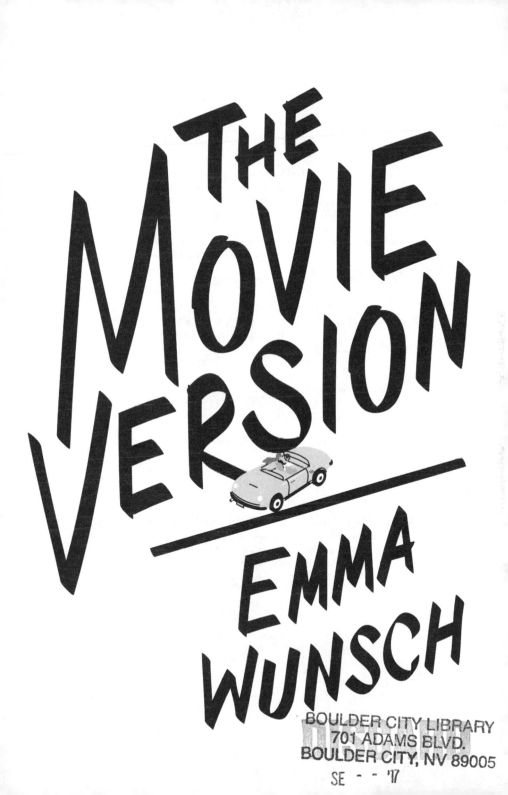

EMMA WUNSCH

Cataloging-in-Publication Data has been applied for and may be obtained from the Library of Congress.

ISBN: 978-1-4197-1900-4

Text copyright © 2016 Emma Wunsch
Jacket and interior illustrations © 2016 Sunra Thompson
Book design by Alyssa Nassner

Printed and bound in U.S.A.
10 9 8 7 6 5 4 3 2 1

Amulet Books are available at special discounts when purchased in quantity for premiums and promotions as well as fundraising or educational use. Special editions can also be created to specification. For details, contact specialsales@abramsbooks.com or the address below.

ABRAMS The Art of Books
115 West 18th Street, New York, NY 10011
abramsbooks.com

FOR MY FAMILY

PROLOGUE

SEE TOBY LIKE THIS: IT'S EARLY JUNE AND THE SUN
reflects on the waxed linoleum floors, through the windows
and onto the light blue walls, which makes everything seem
swimmy and surreal. The halls are empty, so I'm super aware
of the silence around me. Then I see Toby. He's walking towards me in a space that's so drenched in light, it looks like
he's gliding. When he sees me, he smiles. "Meals! Of course
it's you."

"What are you talking about?" I ask my brother.

"I thought to myself, *Whoever comes down this hall is
the person I'm going to share my peace pipe with.*" He opens
his left hand and reveals, in a flash, a joint.

"I'm just going to the bathroom. I need to go back to
French."

"No, you don't."

"I'm just supposed to leave? To get high?"

He nods.

"Leave my books? My bag?"

"Yeah," Toby says, like it's no big deal. "Just leave your
stuff, Amelia. What's the worst that could happen?"

*What will Madame Lapelle say if I don't come back?
What will she do?*

"No one will steal your books. You won't fail your next
test on the indicative past present subjunctive." Toby puts
the joint behind his right ear.

Without thinking, I follow him down to the basement,

past the art rooms, the band room, the locker rooms, and out through a door by a janitor's closet that comes out on the far end of the athletic field.

"What if someone sees us?" I ask as we make our way around the perimeter of the field.

"They won't," he says calmly.

I believe him. I believe that nothing bad will happen to my French books, that no one will catch us leaving school, that we won't get busted for smoking a joint. My older brother is a presence. A force. We smoke in his car, Prudence, and listen to songs from his "Ringo Sings!" Beatles playlist.

When I tell him I don't feel like going back in, that my last class is music and Mr. Whitman will never notice one less soprano, my brother grins. "I knew you'd be awesome-sauce," he says. "Follow me."

Walking back across the athletic field, I feel like I'm moving in slow motion. We cut across the teachers' parking lot and then over the baseball diamond till we get to a small hill overlooking the tennis courts.

I lie down next to him under a big maple tree and stare at the tree branches. "I'm really high," I tell him.

He smiles. "You got enough brain cells to play?"

"Always."

"'I'm trying to decide how stoned I am and just how on the verge of death I am right now. Like, am I seeing shit because I'm stoned or because I have no blood left in my body?'"

I don't even need time to come up with the next line. "'Well, you've been shot like seven times.'"

"Well played, little sis." Toby shakes his head. His wavy

brown hair falls into his eyes and he pushes it away. I've always been jealous of his hair. We have the same color, chestnut brown, but mine is boring and stick-straight.

"*George Washington* is David Gordon Green's best movie. *Pineapple Express* is up there, especially for a stoner flick, but it's no *George Washington* or *All the Real Girls.*"

Toby nods like he agrees, but doesn't feel like getting into another long conversation about movies. "So, Ari asked if I want to go to prom. With her."

"Are you going?" Ari is Arianna Kaufman, one of the prettiest and most popular girls in school. She's a senior. Toby is a junior—but a cool junior. He was a cool freshman even though freshmen are inherently uncool. I'm a sophomore and not especially cool. This is the first time I've ever cut class.

"Proms are stupid." Toby pulls on the rubber from the sole of his black Converse. "They're just another form of commodification of teens, America, popularity." When other people say things like "commodification of teens" it sounds pretentious, but Toby just sounds smart.

"She's really pretty," I say lamely. Ari is prime-time pretty—flawless skin, salon-perfect blond hair, and excellent teeth. She's sort of a smaller, blonder, less-toned Jennifer Lawrence.

Just as I'm craving something sweet, Toby takes a pack of M&M's out of his bag. "It's so much fucking money. For a dance."

"Mom and Dad will help." I shove a handful of candy in my mouth. "These are the best M&M's ever."

My brother nods. "Mom and Dad won't five-hundred-dollars help."

"It's that much? I thought it was, like, seventy-five."

"For the ticket. I'll need to tux up, money up for the limo. Go in on a hotel room." He throws an M&M up in the air and catches it in his mouth. "That's a lot of M&M's, Grasshopper."

I nod.

"Shouldn't I do something more, uh, political with all that money? If I were truly a good person, I'd donate to a school in some politically fucked-up country where they turn their children into human shields and soldiers."

"I guess." When I'm a senior, it's way more likely that I'll have a prom-themed movie night at home than actually go. *Carrie*, obviously, and then maybe *Napoleon Dynamite* and *10 Things I Hate About You*.

"Then again, Ari *is* hot and I guess I'd get to fuck her, which would be cool," Toby says, jolting me out of Prom Movies to Watch on Prom Night. He gives me a look. "Another notch in my belt."

"Gross, Toby," I say, even though I don't really care that my brother will be Ari's date to the prom right now. It's beautiful out and it's a lot more fun to be stoned than listen to my classmates sing off-key.

But then, when it seems like only five minutes have passed, Toby looks at his phone and says, "Holy crap. Shithead and Dipstick!"

Shithead and Dipstick are Sam and David, our seven-year-old brothers. We have to be home for them twice a week when our parents and grandmother can't be. Tuesday is my day and Thursday is Toby's, but he usually pawns it off on me. I look at my phone. It's 2:35. Where did the time go? School got out fifteen minutes ago.

But this is what it's like in Toby's world. Everything else disappears.

"Holy shit," I say. "You're going to be late."

"*You're* going to be late."

"It's Thursday. Your day."

Toby jumps up and does a cartwheel. "Dat vas a perfect ten," he says in a Russian accent.

"We gotta go. The driver won't let them off if no one is at the stop. Can you drive?"

"Can *you* drive?"

"Shut up."

"You actually can drive—you have feet to press the brake and gas, and hands to steer the wheel, and eyes to see. You have the ability to drive, but you're just a scared chicken-shit."

"You got me" I say. "I am a scared chickenshit. I'm going to get therapy. One day. But seriously. We have to go. Are you okay?"

"'I just really want a milkshake.'"

"*The Perks of Being a Wallflower*. Seriously, you can drive?"

"I'm more than fine. I'm perfectly amazingly awesome."

We start walking back to the car. "I'm really stoned," I tell him. "I hope the twins don't notice."

"They won't," he says. "It'll be another Secret Sibling Society secret."

When Toby was nine, he decided that we were copresidents

of the Secret Sibling Society. It was totally silly, but even almost nine years later we both kind of believe in it.

"A Stoned Secret Sibling Society secret!" He does another cartwheel.

And it was. No one knew about the day in June when I skipped French to get high with my brother. It was our perfect little afternoon, especially considering everything that came after.

1

HOMECOMING

WHEN THE CARTERS DROP ME OFF ON THE LAST DAY of August, Sam is sitting on the front porch, poking a stick in the air. He's wearing a puffy blue coat, a pair of unevenly cut jean shorts, and one Croc.

"Hey, Sammy!" I call up.

Sam doesn't acknowledge my existence.

Mr. Carter opens the car trunk, hands me my bags, and gives me an envelope. "A bonus for all your work," he says.

Mrs. Carter rolls down her window. "You were terrific, Amelia. The girls will miss you. I hope you'll babysit once in a while."

The girls are nine-year-old Sabrina and ten-year-old Selena. They roll down the backseat windows. "Bye, Amelia!" they scream. "WE LOVE YOU!"

"I love you guys, too."

"You love EPSTEIN!" Sabrina screams.

Mr. Carter shakes his head and gets back into the car. "Give her a break, girls."

"Goodbye, goodbye, goodbye!" Sabrina and Selena sing as the car pulls out of the driveway.

I drag my bags up to the porch, but even when I'm right in front of him, Sam doesn't look up.

"What a warm welcome," I say. "Did you even know I was gone? For the whole summer?"

He drops his stick.

"What's going on? Where is everybody? Where's Kepler?" Kepler is our chocolate Lab, and while I missed my family, I REALLY missed Kep. It's corny, but the dog just gets me in a way that no one else does. The whole ride back, I was looking forward to seeing her cry with happiness when she saw me.

"MomandDadareattherestaurantDavidisplayingat Ryan'sGrandmaisgettinggroceries," Sam says robotically. "DaddytookKeplertowork."

"Why are Mom and Dad at work?" My parents own a restaurant two towns away. They work insane restaurant hours, but are strict about being home on Saturdays, Mondays, and holidays. "It's Saturday. Mack's running Ginger's today."

"Something broke. I think. Or someone quit. Or someone broke something and quit. Mack quit?"

I should have known better than to think I'd get reliable information from Sam. "Where's Toby?"

"I hate Toby."

"Why?"

"He stole Mr. Mittens. He said he's going to make kitty porn."

I stifle a laugh. Mr. Mittens is Sam's cat and Sam loves Mr. Mittens the way I love Kepler, so I understand his anger on the human–animal level.

"Why did he take him?"

"He was mad because I told Mommy I saw him take money out of her wallet."

Weird. It's not like my brother to steal from my parents, but I'm sure he had a good reason. "Toby hates tattle telling. Hasn't he initiated you into the Secret Sibling Society?"

Sam shakes his head. "Stealing is a sin."

"The Toby code is that siblings must always protect one another. Tattling is a sin. Forever and always."

"Toby is a diarrhea butt fart."

"I see your side, too. Why are you wearing a coat? It's so hot."

"Daddy said I needed a thicker skin. I started crying. David said I was retarded. Daddy said I'm too sensitive. I hate everybody. Mostly Toby."

"Sorry, Sam." I pat his sweaty blond head and open the front door. Music blasts from upstairs. I leave my bags in the mudroom. Sam is acting so pathetic that I feel a big-sisterly obligation to help him. "Do you want to go rescue Mr. Mittens?"

"Toby won't let me in his room."

"He'll let me in. He's got to. I've been gone for weeks." *Has Sam even noticed that I've been gone?* It seems lame that most of my family isn't here. At least Toby could have come downstairs. *I* would've if *he'd* been away for seven weeks. I would've baked him cookies and made him an ironic "Welcome Home" banner. Then again, if Toby had been gone, I would've been stranded and miserable without him. Since Toby has a car and a million friends, he probably didn't miss me that much.

"Amelia," Sam whines.

"Right, here's the plan. I'll start talking to him. Then I'll give you a signal—you hide in the hall. When I hold up three fingers, you come in and grab Mr. Mittens."

He follows me upstairs. When I knock on Toby's door, Sam attempts to hide behind me. I attempt to knock louder than the Beatles are singing "Can't Buy Me Love."

"He's going to go deaf," I tell Sam.

Finally, after much pounding, Toby opens the door. The first thing I notice is that his hair is a lot longer. And it's clear that he didn't spend nearly as much time outside as I did this summer because he's really pale.

"Jeez, Toby," I say. "It's too loud."

"What? What did ya say?" Toby cups his ear with his hand.

"Very funny."

Toby finds the remote from the pile of clothes on his bed and turns the music down to a more comfortable loud. A pungent waft of salt-and-vinegar potato chips and boy sweat floats into my nose.

"Your room smells horrible."

"Nice to see you, too." Toby smiles but blocks the doorway with his body so I can't go in.

"Where's the cat?"

"'You gonna bark all day, little doggy, or are you gonna bite?'"

"I know that one." I close my eyes until it comes to me. "Michael Madsen to Harvey Keitel in *Reservoir Dogs*."

"Aces."

"Sam wants his cat." I peek into his room.

"'You cannot pass! I am a servant of the Secret Fire,

wielder of the Flame of Anor. The dark fire will not avail you, Flame of Udun! Go back to the shadow. You shall not pass!'"

"Gandalf in *The Fellowship of the Ring*. Easy. But come on, Toby. It's not funny. Give Sam his cat." Is he stoned? It would be weird for him to get high during the day—especially when he's supposed to be watching our brother. The twins prefer when Toby babysits because, when he's not catnapping, he'll do fun stuff, like build *American Ninja Warrior* obstacle courses, or invent dishes like microwaved s'mores pie. I usually just let them watch TV.

"Shithead wants his pussy back? A pussy for the pussy?"

"Hand Mr. Mittens over." *This is having brothers*, I think. The girls I babysat would much rather give manicures and look at pictures of boy bands.

"*Un momento.*" Toby steps back in his room and closes the door.

Sam emerges from behind me. "What's he doing? What about our plan, Meals?"

The door opens a crack and Mr. Mittens, with ten little rubber bands attached to nubbins of fur, comes mewing out.

"Mr. Mittens!" Sam screams. "What did he do to you?" The cat takes off. Sam follows him frantically.

The door opens again.

"Amelia," Toby says in a British accent. "What a jolly good pleasure to see you. Welcome back. How was your summer?" He opens the door wider, so, even though it really does stink, I go in.

"Are you stoned?"

He shakes his head. "Town's dry."

"Oh."

"Should be getting some soon, though. My buddy Toast went to Buffalo."

"Toast's your buddy now?" I'm surprised because Toast is a skeevy, sketchy stoner in my grade, and Toby has always been friends with popular people.

Toby shrugs.

"I didn't smoke all summer," I tell him. "Epstein is kind of, like, straightedge." Then I remember that Toby doesn't know Epstein. "Epstein is the guy I met."

"*You* met a guy?"

"Yeah. What's so weird about that?" My heart does a bumpity-bump, because part of me thinks it is bizarre that I maybe kind of have a boyfriend.

Toby gives me a Jim Carrey grin. "It's not *that* weird. You're not completely heinous."

"Thanks a lot."

"What's up with his name?"

"Epstein was his grandmother's maiden name. His last name is Boffee-Barnes."

Toby throws a pair of jeans off his chair and sits down. "That's weird." He spins the chair around. "You like this Epstein?"

"Yeah. I think so. I think I really like him. He's really smart."

"Cool," Toby says.

I can't tell if he means it or not, which is annoying. He almost always has a girlfriend and I'm always nice about them, even if they're kind of annoying and text him a million times a day.

"He lives in New York. Manhattan."

"'Standing on the corner, just me and Yoko Ono / we was waiting for Jerry to land. / Up come a man with a guitar in his hand . . .'"

"Is that from a movie?"

Toby shakes his head. "It's 'New York City' by John Lennon and Yoko Ono."

"Oh."

"'New York City / New York City / New York City! / *Que pasa*, New York?'" Toby sings, playing air guitar.

"Epstein lives on the Upper West Side." I'm kind of annoyed that he isn't more interested in my possible boyfriend.

"Did ya make a lot of cash, Amelia Bedelia?"

"Yeah, Toby Maguire. And I forgot about this." I open the envelope Mr. Carter gave me. "Wow!" The Carters gave me an additional two hundred dollars.

"Nice! 'You are only ever as good to me as the money you make!' Can I have a loan?"

"That's from *21*. Didn't you work?" Last year, Toby worked so many shifts at my parents' restaurant that he was able to buy Prudence, his pre-owned Honda Civic.

Toby shrugs. "Not so much."

"What've you been doing?" All of a sudden I feel like I don't really know what Toby did this summer. Except for a random text here and there, we didn't communicate that much, which is weird for us.

Toby tries to pry a hundred-dollar bill out of my hand. "I've been chilling."

"Yeah. You still seeing Ari?" Toby started dating Arianna Kaufman after they went to prom together. I was only home for ten days after the prom, but it seemed like Toby was always running off with her, in her graduation-gift MINI Cooper, going to beach bonfires, amusement parks, and other cute, memory-making rom-com activities.

Toby shrugs. "Not so much."

"Oh." I wait for him to say something about another girl, because he's usually hanging out with a girl even if she's not technically a girlfriend. Instead, he lifts up his shirt and scratches his stomach. He looks thinner than ever. He could live entirely on ice cream and chips and still be a rail.

"Lend me some ducats, Meals."

"Jeez, Toby. I kind of need this. I *worked* for it." Since I don't drive, I don't have many job options, so it's nice to actually have a little money, for a change.

"'Where's the money, Lebowski? Where's the fucking money, shithead?'" He smiles and without really thinking about it, I hand him one of the hundreds. Toby is very hard to say no to.

"This is a loan, Toby. Not a gift."

"'The best things in life are free / but you can keep 'em for the birds and bees. / Now give me money (that's what I want) / that's what I want, yeah . . .'" he croons.

"Seriously, Toby. You promise to pay me back?"

"You're the best. 'You are the most talented, most interesting, most extraordinary person in the universe.'"

"'You are capable of amazing things,'" I say, even though I'd rather Toby agree to pay me back.

He nods. "I am capable of amazing things. Unfortunately one of them was watching *The Lego Movie* with Shit-head and Dipstick around eighty-three thousand times."

"Sorry. We can make up for it. Let's binge-watch a ton of good movies. How about *Goodfellas*, *Bad Santa*, *Pretty Ugly People*. Get it? Good, bad, and ugly!"

I feel very excited by a possible movie marathon with Toby, but he just picks up his phone. "Maybe later. I gotta call Toast and let him know that I'm in for the good shit."

"You want money for pot?" My brother smokes pot more than I do, but he's not a stoner or anything.

"No judgments, Amelia. No judgments."

"Pay me back," I tell him, turning around. "And clean your room, Toby. It stinks."

"Like roses." He shuts the door behind me.

2

MY VERY OWN ALMOST MEET-CUTE

BEFORE I MET EPSTEIN, IF MY LIFE WERE A MOVIE IT
would've been something in the vein of *Elizabethtown* or *The Family Stone*: good actors, terrible plot. On paper, my family might seem like a great reality TV show: hardworking restaurateur parents, a newly-in-love grandma who lives downstairs, the perfunctory blond twin boys, the handsome older brother and his high-school high jinks. Technically, we don't have actual next-door neighbors, but my best friend, Ray, can definitely compete with famous television neighbors. She smokes cigarettes, is really into clothes and fashion, and isn't scared to speak her mind. Although her home life isn't the best—her dad left when she was three months old, and her mom is kind of paranoid and really overweight—I think my mom thinks Ray is a good friend for me because, unlike me, she's very take-charge. Ray got an after-school job when she was only fourteen, bought herself a car the minute she turned sixteen, and pays for most of her stuff.

The thing is, even with this supposedly interesting cast of characters, most days I hit snooze, stumble into the shower, and exert a lot of energy bumming rides. I'm not debilitatingly unpopular; I don't cut myself, puke on purpose, or spend an unhealthy amount of time texting, gaming, or doing drugs. I don't have a reputation like Jessie Eaves, who, although she's my age, is pathologically obsessed with Hello Kitty. When my mom says I could stand to be more adventurous, maybe watch fewer movies, I say something like "should I take up rock climbing, get a motorcycle, or send a naked picture of myself to the football team?" Then she says, "Jesus, no, Amelia. You're perfect."

My dad says I'm his rock, tells me to hold down the fort, and often calls me a good egg.

I don't know if it's because I'm sandwiched between my very charming older brother and Thing 1 and Thing 2, but I've basically been in the chorus all my life: I've never had or wanted a solo.

Then I met Epstein.

Here's what happened. This mom down the road, Claudia Carter, frantically asked if I'd consider babysitting her daughters in Montauk this summer. Their regular sitter had just quit and she was really desperate and said it didn't matter that I didn't drive. I was kind of nervous about being away from home, but my mom thought I should try being on my own for a change.

It was a great job. During the week, I'd make sure Selena and Sabrina were ready for camp and walk them to the bus stop. Back at the house, I would clean up, do their laundry, and basically just wait around until it was time to pick them up, which is why I was able to text 24/7 with Ray. Ray works at CinnaYum! in the mall and all day she'd text pictures of mall weirdos, vats of disgustingly gooey icing, and things she was bidding for on eBay. I'd text her pictures of the pool, the ocean, and beautiful blue skies, and she'd text back that I sucked.

I also texted with Emily Moffet, aka Muppet. Muppet

started hanging out with me and Ray back in eighth grade. Neither Ray nor I are exactly sure how it happened, but one day we were like: *Wow, we've been hanging out with Muppet for three years?!* Muppet is this slightly spacey girl who just sort of bops along to a whistling soundtrack in her own brain. Ray secretly started calling her Muppet when she realized that she had an uncanny resemblance to a combination of Beaker, Gonzo, and Kermit. But she's not a bad person or anything. She's just kind of there.

After I walked the Carter girls home from camp, we'd hang out at the pool, paint nails, and play Uno. The worst thing about the job was dealing with wet towels and bathing suits every day, which wasn't really that bad. Mrs. Carter, who painted huge, blobby pictures in a studio about twenty feet from the main house, was there a lot of the time and was always telling me to go relax or offering to make me a kale smoothie, which is as gross as it sounds. On the weekends, when Mr. Carter came down, the family would take trips around Long Island or go into Manhattan. They always invited me, but I'm not a city person and felt kind of weird tagging along, so I'd mostly hang out at the house by myself, or walk to the beach.

What saved me from complete weekend boredom was the enormous movie collection. The owners of the house that the Carters rented had practically every DVD from the Criterion Collection. It was heaven. At least, for the first two weeks, when I had a blast with my self-curated themes like: The Wednesday (and Part of Thursday) Wes Anderson Special (*Fantastic Mr. Fox, The Darjeeling Limited, The Life Aquatic with Steve Zissou,* and *The Royal Tenenbaums*), Bonding with Michael Bay (*Armageddon* and *The Rock*), Indie Chick Flicks (*Tiny Furniture* and *Frances Ha*), and My Dad Will Be Happy I Finally Watched Some Hitchcock (*Notorious* and *Rebecca*).

On my third Sunday, when I finished two of my all-time favorite films for the fiftieth time, David Gordon Green's *George Washington* and David Fincher's *The Curious Case of Benjamin Button* (which coincidentally also fit into a Directed by David theme), and literally could not watch another movie, I decided I would jog to the lighthouse, a famous Montauk landmark only four miles away.

I have no idea what I was thinking. Maybe my brain was sun damaged and chlorine-logged and didn't remember that, unless it's a leisurely walk with my dog, I hate exercise. I set off "running" at 12:30 PM, and by 12:45 PM I was completely dripping with sweat and cursing myself for not bringing any water and for wearing Ray's hand-me-down pink slip-on Onitsuka Tiger sneakers, which are not meant for running. I must have been totally dehydrated, because it took me over two hours to get there. I Instagrammed a selfie by the stupid lighthouse, which took up about seven seconds. Then I remembered that I had to actually get back to the Carters. I would've cried, but my tears were all evaporated, so I sat there for an hour, beyond thirsty, in this weird spaced-out denial funk where I was only able to come up with two running-themed movies: *Forrest Gump* and *Unbroken*. This was a personal low. I texted Toby, Ray, and Muppet my sad story, but only Muppet wrote back with a weird string of emojis. Eventually, I started to walk back, cursing myself each step of the way.

It started to rain, which was actually kind of nice since I was so hot. I even opened my mouth trying to catch some drops. But then the wind picked up and I could feel my blisters getting bigger with each step. Cars full of disappointed beachgoers kept whizzing past me. When I was still about three miles away from the Carters' house, a red Honda Fit pulled over. And the driver rolled down the window.

I know. You never get into a car with a stranger. When it comes to important life stuff, I'm not an idiot. In addition to being forced by Toby to watch horror movies, I hear enough news to know that there are a lot of sickos out there.

But the guy who was driving looked around my age with red hair that fell in his eyes, freckles on his tan arms and face, and rectangular brown glasses. He was wearing a green T-shirt that said "Reading Is Sexy" with a picture of a girl with big glasses on it. He looked like the opposite of a killer/rapist. It's a stretch, but he looked like a combination of Ansel Elgort and Jason Segel but with bigger ears. Much bigger ears. His ears seemed unusually big, and I stared at them until he said, "Hello. I know you never get into the car with a stranger. It's one of the stupidest things to do. Your mother would probably kill you for even considering it. *My* mother would kill *me* for sure. But, listen. My name is Epstein Boffee-Barnes. Boffee has two *F*s and two *E*s. Barnes has an *E*, too. I'm seventeen and not a killer. I don't like horror movies. I've been a vegetarian since I was nine. You look *really* wet and really tired and I saw you walking like three hours ago. Um . . . I have a car."

I couldn't speak because my brain felt like it had been submerged in water. It felt good not to be moving, but even though this guy didn't look or sound psycho, how could I know for sure?

"I'm not a rapist," Epstein said, reading my mind. "I think rapists should be killed. Except I'm against the death penalty so it's actually a little confusing. But really, I'm not a killer. I teach kids to sail."

I put my hand on the rear door and hesitated.

"You're soaking wet. Rain is coming into my car. Let me drive you where you need to go."

I thought about the girls in Cleveland who had been locked up for ten years, which made me think about *Unbreakable Kimmy Schmidt*. Then I wondered what Tina Fey would think if her daughters got in a car with a guy named Epstein Boffee-Barnes. That made me wonder about Amy Poehler, but then I remembered that she has sons, so I wondered what Toby would do. I knew right away that he'd get into a car if a cute girl offered him a ride in the rain. He wouldn't for a second consider the dangers, because in the movie version, you get in. So, even though my heart was pounding, I got in. But, even though I knew it wasn't the movie version way to do things, I got into the backseat, figuring I'd have a better chance of escaping.

I told him where the Carters lived, that I was a babysitter for the summer, and that I'd never been to Montauk before.

He told me he'd spent every summer in Montauk with his aunt and uncle who had no kids, that he worked at the sailing camp he used to go to, and that he lived in Manhattan.

I told him my summers were normally spent making sure that my twin brothers weren't inventing new forms of psychological torture tactics on each other, or burning the house down. Sometimes, I'd bus tables at my parents' restaurant, and, since I didn't drive, I'd watch a lot of movies with my dog.

"Does your dog like movies?" Epstein asked.

I nodded. "She has her own Netflix queue."

He laughed. "What's on it?"

"*101 Dalmatians, Bolt, Space Dogs.*"

He laughed again and told me he had a cat, loved sesame bagels, comedy podcasts, and jam bands.

"Jam bands?" I asked, kind of surprised, since he didn't have a hippie vibe.

"Don't judge."

"Okay. I won't judge." I smiled so he didn't think I was a judgey music snob. I pretty much listen to whatever pop music Ray puts on, and the Beatles with my brother because he's obsessed with the Beatles.

I told Epstein I was a junior at Washington Lincoln High School. I didn't mention that I have never listened to a comedy podcast.

Epstein said Washington Lincoln was a weird name for a school. "They couldn't decide which president to name it after?"

"No, they couldn't decide so they named it after both."

"What's your name?"

"Amelia."

He pulled into the Carters' driveway. "I like watching movies too, Amelia," he said, as if it was an unusual thing for two American teenagers to like.

I liked the way Epstein said my name even though he pronounced it totally normally.

Epstein Boffee-Barnes tapped on his iPhone. "I don't only listen to jam bands," he said. "This is my current favorite song." In the movie version we would've listened to the entire poppy-indie song so the director could make it clear that I, the main character, felt totally comfortable listening to a song with a guy she'd just met. What really happened was that ten seconds in, I realized that I needed to pee and that the Carters were home. I wasn't sure how I would explain sitting in the car with a random guy after trying to run in the rain. I didn't think they'd be mad, but the whole thing seemed random. So I awkwardly mumbled thanks to Epstein, ran out of his car, and burst into the house to get to the bathroom. But in my awkward hurry to flee, I left my phone in his car. Luckily, Epstein brought it back a few hours later.

"You get a lot of texts," he said. "I didn't read them, but your phone has been vibrating like crazy."

"My best friend hates her job," I told him. "It's in a mall. We text a lot."

He smiled. His smile made his ears look smaller, which made him cuter.

"I didn't leave it on purpose," I explained. "In the movie version I would've left it intentionally, but I didn't."

"What's the movie version?" Epstein asked.

"It's the better version," I said, which I immediately regretted. Except for Toby, who kind of invented the idea, I don't think I've ever really told anyone about the movie version.

"Better?"

"Better like the audience is willing to pay ten dollars to see it. Not better like happy. There are plenty of sad movies, like *The Fault in Our Stars,* which was amazing, or *If I Stay*, which I didn't like. But movie-sad is way better than non-movie-sad. For one thing, there's a soundtrack, which helps you get right to the heart of the sadness. Violins and stuff."

Epstein smiled, and even though I was talking way too much, I kept going. "In real life when someone gets a cancer diagnosis, there's tons of time just waiting. You have to wait for weeks to get results for like a million terrible tests. My grandfather was sick with cancer for three years. In the movie version you never see the bedpans."

Epstein laughed. "That's a great line."

I was shocked. This guy was standing on the porch, and even though I was talking nonstop about nonsense like bedpans, he seemed kind of interested. I couldn't believe it. That stuff doesn't happen to me. I wondered what Ray would think of Epstein. She has a lot more experience, and at least once a week some random mall weirdo asks her out.

When the cute big-eared guy asked me out, I stopped wondering what Ray would think and said yes.

We went to a movie.

Of course.

3

A WONDERFUL REST OF THE DAY

THE DAY BEFORE THE OFFICIAL START OF MY JUNIOR year, I beg Toby to drive me to the mall. Oddly he says he doesn't want to go, that he doesn't need anything. It's weird that he'd prefer to be holed up in his room. Normally he is pretty into clothes for a straight guy.

"Ray's at work," I tell him. "If her manager isn't around, you can get free CinnaYum!"

"That shit is full of cancer."

"But they're just so gooey and sweet and I haven't had one all summer."

"You're better for it."

"Please, Toby. Muppet is there, too, and I haven't seen her in ages."

"Muppet's at the mall?" He looks slightly interested. "I thought she was with Toast . . . I can't find Toast."

"Why would Muppet be with Toast? Why do you want to find him? Please, Toby, I won't spend that long with Muppet and Ray. Please please please!"

"You *need* a license," he says, putting on his shoes. "You need to get over your silly shit and drive."

"I know." I follow him out of his room, down the hall, downstairs, and out the back door.

"There's no reason for you not to be driving. Like my good friend Jake Gyllenhaal says in *Nightcrawler*, fear is only 'False Evidence Appearing Real.'"

"Christian Grey says to Anastasia Steele, 'Most of the fear is in your head.'"

Toby makes a face. "You're quoting *Fifty Shades of Grey*?"

I slide into the passenger seat. "Ray wanted to see it."

He shakes his head. "Well, it's true. Your driving fears are only in your head. You'd be fine behind the wheel."

I nod.

"I'm enabling your not driving by chauffeuring you."

"Just imagine I'm Miss Daisy. I'll call you Hoke."

"I'd like to imagine you in Driver's Ed."

"You sound like Mom."

That shuts him up. He puts on his "Yesterday, Today, Tomorrow!" Beatles playlist and drives off.

Once we get to the mall, instead of going into the garage, Toby pulls in front of Macy's.

"You're not parking?" I ask.

"I don't want to go in. Too oppressive in there. Let me know if you see Toast."

"You're just going to wait for me?" I'm surprised. I thought once Toby actually got here, he'd get into it and make things fun by ordering made-up foods from Ray and suggesting atrocious clothes for me to "try on."

"I'll wait," he says.

"In the car?"

"I got my book." He holds up *The Lord of the Rings*.

"Sit and read in the food court. At least it'll be air conditioned." It has to be at least ninety-five degrees out. "Ray says mall cops ticket like crazy."

"Just go expend your personal consumption."

"I think you should park in the garage."

"Avoid the food court at all costs," he whispers. "Lots of secret ops in there."

"What movie is that from?" I open the door. "I think you got me."

But he's already reading and doesn't answer.

There's a long line at CinnaYum! but Ray comes flying out from behind the counter and screams my name. "Ahhhhh-meeellllliiiiiiaaaaaaaahhhhhhhh!" She gives me a huge hug.

I kind of love it because it's very movie version, but it's also a little embarrassing because all the people in line look at me like I'm the one to blame that they'll have to wait for their Yums!

"I missed you, too," I tell Ray.

"Bullshit. You were living it up in the Hamptons with your infinity pool and ocean views."

"Montauk isn't like the rest of the Hamptons. I didn't see a famous person all summer. Well, Mr. Carter thought he saw Alec Baldwin at the grocery store, but it couldn't be verified. Mrs. Carter thought he was too short. And the pool was nice, and the view was too, but I still missed you."

"Excuse me," a woman with a little girl wearing fairy wings says sharply. "But I'd like to order."

Ray shuffles back to the stand. I follow and wait by a large fake tree next to her.

"My bestest friend was away for, like, the last one thousand hours," she tells the old man at the front of the line. "She hung out in a mansion and got herself a boyfriend with seven names."

He ignores her and orders an XL Yum! stick.

"It wasn't a mansion," I tell her. "It was a really nice house, but not a mansion. And Epstein doesn't have seven names. I don't even know if he's my boyfriend."

Ray grins and rings up the old man. "You haven't had your DTR, yet?"

"My what?"

"Your Defining the Relationship convo."

"No. Not really."

"You need to DTR it, girl."

"We're going to visit each other. Hopefully he can come up soon. The train ride is only about two hours."

"But is he your boyfriend?" Ray grins. "Have you said, 'My dear Epstein Lepstein Fenstein Benstein, are you my boyfriend? Or just my lover?'"

"I thought Muppet was here," I say, changing the subject. "Lover" seems like such an adult thing to say.

Ray points down to the other side of the food court where I see Muppet in a bright magenta and yellow dress looking up at the ceiling.

"What's she doing?"

Ray shrugs. "I have no idea." She takes the order from the mom of the fairy-wing girl.

"I thought maybe she'd want to say hi since she hasn't seen me."

"Total weirdo," Ray says. "I think she might have gotten even dingier this summer."

"Impossible. Is Toast here?"

"Toast?"

"Toby was looking for him. He thought maybe Toast would be with Muppet."

"Is Toby here?" Ray asks. Her voice seems to go up an octave.

"He's in Prudence. Outside Macy's."

"Really? Why?"

"He's being weird. Wants to read. Didn't want to pay to park."

"He's going to get a ticket. Even if he's in the car, they'll ticket. Mall cops are vicious."

Ray seems unusually concerned about my brother's parking situation.

"I told him all that. Anyway, I should go buy something to wear for school. I seriously have no clothes. If I'm unsure, I'll send you a picture."

"Stay away from the moccasins, girl."

"That was one time, like three years ago," I mutter mostly to myself as I walk toward Muppet.

Muppet's reaction to seeing me is the opposite of Ray's. She glances at me and says, "Hey, Amelia. How do you spell cucumber?"

"Cucumber?"

She nods.

"C-u-c-u-m-b-e-r. Why? Actually never mind. I don't want to know. How was your summer?"

"Good. It's nice to see you, too."

Muppet kind of reminds me of Sam. I chat with her a little, but then tell her I need to go shop because Toby's waiting for me.

Unlike Ray, Muppet doesn't seem to care that Toby isn't in the mall.

Unfortunately, my shopping isn't a success. For one thing, I feel rushed since Toby's waiting, and also because I'm not that confident without Ray. While I'm content in a pair of Gap jeans and a plain tank top, Ray is always saving up for expensive things like polarized Ray-Bans and Hunter rain boots. She spends a lot of time looking for deals and bidding on eBay, which I don't really get. Sometimes she'll be super psyched to tell me that she won a $400 Chanel wallet for $150. But I think $150 is still a lot to spend on a wallet. Since she makes her own money, I guess it's her prerogative. But she's really helpful when we shop together. She always knows what's on clearance and steers me away from bad fashion choices.

I get two new bras and five pairs of underwear at Victoria's Secret, and Sperry Top-Siders that look just like my old ones, but without Ray, I get stuck at Express and take pictures of two potentially ugly sweaters and then walk back to CinnaYum!

"Are these ugly?" I show Ray the photos.

"Yes," she says without hesitating. "They would make an Olsen look fat. Do not buy them. Under any circumstances."

"Ugh. I don't have time to really shop."

"Toby still hasn't come in?"

I shake my head.

"Weird. Does he want free Cinnacrack? We can go give him one."

All of a sudden something in my brain clicks on. Ray tried to sound casual when she asked if Toby wanted a free Cinna-Yum!, but she didn't, which means she wants to give him one because she was bummed he wasn't in the mall, and she also cared a weird amount about his illegal parking. Which must mean that she likes him, because why else would she care? I know they texted about parties this summer, but something doesn't feel right about Ray liking Toby. It doesn't make sense, because I love Ray *and* my brother. So why wouldn't I want them to go out?

"He doesn't want one," I say. "He said they're full of cancer."

"He's probably right."

I can't tell if she's disappointed or not, but then Ray's manager, Jason, comes back so I give her a wave and make my way back towards the mall entrance.

As I step into the sultry, non-air-conditioned air, my phone buzzes.

Epstein!

"I'm in the mall," I tell him. "Actually I'm just leaving."

"The mall?"

"Yeah. You know, the oppressive place for consumption."

"Consumption is another word for tuberculosis."

"It sounded better when my brother said it."

"Consumption is the disease that killed Emily Brontë and John Keats."

"Did you Google that or do you actually know it?" Epstein knows a lot of random facts about a lot of different subjects. Most of the time, I find it cute, but sometimes I just feel dumb.

"I knew it. Back in fifth grade, I was interested in the diseases that killed famous writers."

"When I was in fifth grade I was into Adam Levine. You must have been a really fun fifth grader."

There's an awkward pause and I wonder if I've insulted Epstein. Sometimes we have weird pauses, which isn't very movie version. Whenever Toby has a girlfriend they seem to always be laughing, kissing, or speaking in annoying baby talk.

"I was a weird fifth grader. I'm still weird. What are you doing in the mall?" Epstein asks. I'm happy that he doesn't sound hurt.

"School shopping, although I didn't do much of it. Toby didn't want to come in so I had to do it quickly."

"What did you get?"

"Shoes. Bras." My face flushes and I swallow hard. I did more with Epstein than any other boy, but we didn't have sex or anything. I wonder if we do need to have the DTR talk.

"Oh," Epstein says. "That's exciting. The bras, at least."

I'm not sure what to say to this so I awkwardly cough.

"I miss you," Epstein says.

"I miss you too." I picture his cute freckled face and, unfortunately, his big ears. But then I see Prudence, and there's a cop car next to it. "Hold on," I say.

A cop is talking to Toby through his rolled-down window.

"Oh no," I say to Epstein. "I gotta go. I'll call you later."

Shit. Mall tickets are big. Toby is going to be mad.

Except when I get close to the car, I hear laughing.

I walk closer.

The cop, a short, young Latina woman, is laughing.

Toby is making a cop laugh!

And they're listening to the Beatles.

My brother so lives the movie version, I think as I walk up to the car.

"Here she is," Toby says. "Lucy in the Sky with Diamonds, herself."

"Hi?" I say, not meaning for it to come out as a question.

Toby gives me a what-were-you-so-worried-about smile.

"Shopping success?" the cop asks.

"Not really."

"I should have helped her," Toby says. "'Give a girl the right shoes, and she can conquer the world.'"

"Huh?" I say.

"Marilyn Monroe!" the cop says. "What about 'You're never fully dressed without a smile'?"

"Good one, Officer Martinez!"

I feel like I've entered an alternate reality. Only my brother could charm his way out of a mall ticket. I get in the car and put my seat belt on, even though Officer Martinez doesn't seem to notice. She's still laughing with my brother.

I don't know why Ray was so worried about Toby. Of course the cop doesn't give him a ticket. She gives him, totally unprofessionally in my opinion, a high-five and tells us to have a wonderful rest of the day.

Act I: Scene 3

AMELIA is nine years old

TOBY is eleven years old

FADE IN:

INT. AMELIA'S ROOM. MORNING. A CLOCK ON THE
DRESSER SAYS 7:30 AM.

AMELIA wakes and notices dozens of leis and
white lights all around the room. There are
plastic palm trees and plastic flamingos poking
out from the bookcase, the desk, etc.

TOBY walks in with a yellow, sun-shaped cake.

TOBY
singing
Happy beach birthday to you,
happy beach birthday to you!

AMELIA
Huh? What?

TOBY
You always said you hated that your
birthday was in the dead of winter.

Well, now it's summer.
in an Australian accent
Welcome to Australia, mate. I'm pleased to
inform you that it's a whopping 25.5 degrees,
mate.

Toby hands Amelia a stuffed kangaroo.

AMELIA
cuddles kangaroo and yawns
That sounds cold.

TOBY
grinning, still in an Australian accent
Don't be silly, mate. That's Celsius. In your
silly American Fahrenheit, it's a lovely 78
degrees. Come on, love. Up you go. Let's celebrate
this summery birthday of yours at the beach.

Amelia gets up, still holding
her stuffed kangaroo.

TOBY
Here you go.

Toby hands Amelia a pair of pink flip-flops.

AMELIA
Thanks, Toby. These are great.
This is pretty funny.

TOBY
That's not all, mate. Step inside to the
beach.

Toby leads Amelia into her bathroom, which
has been transformed. The tub is full of blue
water and there is a child's sandbox filled
with sand and beach toys. Next to the "pool"
is a small plastic beach chair and rows of
plastic palm trees. Hanging sunshine lights
line the perimeter of the ceiling.

AMELIA
amazed
Toby! This is amazing. How did you do all
this?

TOBY
shrugs
I just wanted you to have a warm birthday for
once. Happy beach birthday, Amelia.

Toby hands Amelia a bottle of sunblock and a
pair of sunglasses.

FADE OUT.

4

LADIES' LUNCH

THE FRIDAY AFTER MY FIRST WEEK OF SCHOOL I'M
standing on the front porch, trying to get my keys out of my
bag, when my grandmother and mom burst out of the house.

"Jeez!" I say. "You scared me."

"We were waiting for you," my grandmother says.

My mom nods. "We're whisking you away for an LL."

LL stands for Ladies' Lunch, which is this corny thing
me and my grandmother and my mom used to do a lot. We'd
go out, just the three of us, for lunch. My mom started it
when my grandfather got sick so my grandmother could have
a little break. We kept doing it after my grandfather died,
because other than taking care of the twins, my grandmother
didn't have that much of a life for a while. But two years
ago at the senior center, Grandma met a widower named
Harry and things have been hot and heavy ever since. Joke.
But Grandma does spend a lot of time with Harry—they're
always going off to inns in New England and taking classes
at the community college.

"In lieu of lunch, we thought we'd have an early-bird
dinner at the diner," my mom says, opening the car door.
"Grandma has tickets to a play with Harry tonight."

I get in the backseat.

"Your dad said he'd feed the twins," my grandma

says. "I told him there's some stuff in the freezer . . ." She sounds worried, which is funny since his job is feeding people.

"Where's Toby?" I had to take the bus home because Prudence was gone. I don't know if it's because he's a senior, but all week, I was stuck on the bus because Toby left before me. Last year, he'd usually wait for me, but now, he's always gone when the final bell rings. Between that and Ray getting more hours at CinnaYum! I'm resigned to the dorky yellow schoolbus.

"He's studying at the library," my mom said. "He won't be home till later."

"He is?" I wish I didn't sound shocked but when I saw Toby after lunch he was lying on a picnic table with skeevy Toast and some stoner sophomore girls, looking as unlibrary as you can get.

My phone vibrates with a text.

Epstein: i miss u.

Me: me 2. What r u doing?

Epstein: @starbucks listening to new wtf podcast. U?

Me: in car 4 early dinner w mom & grandma. wtf?

Epstein: What the fuck with Marc Maron. Amazing podcast! Listen!

Me: u say all podcasts r amazing! I've been listening to a lot! Nerdist! Comedy Bang Bang!

Epstein: ☺

Me: Not really into the jam band ones though. Sry.

Epstein: You can be practically perfect.

Me: Mary Poppins wouldn't be into jam bands either. ☺

Epstein: Sure she would! Laughing on the ceiling? Jumping into chalk.

"Amelia." My mom glances at me in the rearview mirror.

"I'm texting Epstein."

"Grandma asked you a question."

"It's okay," Grandma says.

Me: Gotta go.

I put my phone in my bag.

"What, Grandma?"

"I can't remember."

I try not to feel annoyed. I love my grandmother. She's really sweet, doesn't ever boss me around, and without her, I'd be stuck doing tons more babysitting.

"I can't believe you have a boyfriend, Amelia," Grandma says. "Where does the time go? Just yesterday you were on the baby swing."

I blush. "I don't know if he's exactly my boyfriend." I still haven't had the DTR convo Ray suggested. I'm not sure how I'd write something like that in a text, and having the talk on the phone would be weird and maybe too grown-up. That's the kind of thing they do in movies but not in a good way. I don't want to scare Epstein off by talking about what we're doing. I wonder if Toby has DTR talks with his girl-friends. The girls he goes out with always seem like they're SO into him. I remember when Kate, a girlfriend his sophomore year, brought him a dozen balloons and cupcakes to school on his birthday.

"How's Harry?" I ask, because it's rude not to ask my grandmother about her boyfriend. Man. Companion. Friend.

"He has a cold," my grandmother says. "The theater was chilly on Saturday. I'm going to remind him to wear his wool sweater tonight."

"Oh," I say. Harry seems nice, but there's not that much to say about a sweet old guy who wears sweaters all year.

After we've eaten and my grandmother is sipping her decaf, supposed-to-be-in-the-library-studying Toby comes into the diner, laughing his ass off, followed by Toast, Muppet, and two popular senior girls. Abdi Osman, a guy who moved here from Somalia in fifth grade, follows behind them, filming with a big camera.

I can't imagine a more random group of people. I think the only thing they have in common is that they all look high.

My grandmother waves at my brother. "Well, look who it is!"

I look for the panic on Toby's face when he registers that he's busted for lying about the library, but he just smiles at us. "Mom, Grandma, Meals. Hey." He sounds like he's genuinely happy to see us.

Muppet grins at me. "Hello, Ah. Melia." Her eyes are bright red and she looks extremely high.

"Hi," I say, kind of embarrassed. Although I'm not sure if I'm embarrassed for her or for me.

Muppet grins at me more. "What. Are. You. Doing?"

What a wacko. I can't wait to tell Ray about Muppet on drugs. "Just hanging out with my mom and grandma."

"I thought you were studying," my mom says to Toby.

"We did study," Toby says. "We studied so much algebraic geometry that we got hungry. We're just taking a break. We're headed back to the library after we nosh on a little something."

Nosh on a little something? There's no way my mother is going to buy this! Who does he think he's kidding with algebraic geometry?

"Toby has a lot of really interesting theories," Muppet says.

I hold my breath, because no one in their right mind would believe these stoned nut jobs have been at the library!

But I am so wrong.

"Well, I'm impressed that you're working so hard," my mom says. "And on a Friday afternoon, too."

"Geometric string theory isn't easy," he says, smiling at me. "'They've done studies, you know. Sixty percent of the time, it works every time.'"

That's from *Anchorman*, my brain screeches! But my grandma nods like Toby makes perfect sense. "Are you eating?" she asks.

Toby shakes his head. "Just coffee. We have to study more."

"I think you should get something to eat," my grandma tells him. "You look thin, Toby. Don't push yourself too hard, honey." Then she takes her wallet out of her purse and hands him a twenty!

I have to admit that he's the best. I hope Abdi got this on film because in a million years, no one will ever be half as cool as Toby.

5

EPSTEIN EPSTEIN EPSTEIN EPSTEIN EPSTEIN EPSTEIN EPSTEIN

EVEN THOUGH IT'S POURING ON THE LAST FRIDAY IN September, and even though I got drenched waiting for the bus after I shook Toby senseless trying to wake him up, but he *just doesn't feel like going to school today*, I'm in a fantastic mood because Epstein is coming. Today! In six hours, then five hours, and then I get a text that he's leaving school, that he's getting on the subway, that he's sitting on the train. He's so close, and it's important that I somehow pick him up at the station. My mom said she could pick him up, but that would be so incredibly lame that I spend most of school convincing Ray to:

1. Drive me to meet Epstein's train.
2. Drive Epstein and me to Ginger's for dinner.
3. Drive us back to my house.

"Come on," I say as she shoves her books into her locker. "It'll be fun."

"Fun?" She gives me a very Ray look. "Chauffeuring you and your boyfriend all over town?"

Boyfriend! I think. Not that we've had the DTR yet, but am I the one with the boyfriend? Since middle school, Ray's always been the one with boy drama. I've had the occasional crush and technically Leo Kavanaugh and I went out for three days in eighth grade, but that's been pretty much it. And now I have someone I talk/text with almost every night! Someone who's coming to visit! Me! That must make him my boy-friend, even if we've never actually said it.

Ray slams her locker and I'm jolted back to the reality of being carless and desperate for rides.

"I really want you to meet Epstein. You'll be the first person to meet him."

"Lucky me," she says a little sarcastically, picking up her bag. "I should just call Cinnafuckincrack and see if they have any open shifts tonight."

Ray calling for work when she's not scheduled is as likely as me overcoming my fear of driving, getting my license, and buying a car. Today. I follow her down the hall.

"Please, Ray. I'll give you gas money. And buy you cigar-ettes. We'll eat at Ginger's and hang out at my house later."

"I don't want to be a third wheel. And speaking of wheels, there's no reason you can't get your freaking license."

"You won't be the third wheel," I tell her, ignoring the license talk. "Come on, Ray, I hung out with you and Jake all the time." Jake Sweeney was Ray's boyfriend most of last year until he cheated on her with a freshman. He's on our Enemy List so we don't usually talk about him. I look to see if she's mad that I brought him up, but she seems okay.

"What about at your house?"

"Toby will be there. He's watching the twins, but once they go to bed, we'll all hang out. It'll be fun."

Ray gives me the look that means she's going to go off on how I need to learn to drive.

But instead, she asks, "So you want me to hang out with Toby?"

I'm surprised but shrug, trying to seem casual. "Well, yeah. We'll all chill, drink some beers." *But Epstein doesn't drink, I remember. Will this be weird? What if this is a disaster? What if everyone is awkward?*

"You don't mind me hanging out with your brother?"

"Why should I care?" I ask, even though my heart goes chug-chug-chug. "You're friends."

"I thought maybe you didn't want me to."

"Hang out with Toby," I say. "Be my guest. I just don't know why you'd want to. He's been a total bum lately. I think he skipped most of his classes this week." I immediately feel bad after saying that. *Siblings never tattle. Toby and I are members of the Secret Sibling Society.*

"And I think he's still into Arianna Kaufman," I say randomly. "I think they text a lot." I have no idea why I just said that. Toby *could* text Ari but I don't think he does. Now that I think about it, he's actually not on his phone that much lately.

I feel relieved that Ray agrees to drive me to the train station and even more relieved when she and Epstein get along right away. I know as soon as he calls her "the very famous Ray" and she calls him "the supremely famous Epstein" that they'll get along. It's petty, I know, but I'm happy that his hair is longer because it covers his ears more.

In the car I wonder what Ray thinks of him and if she's noticed the size of his ears. I wonder if Epstein thinks Ray is pretty. She's got bigger boobs than I do and almost-black hair that's long and shiny. But then we walk up to Ginger's and Epstein takes my hand! I get extra lucky when a huge party comes in, and my parents can't spend too long grilling him.

When we get home, Sam, shirtless with *Minecraft* pajama bottoms and pink goggles, meets us at the door. "Who are you?" he asks Epstein.

"Epstein," Epstein says. "Are you Sam?"

Sam nods.

"Cool house," Epstein says, putting his bag down.

Trying to see the house through Epstein's eyes, I guess maybe, if you can see past the mess of toys, shoes, and dog hair, it is kind of cool. There's a wall of windows in the dining room, which opens into a big kitchen that has a long wooden farm table, a wood-burning stove, and a skylight. There are open ceilings with high beams and neat things like window seats and built-in shelves. There's also the unfinished mudroom and an "office" that's a dumping ground for random stuff. Most of the upstairs is covered in floral wallpaper, which my mom complains about but never changes.

"David and Toby keep calling me Samwise Gamgee," my brother whines. "They're being mean."

"Samwise Gamgee is very cool," Epstein tells him.

Sam scowls. "I don't like all that *Lord of the Rings* stuff."

"Let's go find them," I say.

We find David and Toby downstairs in my grandmother's part of the house. It's a fully functional apartment with its own entrance. My dad renovated it when she moved in, but she never uses the kitchen, and once she met Harry, Toby and

I started hanging down here to escape the twins. Now, when we find them, David and Toby are so engrossed in watching *Lego Ninjago* that they barely look up at us. There are bowls of mushy cereal and an empty pint of Ben & Jerry's ice cream on the table.

"Toby, David, this is Epstein," I tell them.

"Nice to meet you," Epstein says.

David doesn't look up.

Toby looks at him. "Nice. To. Meet. You. Too." Then he turns back to the TV, which seems unusually loud.

"Hey," Ray says.

"Hey," Toby says more to Lord Garmadon than anyone in the room.

What is wrong with my brothers? David needs a lesson in manners, but he's seven. Toby, on the other hand, is nearly eighteen and is being totally rude. Why is he watching this dumb cartoon?

"Want to buy ice cream?" Ray asks Toby. This is code for buying beer. Ray has her cousin's ID and can usually get a six-pack.

"We have ice cream," David tells her.

"Not the kind I like," she tells him. "I like root BEER flavor." She looks at Toby.

"Okay." Toby sounds kind of bored. "Can we stop by Toast's? I need to pick up some stuff." He rubs his hands over his eyes.

You smoked all that pot already? I think. I don't say anything because I don't want to give Epstein the impression that my brother is a fuck-up. Plus, David is totally listening.

"Sure," Ray says agreeably. "I'll drive."

Toby stands up. "Good. I don't know where my keys are."

Once they leave, I bribe David with extra screen time to go upstairs with Sam.

Finally Epstein and I are alone, and we kiss until Sam runs down complaining that David hit him three times, called him retarded, and keeps changing the channel to something "very very very very very scary."

I run upstairs, tell David to stop being mean, give them a bag of Pirate's Booty, and turn on Nick Jr. "Don't even think about changing the channel," I order David.

When I return, Epstein smiles and wraps his arms around me. "So . . . When do you think your brother and Ray will be back?"

I silently calculate driving to the Mobil Mart that is lax about IDs, driving to Toast's for weed, smoking a joint there, Ray realizing that she's out of cigarettes. "Forty minutes. Give or take."

"So . . ."

"Just a sec." I slide out of his arms and latch the door at the top of the stairs.

The one positive thing about not getting to see your probably boyfriend for more than a month is that hooking up feels more good than awkward. I don't even feel bad that I give my very first blow job right on the couch where my grandmother watches the evening news.

In the movie version, you never see the main character wondering what to do with a mouthful of semen. I don't want to swallow it, but I also don't want to insult Epstein by spitting it out. Also, I'm not exactly sure where to spit it. It's so not the movie version, but I grab one of the twins' juice boxes and half spit, half sip the juice and try not to think about the sperm in my mouth.

I wonder if Epstein will want to go down on me. I'm curious, but the idea that my brothers or Ray could discover the locked door makes me pull my pants back on before Epstein can move anywhere near there. It's a good thing I did, because three minutes later we hear Ray's Frye boots clomping around upstairs. I'm surprised that they're back so soon. Now that Toby is hanging out with Toast, it seems like he can be there all day.

When I run up and unlock the door, Ray grins. "What's up?" she asks in a lilting singsong voice. I know she's wondering if we had sex. She's hooked up with a lot of guys, and she's had sex with Jake and a random college guy she met at the mall after Jake cheated on her. I've promised to tell her the minute I lose my virginity.

"Um . . ." I feel myself getting red.

"Yes?" Ray prods, following me downstairs with Toby.

I swallow.

"Well until you came in, Amelia and I were just discoursing about *The Origin of Consciousness in the Breakdown of the Bicameral Mind*," Epstein says matter-of-factly.

We all stare at Epstein.

Epstein smiles. "It's a book on my parents' shelf. I always see that pretentious title, and I don't know, I guess I memorized it. Neither of them has read it, as it turns out."

When Ray and Toby laugh, I start to relax. I wonder if it's normal to be sort of nervous about your friend/brother liking your maybe boyfriend so much. But Ray and Toby don't make a big deal when Epstein declines a beer and passes the joint. I drink one beer, but don't smoke. I know Epstein doesn't care, but I want to be myself.

Ray tells a long, rambling story about Toast and Muppet, which somehow turns into Toby talking about some conspiracy involving Peter Jackson. When I realize that I've left the twins unattended in front of the TV for hours, I go up, since Toby seems too fucked up to handle bedtime. I'm shocked when Epstein follows behind me and asks to help. I know it's cheesy, but there's something sweet about the way Epstein reads them a chapter from *The Goblet of Fire*. I imagine Epstein and me with our own kids, but then the craziness factor kicks in and I remember that we're in high school and have only been going out for two months and haven't actually had sex yet.

While Epstein is reading, my mom calls to say they won't be home till one at the earliest. "The boys are asleep?" she asks.

"Just about."

"Dad and I really liked Epstein. He seems really smart. Is he all set in Toby's room?"

"Toby's room is kind of gross. Can he sleep on Grandma's pullout? She's at Harry's."

"That's fine. Love you, Amelia."

"Love you too."

I walk back into Sam and David's room and listen to Epstein finish the chapter.

"Will you read to us tomorrow?" David asks. "You do the voices way better than Amelia."

"Don't close the door all the way," Sam says.

"You say that every night, Samwise Gamgee," David says as Epstein and I walk into the hallway.

"Shut up," Sam says. "Toby always calls me that. You just want to be like him. My name is Samuel Aaron Anderson."

"Okay, poop fart butt."

Epstein laughs. "They're funny."

"They have their moments."

Even though we're planning to go back to the basement, Epstein and I end up staying in the living room where, in between kisses, we start looking at my grandmother's scrapbooking albums. He must be my boyfriend because it's amazing that I'm not too embarrassed to show him pictures from my toothless-wonder stage or the time I was covered with poison ivy.

I'm so happy to be alone with Epstein that I'm totally unfazed by the fact that Toby and Ray are drinking and alone downstairs.

But then Ray comes sprinting up. "Can you guys come down? Toby got kind of fucked up. I don't know what to do."

I follow her down to find Toby in the unfinished room in the back of the apartment, where the boiler and washing machine are. He's cross-legged and rocking back and forth.

"Hey," I say. "What's up?"

He ignores me and keeps rocking.

"He's been like this for, like, I don't know." Ray looks at her phone. "Shit—twenty minutes?" She sounds worried, which scares me because Ray is good at taking care of drunk people.

"Toby?" I say softly. "Are you okay? Do you want help getting up?"

"He won't answer," Ray says.

"How much did he drink?" Epstein sounds concerned.

"Not that much. Three beers, maybe. Probably less. This doesn't seem like drunk," Ray says.

Sweat pours off my brother's forehead even though he's only in a T-shirt and it's cold down here. He continues to rock like we're not even here. I look at Ray who looks back at me. I look at Epstein who looks at my brother.

Then Toby screams. "AIEEEEE!" and rocks himself so vigorously that I think he might crack open his head. "Leave me the fuck alone!"

"Toby," I say. "You need to calm down. This isn't funny."

"Shit ass fucking fuck. They want to make me eat shit. I won't eat shit you fucking fucks."

"No one wants you to eat shit," Ray tells him. "It's okay, Toby. You're with your friends."

"They're here. They're listening. I need to make it stop before it can go. All those orcs. You know." He pulls his dirty T-shirt off so forcefully that the sleeve rips.

I look at Ray. "What's wrong with him? Did he take something at Toast's?"

She shakes her head. "One bong hit."

Toby flings his sneakers across the room. They hit the dryer and bounce off.

"Should we call someone?" Epstein asks.

"No!" I don't mean to snap, but I do. "We can't call anyone."

"He might need help, Amelia," Epstein says quietly.

I remind myself that Epstein just doesn't get how we do things up here. My parents are going a mile a minute at work, and I wouldn't call them unless someone stopped breathing. And that would probably be from the back of an ambulance since I'd call 911 first. I can't call my grandmother—I'm not about to wake her and Harry up to explain that her grandson is drunk or something.

While I imagine the preposterousness of calling someone, Ray walks over to Toby, picks up his hand, and gently strokes it. After a while, Toby stops rocking and starts swatting invisible nothings in front of him. He keeps babbling nonsense about people wanting him to eat shit and orcs and Sauron, but Ray just nods sympathetically. Sweat still drips off his forehead, but he eventually gets quiet.

None of us say anything. After a bit it's Epstein who walks over to Toby, puts his hand on Toby's shoulder, and says, "Hey, man. You okay?"

Toby doesn't say anything.

"You want a hand?" Epstein holds onto Toby's shoulder and together with Ray, who's still holding his hand, they help him up. Very slowly, they guide my brother back through the apartment, up the stairs, through the kitchen, and up to the second floor. Dazed, I follow behind them.

When we get to Toby's room, Ray says, "I can hang out with Toby if you want."

"You think he's okay?"

"He seems better." She sniffs loudly. "Stinky, but better."

"Stay here tonight," I tell her. "You can't drive." I also want someone else around.

She nods. "That episode just sobered me up, but yeah, I'll crash here. I'll text my mom."

"Sleep in my room. Epstein's sleeping downstairs."

"I'll come in a bit. You and Epstein should hang out. This is a shitty way to end your big night."

Epstein follows me into my room and we lie down on my bed. I can't believe it's almost midnight. I feel drained and tired and relieved that Epstein doesn't try anything.

"That was weird," I finally say.

"Has that ever happened before?"

"Never!" I sound angrier than I want, but I can't believe that the first time Epstein meets my brother, Toby is so not himself. "Toby's an awesome guy. Even when he's drunk or stoned he's usually just really funny and smart."

"Do you think he was hallucinating?"

"Hallucinating? From smoking pot and drinking beer?" I look at Epstein. "Is that possible?"

He shrugs.

"This is really weird. Toby is like, he's just like . . . he's just really cool," I say lamely.

"Well, you never know how alcohol or pot can affect you. If he didn't eat a lot . . . you never know."

"Maybe you're right." Cereal and ice cream isn't enough for dinner. Knowing my brother, that might have been his only meal of the day.

"I was at a String Cheese Incident show and this girl went blind after smoking pot."

"Really? Blind?"

Epstein nods. "She took one puff and said, 'Uh, I can't see.' I literally had to lead her to her seat because she couldn't see."

"Weird."

"Yeah. Her sight came back after a few minutes, but she was really blind for a while."

I feel a little better. Epstein's right. Toby's weird combination of no food, funky pot, and beer must have made him freak out. "I'm sorry you have to sleep downstairs. It's a mess down there. Crap. I need to get rid of all those beer bottles . . . Ray's cigarettes."

"No worries. I'll do it."

I stand up. "Really?"

He hugs me. "I will totally hide the illicit booze. Where should I put it?"

I explain where Epstein should hide the empty cans and where the Febreze is. "Thank you so much. I'm really happy you're here." I give him a quick, no-tongue kiss good night because hooking up just doesn't seem fun right now.

After Epstein leaves, I brush my teeth and wash my face. I'm tired but I can't sleep. At some point, I hear my parents come home, but I don't see Ray until, after a terrible, noisy sleep, I drag myself down to the kitchen, where everyone—

Toby, the twins, my mom, my dad, Epstein, and Ray—are all eating breakfast.

"Morning, sunshine," Ray says.

I stare at her. She spent the night in my brother's room while Epstein spent the night on my grandmother's lumpy pullout couch? Did she and Toby hook up?

"Hi, Amelia," Epstein says. "How'd you sleep? I slept great." He sounds like he's telling the truth.

My mom smiles. "It's nice and dark down there, isn't it? I nap there sometimes."

"Pancake, Meals?" My dad holds up one of his famous giant pancakes.

"I don't know how you two girls shared Amelia's bed all night," my mom says.

Ray shrugs. "It wasn't so bad."

I look at Toby. He's pale, but looks showered and fine. You'd never know what a mess he was last night, which makes me kind of mad at him. *He never gets in trouble.* I remember when he was so stoned in the diner and how he charmed his way out of the parking ticket at the mall. If he's so great the other 364 days of the year, why does he have to freak out the one time I have a guy visit me? I'd never do anything like that if one of his girlfriends spent the night! I'm always nice and normal to his girlfriends!

After breakfast, Ray goes home and everyone else except Toby, who says he's writing a college essay, goes apple picking at an orchard about thirty minutes away. At first I don't think Epstein and I should go because it sounds so dorky. But since I can't drive and don't want to stay in the house with my brother—who's probably just going to barricade himself in his room, get high, and blast music—I decide we should go.

As we pile out of the car, the twins fight over Epstein.

"Let's do the corn maze first," David tells him. "It's *really* hard!"

"Horse rides," Sam says. "Don't you think that will be fun, Epstein?"

"Yeah," he says enthusiastically. "It all sounds awesome."

"He's great," my mom whispers. "He's so sweet to the twins, so mature. Maybe it's growing up in Manhattan."

"Yeah." I feel happy that my mom likes Epstein. I wonder if his good manners make his ears look smaller.

"Alright. I'll go round up the twins and give you guys some space."

"Thanks, Mom."

I run up to Epstein, who says, "I love this. It's so nice to be out of the city."

"Sorry we have to hang out with my family. I really need to learn to drive."

"I'm having a great time." He smiles and I realize that the air feels especially crisp, the sky is a bright cloudless blue, and even the apples, which I've picked here every fall, seem brighter. Suddenly it doesn't matter that we're spending the day with my parents and brothers or that Toby freaked out last night. And Epstein is smart and cute! I imagine Ray whispering to me to go freaking ask him already if we're boyfriend-girlfriend. If it were Toby, he'd run over to someone like Arianna Kaufman, kneel before her with an apple, and say in a British accent, "Do you want to be my girlfriend?" Naturally, she'd crack up and say yes. Ray probably asked Jake if they were boyfriend and girlfriend after they had sex and were smoking cigarettes in bed. But Epstein and I have never had sex and my family is fifty feet away. I'm too nervous to ask him and so I just take his hand and lead him to the raspberry bushes on the other side of the orchard.

And then on the way home, because miracles do happen, my parents say they're taking the twins to a movie and won't be home till eight.

"We'll drop you guys off," my mom says, as if it's the most natural thing in the world for me to be home alone with a guy. I'm thrilled that Prudence isn't in the driveway and, since my grandmother is still at Harry's, Epstein and I are all alone.

This time, since the house is empty, I let Epstein go down on me. At first I can't help laughing because it feels weird and ticklish. Then it's awkward because Epstein looks up at me through my open legs.

"Are you okay?" he asks.

I almost say, Are you my boyfriend? but I stop myself and just nod.

"Should I keep going?"

I nod again and then bite my bottom lip so I won't laugh anymore. When I finally relax enough the licking starts to feel pretty good, but then Epstein stops and just lies on top of me. I guess maybe his tongue is tired. I remind myself to ask Ray how long guys usually go down on her for, and then I wonder why I'm thinking about Ray when I'm half naked with a city boy on my bed. I wonder if Epstein will want to have sex, and if I want to have sex, but then we hear the back door open and Toby starts singing "I Am the Walrus" at the top of his lungs, so we stop doing what we're doing and get dressed.

Sunday means brunch at Ginger's, so my grandmother is home and my parents are gone super early. And I don't believe it, but Toby actually volunteers to drive Epstein to the train. He pockets the money my mom left so Epstein could take a taxi, but I ignore it because I'm thrilled that he's acting normal again.

"You get shotgun," he tells Epstein.

"Hey!" I joke.

Epstein chooses one of my brother's playlists and it's great to see them both bopping their heads to the opening of "Come Together."

"It's amazing how much the Beatles did in just seven years," my brother says.

Epstein nods. "They revolutionized recording for sure."

Toby bops his head happily. "Those hippie jam bands wouldn't be around without the Beatles."

When Epstein nods in agreement, I feel like he and my brother have been friends for a million years.

Toby gets Epstein to the train with four minutes to spare. Epstein jumps out, grabs his bag, and kisses me quickly. Toby shakes Epstein's hand in one of those ridiculously complicated ways, and they both laugh, and I feel incredibly happy that Epstein finally got to see Toby as Toby.

6

A FEMA SITUATION

WHEN I GO DOWN TO THE KITCHEN LATE THE FOLLOW-
ing Saturday morning, Sam and David are slurping cereal, my
dad is reading the paper, and my mom is standing by the window, cereal bar in hand, looking at a tree in the yard.

"I can't believe that's a robin," she says. "It's October.
Something weird is going on. Morning, Meals."

"Goddamn Mets," my father grunts, turning the page.
"Morning," he says to me.

"Daddy cursed," Sam says. "Cursing is a sin."

"Don't be a tattletale," David says.

"I'm not," Sam whines.

David scoffs.

Sam scowls.

"Boys," my dad says in his this-is-my-day-off-so-don't-
make-me-mad tone.

"I'm not a tattletale. I'm really good at keeping secrets. I
never told Mom that I painted her a candleholder for Christmas, and I didn't tell Daddy about the mug. Did I?" Sam looks
at our parents.

My mom nods. "You're good at secrets, Sammy."

"See!" Sam glares at David. "And I didn't tell on Toby for
letting you play *Grand Theft Auto* last night."

My mom looks at David. "He did? He let you play that
violent game?"

"Sam! You idiot!"

Sam bursts into tears and runs up to his room.

My mom looks at me.

"Don't look at me," I say. "I didn't have anything to do with the video games. I was at Muppet's last night." Muppet's was a bust since she spent most of the night texting Toast. Sadly, the best part of the night was watching the last half of *Trainwreck* with her stepmom.

"Lou?" My mom looks at my dad.

My dad sighs loudly and turns the page of his paper.

Wails ring out from upstairs. My mom leaves to comfort my brother.

"Sam's such a scaredy-cat," David tells me. "He couldn't even watch *Pan's Labyrinth*."

"You watched *Pan's Labyrinth*?"

"It wasn't scary. Sam's a wimp. Toby said I'd be fine and I was. I am."

"Guillermo del Toro is a great director," I say, horrified and impressed that Toby showed that movie to the twins. Poor Sam might be traumatized for life. "I was creeped out."

"I like *Star Wars* more," David says as my mom comes back into the kitchen. "*Star Wars* is the best movie ever."

"Where's Toby?" she asks me.

"Sleeping, probably," I say.

She shakes her head. "He's not in his room. I went to tell him that it's inappropriate to let seven-year-olds play that game, but he's not there."

My dad puts down the paper and looks at me.

"I was at Muppet's till eleven. Her stepmom drove me home and I went to bed."

My dad walks out of the kitchen and down to my grand-mother's apartment. In less than a minute, he silently walks back through the kitchen and upstairs.

"He hasn't texted?" my mom asks.

"No." My most recent text was from Epstein last night.

My dad barrels back into the room. "He's not here," he booms. "And his room is a FEMA situation, Meg."

"I told you that," my mom snaps. "Did you think I just didn't see him?"

"What's FEMA?" David asks.

"Federal Emergency . . . it's not important, David. Go play, okay?"

David slides off his chair and shoves it forcefully under the table. "You *always* make me leave during the good parts."

"Upstairs," my dad says. My brother books it. My dad is not someone who tells you to do something more than once. He's very tall, has a bunch of tattoos on his arms, and has a shaved head. When he wants to be, he can be really intimidating.

"Amelia," my mom says. "What do you know? Were there any parties or anything?"

"I think Toast had people over. I'll text him."

have u seen/heard from toby? I text Toast and Ray.

Ray: No. ??????

Me: just wondering

Toast: Not since 6th period Fryday

"They haven't seen him," I say.

My mom rubs her palms over her eyes. I feel terrible. My parents are the hardest-working people I know. They probably weren't home till like 1:00 AM and then up early with the twins. How could my brother do this?

"I'm sure he's just at someone's house, Mom."

"But he knows to check in," my mom says. "It's always been the house rule. Just tell us where you are and when you're going to be home."

My dad nods.

She looks at me expectantly. "What's going on with Toby, Meals? He's been so . . . so *distant*. He's in his room *all the time*. Has he seemed distant to you?"

"He's probably got senioritis. A lot of them do."

"You're supposed to get senioritis when you've gotten into college." My mom picks at her cuticle. "You'd tell us if Toby were in trouble. Drugs or something."

I think back to the night after the eighth grade dance when Ray and I drank peach schnapps. Toby snuck us into the house and stealthily cleaned up gallons of our vomit. He wouldn't tell on me in a million years. How can I tell them he owes me more than a hundred dollars, which I think he's spent all on Toast's pot? "Yeah, I'd tell you," I say, crossing my fingers like I'm five.

"He's a teenage boy," my dad says. "Teenage boys don't want to talk to their mothers. I was the same way. Not that leaving like this is in any way excusable. He's working the next ten weekends. We can always use another busser."

"Maybe we shouldn't have made Ginger's a full restaurant," my mom says. "If we'd kept it a coffee shop, we'd be home more. I could have taken Toby to look at more colleges over the summer."

"He probably fell asleep at a friend's house," I tell her. "It has nothing to do with Ginger's." A few times a year my mom gets on a running-a-restaurant-takes-me-away-from-my-children kick. "You guys are here. You really are."

"I don't know." She doesn't sound convinced. "It's so much work, Meals. Something is always going wrong. The dishwasher is on the fritz. A waitress quits. It was simpler before."

"But it was boring," I remind her. "You and Dad were miserable just making muffins."

"Your dad was miserable. *I* was okay. *I* like making muffins." She looks at my dad.

I'm not sure what to say. And I guess my father doesn't either because he just picks up the paper again.

"Well, Prudence is here, so at least he's not driving," my mom says. "It's the driving that really scares me. There are so many accidents on these dark roads."

"Amelia doesn't drive," my dad reminds her.

I actually hope that my parents will have another why-won't-Amelia-get-her-license-already conversation because at least then they'll stop talking about Toby. But they don't tell me to get my license. They just sit there looking at me, as if I know something I'm not telling them, until my mom says that when Toby comes home, they'll talk to him about being a responsible member of the family, which means, in addition to checking in with his whereabouts, not letting the twins play violent video games and keeping his room cleaner. Then she asks me to write down the phone numbers of all his friends so she can call them herself.

"What's up?" Epstein says when he answers his phone an hour later. He's spending the weekend at Brown University.

I think about how my mom just called practically every senior at Washington Lincoln, but none of the ones who answered had seen Toby. Epstein is a senior, too. If he went to school here, my mom would have called him. Should I tell him? But Epstein doesn't go to school with my brother, has no idea that Toby played Peter Pan in sixth grade or got asked to the prom by three girls his sophomore year. Epstein barely knows anything about my brother so I don't want to tell him this.

When my pause is just a bit too long, I say, "Nothing. How's Brown?"

"Pretty awesome. I'm definitely going to apply. You sound kind of weird."

"I'm tired."

"Me too. I stayed up late at this improv comedy sketch thing last night. It was really funny."

"Sounds fun," I say.

"I miss you."

"You do?"

"Horribly."

"My parents loved you," I tell him. "So did the twins and Ray and Toby—"

"Hey, Amelia. I have to go. An informational thing is starting. I'll call you later."

After we hang up, I lie down on my bed and look at the ceiling. Out of nowhere I get a sour feeling, like a piece of ice is slowly and painfully melting in my stomach. *Why would Toby just leave? My parents aren't strict about curfew. Most of the time, especially on weekends, they're home later than we are. Is he a drug addict? Owes the Mafia money? What if he killed someone?*

When I can't get past the cheesy movie plots, I go into Toby's room and dig through mounds of clothes and crumpled potato chip bags like I know what I'm looking for. I find: three legal pads with lots of random things written on them, a Bible, four empty packs of M&M's, two black-and-white composition notebooks with some poems/lyrics written in them, a bong, three Sharpie markers, a half-eaten Snickers bar, two crushed Budweiser cans, a bunch of socks, and a family-sized bottle of laundry detergent. There's a Blu-ray of *The Lord of the Rings: The Two Towers*, a beat-up copy of *The Silmarillion*, and a pile of T-shirts and jeans heaped on the floor. I also find two old flip phones that have been taken apart.

Like my dad said, his room is a total mess, but I don't discover any drugs, duffel bags of money, or, thank goodness, dead bodies.

By lunch, my parents are borderline frantic. They don't talk about it in front of the twins and I know they haven't told my grandmother because she would have come back from the weekend she's spending with Harry in Montreal, but my mom is glued to her phone and my dad shovels handfuls of potato chips into his mouth. After lunch I paint my nails, send Epstein a photo of my freshly painted nails that he doesn't respond to, take Kepler on a walk, and then, out of desperation, watch *The Lego Movie* with Sam, David, and Kepler.

When we sit down to dinner, my dad dumps a mountain of mashed potatoes on his plate and barks, "Everyone eat."

"Did Toby run away?" Sam asks. His eyes get big and buggy.

"Shut up," David tells him.

"David told me to shut up, Mommy."

"Boys!" my father barks.

My mom gives my dad a look and then says, "I want you both to think good, happy thoughts that Toby comes home safe very soon. Okay?" My mom sounds like she might cry.

I realize that my parents haven't said that Toby *isn't* missing, that he *hasn't* run away, and I feel sick.

When Epstein calls back later that night he tells me he might apply early decision to Brown and all this other random stuff that I sort of listen to.

"Did you watch seven movies already this weekend?"

"Just one. *The Lego Movie* with the twins."

"That was nice of you," he says. "You don't seem like the *Lego Movie* type."

Not really, I think, wondering if I should tell him what's going on. *You gave him a blow job. He licked your vagina! You're 99.9 percent sure he's your boyfriend.*

"Well, Toby is, uh, kind of, uh, missing," I say. "He's been gone all day. That's why I watched the movie with my brothers. I needed something mindless."

"Oh no, Amelia. That's terrible. You must be so worried." Epstein sounds alarmed, which isn't the reaction I wanted. I'm not sure what I wanted but definitely not alarm. "I'm sorry, Amelia. That's really . . ." He trails off.

"Scary," I say. "It's really scary. Toby wouldn't do this. It doesn't make sense."

"I heard once that one in five teens under the age of eighteen will run away at least once."

"Oh." I'm not in the mood for a list of Random Epstein Facts. Especially when they're about runaway teens. "He hasn't run away. It's not like that."

"Did you ever tell your parents about what happened?"

"About what?"

"The stuff by the washing machine that night? His hallucinations."

I feel annoyed that Epstein's bringing up that night. Is this how he sees my brother?

"Amelia?"

"I gotta go."

"Keep me posted."

As soon as I end the call with Epstein, Ray calls.

"Toby home yet?"

"No."

"Your mom left me two voicemails."

"I know. She's been calling everyone. It's embarrassing."

"It's not embarrassing. She's worried. Where could he be?"

I close my eyes, trying to connect with Toby's spirit, but that's ridiculous. "What if he was kidnapped?"

"Why would he be kidnapped?"

"I don't know. Do you think he's a heroin addict?"

"No."

"A lot of people secretly do heroin. You have no idea they have a drug problem until you read that they're dead on PerezHilton.com. Philip Seymour Hoffman, Heath Ledger."

"You watch too many movies."

"He's been smoking tons of pot, Ray." Philip Seymour Hoffman was a pothead in *Boogie Nights*. And a drug addict in *Before the Devil Knows You're Dead*. And Plutarch Heavensbee in *The Hunger Games*, which doesn't really work with the drug theme.

"Pot isn't heroin," Ray says. "It's mostly legal."

I want to stop thinking about Philip Seymour Hoffman. "I know. Toby is probably at some girl's house. He wouldn't run away, would he?"

"No."

"I know," I say, feeling relieved. Silly Epstein and his silly stats.

"Should I come over?"

"Nah. I think I might go to sleep."

"Really? It's not even eight o'clock."

"I'm tired."

"Okay. Text me the second you hear something."

"I will."

I call Toby twice more after Ray and I hang up, but it goes straight to voicemail each time.

I lie on my bed, thinking that I'll get up to brush my teeth and put on pajamas, but surprisingly I really do fall asleep because the next thing I know my mom is gently shaking me and I'm still in my clothes. "Amelia," she says softly. "Sorry to wake you, but Dad and I are going to work."

"Is . . ." I look at my clock, totally shocked that it's already 6:00 AM.

"No," she says, sitting on the edge of my bed. "Toby's not home. I left last year's yearbook and three recent pictures of him on the table . . . The cops need a picture. Someone will stop by. *Jesus*."

"It's going to be okay," I tell my mom. "He's not *really* missing." It doesn't surprise me that my dad is going to work, but I'm surprised that my mom is going, too.

"I'll leave work as soon as I can. Dad thinks it's better for me to be busy, and we're really short-staffed." She sighs and I feel mad at my dad. If my mom wants to worry about Toby at home, why can't she?

"Honey, I didn't call Grandma yet. I don't want her to worry or rush back from Montreal. Can you stay here? She'll be back this afternoon." My mom sighs deeply.

"I can be here all day."

She hugs me.

After my mom leaves, I can't fall back asleep so I go downstairs where the twins are on the couch, head to head, already glazed over by TV. A box of cereal and a gallon of milk are on the coffee table. Spoons and bowls are noticeably absent. Such a Toby move. I look at the clock. 6:55. *Come on, Toby—come home.*

"Scoot over," I say, standing over Sam and David. Grudgingly they make room for me. I sit in between them, vaguely comforted by their matching Halloween pajamas and comatose presence.

"Did Toby run away, Meals?" Sam asks.

David flicks Sam in the head with his fingers. "Probably from your tattle-telling, Shithead."

Sam howls.

"Apologize," I tell David.

David says nothing.

"Say you're sorry," Sam demands. "That hurt."

"I'm going to turn off the TV if you can't get along," I say. "You're taking total advantage. You're never allowed screen time this early."

"Sorry, Sam," David says robotically.

"When I was your age I went to church," I say, knowing I sound like a boring grown-up. "Grandma took me and Toby every Sunday. And Toby didn't run away. There's a simple explanation." *Please let there be a simple explanation.*

They nod, back in the trance of *Phineas and Ferb*, so I get up and walk into the kitchen, sit at the table, and look at the pictures of my brother. In one picture he's holding up a jar of applesauce and grinning. Another picture is of the four kids sitting on the porch. The twins are on Toby's lap and Kepler is on mine. The picture in last year's yearbook is the best, though. Most guys wear button-downs or sweaters for picture day, but last year Toby wore my grandfather's porkpie hat and tight pin-striped suit, with an enormous wing-tip-collared shirt he bought at the Salvation Army. He looked so outrageous that even the teachers talked about it.

"Where is he?" I ask Kepler as I let her out. I wipe a

trail of crumbs off the table and into the garbage. How did it get to be 8:15? I sit back down at the table. I look at my fingernails. I kick my left slipper off with my right foot. Then I bend down and put my slippers back on. I can't help but think of *12 Years a Slave, The Call,* and the stupid Michael Bay one with Mark Wahlberg. Plus there's *Changeling* and *Gone Baby Gone* and *Argo* and *Gone Girl. Ben Affleck is kind of into kidnapping.* I let the dog back in. *Come on, Toby.* I squeeze my eyes shut. *Come home, come home, come home.* I pick up the landline, hang it up. No more movies, I tell myself. *Come on, Toby.* I will my thoughts to travel into his brain. *Come home.*

The doorbell rings.

"I'll get it!" Sam screams.

Please don't be the cops. The cops only come for the picture of the missing teenager in the movies. And they never find them alive and well.

"Toby!" David howls. "Toby's home!"

I call Ginger's. My mom picks up in half a ring.

"He's home!"

"Thank God," my mom says. I can practically feel her relief pulsing through the phone. "Is he okay? Put him on."

"Yeah. Okay." I walk into the living room, where Toby is sitting on the couch. He looks terrible. His sweatshirt is ripped in the back; there are dark bags under his eyes. The twins stand five feet in front of him, like they're afraid to get too close.

"He'll call you back." I hang up before she can say anything.

"I can't find my keys," my brother says. "I've looked everywhere."

"Toby! Where the——? Where have you been?"

"Looking for my keys," he says calmly.

"Where are your shoes?" Sam asks.

I look at my brother's feet and see that he's only wearing filthy socks.

"Lost 'em," Toby says, as if it's the most natural thing in the world to come home without shoes.

"Sam, David, go get . . . Go get Toby a juice."

"Can I have one too?" David asks.

I nod. "Yeah."

They run into the kitchen.

"What the fuck, Toby? We've been totally freaking out. Why didn't you answer your phone or leave a note? I sent you like fifty texts."

"I didn't have time to leave a note."

I shake my head. "What are you talking about? It takes two seconds. You've been totally unreachable. Mom and Dad called the freaking police! They were going to come over for your picture!"

"I thought I wrote a letter," he says.

"Now that they know you're alive, Mom and Dad are going to be super pissed."

I shut up when David comes back in with Toby's juice.

"I don't know where my keys are," Toby tells us again.

"Yeah. You said that. It's okay." I take a deep breath. "Thanks," I tell Sam and David. "Why don't you go up to your room now."

"Can I use your iPad?" David asks.

"Yeah."

The house phone rings. I know my parents want to talk to Toby. But is he just going to tell them he couldn't find his keys?

"Don't answer it!" I yell upstairs as loudly as I can. "Don't pick up, guys." I feel guilty, but it's better to protect my brother.

"Who picked you up?" I ask, pretending not to hear my cell phone ringing. "Who were you out with?"

"It's not important, Amelia. What's important is the keys. Anyone could find them."

"They'll give them back. Everyone knows your yellow submarine keychain."

"Will you help me look for them?"

I remember the time when I was around the twins' age and tried on my mom's diamond earrings. Then I forgot about them and went scootering. When I discovered I'd lost one, instead of ratting me out, Toby helped me look for almost two hours until we found it inside my sweatshirt hood.

"I'll help you look," I say. "But what are we going to tell Mom and Dad?"

He looks at me.

"You need to say something more than you lost your keys. You've been gone for more than twenty-four hours! Where were you?"

He shrugs. "I can't really tell you at this time."

"What? What do you mean?"

"I will tell you. When the time is right."

"When the time is right? Are you stoned?"

"Maybe a little?"

"Jeez, Toby." I glance at his arms to see if there are any track marks, but I'm not even sure I'd know what a track mark looked like. Besides, Toby's arms look normal.

"Sorry." He gives me a sheepish Toby smile.

The phone rings again.

"It's not me you have to apologize to," I say, although I do feel like I deserve an apology. "How are you going to explain all this?"

"My foot hurts," he says, ignoring everything I've said. He holds up his left foot and I see there's a hole in his sock and a blistery wound under his big toe.

"That doesn't look good. Where are your shoes?"

The phone rings again.

"Can I answer it?" David yells down.

"No," I say. "Toby, look—I *have* to call Mom and Dad back. They're so worried. We have to tell them you're okay. But, Toby—"

"I had no choice, Amelia. I had no choice. I had to get out of here."

That doesn't make any sense. Nothing makes sense. For a second I consider telling my parents how much pot he's been smoking, how most mornings he doesn't bother to get up in time for school, and how he only seems to be hanging out with stoner Toast. But what good would that do? My parents will come flying back from Ginger's, and Toby will be grounded for life and furious that I hadn't helped him out the way siblings in the Secret Sibling Society are supposed to.

"We need an explanation," I tell him. "We need a version that makes sense. A simple explanation."

He looks at me intently.

"Okay . . . We'll say that you woke me up super early Saturday morning and told me you were leaving. You were going . . . camping? No, too cold. How about you went skiing . . . it has to be with someone they don't really know. I know! Arianna. Arianna Kaufman. Ari came home from school and you guys went skiing in Vermont. You lost your phone on the slopes. We'll say that you told me early in the morning that you were leaving, but I was half asleep and completely forgot. You couldn't call because you had no phone."

He yawns.

I can almost picture it. Me, half asleep, cool Toby dressed in hip snowboard gear, whispering to me that he was going with Ari to learn how to snowboard.

Toby coughs deep and rattly.

"Shower before Mom and Dad get home. Clean your foot. You don't want an infection."

He slowly stands up. "And then we'll look for my keys, right?"

"Yeah," I say, even though I have no idea where to look since he hasn't told me where he was. "I'm glad you're okay, Toby." I go into the kitchen to call my parents. My mom answers right away, answering with, "Amelia!" instead of "Ginger's."

"He's fine," I tell her. "He just came home. We don't need the police."

"You're sure? How come no one answered the phone? It's been ringing and ringing. I almost called the police."

"We don't need the police, Mom. Toby is here."

"Thank God. Here's Dad."

"Put him on," my dad says. Unlike my mom, he sounds more angry than relieved.

"He's showering."

"Why did you hang up?"

"Sam broke a glass." I look at the dishes in the sink. "I had to clean it up before someone cut an artery."

Please don't let him ask me any questions, I pray. *Please just say you're happy Toby is home and the restaurant is busy so I should be a good egg and hold down the fort.*

"Where the hell was he?"

Shit. "Well, see, it was kind of my fault, Dad."

"*Your fault?* What the hell do you mean *your* fault?"

I need to just say it and say it quickly. "He went snowboarding. With Ari, his kind-of girlfriend. Remember her? She came back from college. Toby came into my room really early Saturday morning to tell me, but I totally forgot because I was half asleep. He didn't want to wake you guys. Then he, like, lost his phone on the slopes but he didn't think it was such a big deal since he figured I would've told you." I take a deep breath. "I'm just mad I didn't think to text Ari . . ."

My dad breathes heavily. "He doesn't ski."

"Snowboarding. He's good at it—you know, from all his skateboarding." *This isn't really a lie,* I tell myself. Toby is definitely the kind of person who could be an excellent snowboarder.

"This sounds a little far-fetched, Amelia."

"It's true, Dad. It really was my mistake."

"He went skiing? With his prom date?"

"Yeah. Snowboarding."

"In Vermont?"

"Yeah."

"And he lost his phone?"

"Uh-huh."

"Really?"

"Yeah. And his keys, too. I guess he had some terrific wipe out and everything in his pocket just went sailing into a crazy snowbank." *You're talking too much.* I glance over at the hooks on the shelf and see Toby's keys. *They were here the whole time?* Toby is going to be so happy!

"You're not lying, are you, Amelia? You're not trying to cover up for Toby?" My dad's questions jolt me back to reality. *Am I lying for my brother?* I wonder. Nothing he wouldn't do for me.

"Amelia?"

"No. I'm a terrible liar, remember?"

He grunts into the phone. "He's there now?"

"Yeah. In the shower."

"Alright. Mom's coming home. Hold down the fort till she's there, will ya?"

"Sure, Dad," I say, incredibly relieved. I hang up and pick up my brother's keys. Having the yellow submarine keychain in my hand makes me feel a million times better. Toby is home. I've got the keys. I'm pretty sure my parents believe me. Everything is fine.

Act II: Scene 3

AMELIA is twelve years old.

TOBY is fourteen years old.

FADE IN:

INT. AMELIA'S ROOM. NIGHT.
A CLOCK ON THE DRESSER SAYS 9:30 PM.

AMELIA is lying on her bed with her head in her arms.

TOBY knocks on the door.

Amelia, looking miserable, opens it.

                    AMELIA
                    What?

                    TOBY
What's wrong? I thought I heard you
crying or moaning or something.

                    AMELIA
I have a book report due on stupid
C. S. Lewis. I have to compare

and contrast *The Voyage of the
Dawn Treader* and *Prince Caspian*.

TOBY

And? You haven't finished?

AMELIA

I haven't even read them and Mrs. O'Brien
is going to kill me. She hates me
and Mom and Dad will kill me and—

TOBY

Calm down. I'll help you.

AMELIA

Did you read them? Even one of them
would be good. Do you have a report on it?
Do you think Mrs. O'Brien will remember
that you wrote it?

TOBY

Dude, relax. I don't have a report. I didn't
read those books. But I'll help you.

AMELIA

But they're long books. And Mrs. O'Brien
is a hawk for stuff on the Internet.
She flunked Matt Daley for the
whole quarter when he did it!

TOBY
We don't need to steal anything.
Relax, you look up biographical information
about the author. Don't use Wikipedia.
Use sites from colleges.

Amelia shrugs.

TOBY
It'll totally work. You read the first
half of *Voyage*. That's only seven chapters.
Maybe read the last five pages, too. I'll
read the first five pages of *Prince Caspian*
and the last seven chapters. That'll give
us plenty to write about.

AMELIA
We're still going to be up so late.

TOBY
You have a date or something?

FADE OUT.

FADE IN:
INT. AMELIA'S ROOM. CLOCK SAYS 2:30 AM.
The report is in Amelia's backpack. Both
kids are yawning.

AMELIA

Thanks so much, Toby. That was so nice
of you. I feel like I actually read both
books!

TOBY

No problem. You should go to bed.
School starts in five hours.

AMELIA

Aren't you going to bed?

TOBY

I have to study for a math test.

AMELIA

You stayed up to help me when you have a
test? Are you crazy?

TOBY

It's not a big deal. You seemed really
upset. And you're my sister.

FADE OUT.

7

BAD SCENES FROM A MALL

MONDAY AFTER SCHOOL, FOR NO REASON OTHER than not wanting to take the bus since Prudence is already gone from the parking lot, I tell Muppet I'll go with her to the mall. Unfortunately I forgot that since she and Toast are bizarrely going out she no longer drives, so I have to sit in the back of Toast's car listening to them talk to each other in grossly cute baby talk. Toast parks in a super-faraway spot because he wants to smoke a joint. There's no way I'm getting high with them, so I tell them to come find me at CinnaYum!

"Work got even more sucky," Ray says when I walk up to her stand. "Corporate says we have to wear hairnets. I just got a company-wide email about it." She makes a face. "As if these stupid hats aren't bad enough." Ray's work uniform is a ponytail under a blue baseball cap, a blue-and-white-striped blousy thing, and a high-cut blue vest. Even a non-fashionable chick like me knows it's horrendous.

"That stinks," I say, trying to decide if I want a Cinna-Yum! stick or bun.

"Did you come with Toby?" Ray asks.

I ignore the lilt in her voice when she says my brother's name. I shake my head. "Muppet and Toast."

"Random."

"Me going with them or them hanging out together?"

"Both."

"Yeah . . . I don't know. Why did she stop driving once they got together?"

Ray shrugs. "The world is probably a little safer without Muppet driving."

"Yeah, I guess you're right. Toast does seem like a better driver, even if he's perpetually high. I wouldn't stop driving just because I got a boyfriend. It's not very feminist of Muppet to take the backseat in the relationship. Ha. Get it. Backseat."

"You didn't start driving when you got a boyfriend, either," Ray says.

Epstein is totally my boyfriend. He has to be. I should have asked him when we were picking apples. I hate not knowing 100 percent. *But what if he says no? What if he doesn't want a girlfriend?* "Yeah. Well. How did Muppet and Toast even happen?"

"I have no idea," Ray says. "But here they come."

We watch Muppet and Toast glide toward us.

Ray gives them her fake work smile. "Hi! Your day is about to get CinnaYummy! How can I help you?"

Toast grins. "I'd like a dozen of your biggest buns."

Ray hooks him up with four free ones. "Don't sit too close or my manager will be suspicious."

We watch them float hand in hand to the far end of the food court.

"Freaks," Ray says. "If you don't mind sticking around I can drive you home. Unless you want to go with Muppet and Toast."

"I'll go with you. Do you think Toast has ever not been high?"

She shakes her head. "I think he came into this world smoking a doobie."

Five minutes later, Muppet saunters over. "Those were the best buns ever in my whole entire life," she says.

"You're very welcome," Ray says.

"We're going to Hot Topic. Do you want to come, Amelia?"

"Seriously?" I ask. "Hot Topic?"

"You want to come?"

"No, thanks. I'm kind of broke. I'll wait here."

"We'll come back before we leave."

After she's gone, I say, "I would really hate to be stoned in the mall. It's kind of fun at someone's house, but I would be so paranoid here."

"That's why we're not complete burnouts."

"It seems lonely to spend your whole day just out of it."

"Yeah. So . . . don't get mad, Amelia. But where *was* Toby last weekend?"

"I told you. Skiing with Ari. In Vermont."

Ray gives me a look. "The thing is . . . I'm Facebook friends with Ari. It's random but I happened to see her post about homecoming on Saturday. A bonfire football thing. Nothing about skiing."

Shit, shit, shit. Why did I lie to Ray? And Epstein?

"Don't tell my parents," I say.

"I can't believe you think I'd do that. I'm seriously offended."

"Sorry. I know you wouldn't."

"So where was he? Really?"

"I don't know," I admit. "He never told me."

"That's weird."

"I guess. But he couldn't find his keys . . ." *But they were at home the whole time, which is definitely weird.*

Ray shifts her hat. "Your brother has been acting really strange lately."

"No, he hasn't," I say without thinking. "I mean, no stranger than usual." I close my eyes for an extralong second and then open them. *The Secret Sibling Society protects siblings above all.* Ray's an only child—it makes sense that she wouldn't get it.

Ray shrugs and scrapes icing off a knife. "He wasn't in gym again today."

"Ms. Fenster loves him," I remind her. "Remember how he convinced the boys' soccer team to share the field with the girls' when they went to State?"

She nods. "That was cool. But I don't know how many classes he can miss without failing."

"He's not going to fail gym." I laugh. "Don't worry, Ray. Toby is totally fine. We watched *Skyfall* last night." I sound a lot more defensive than I'd like.

"I guess." Ray doesn't sound convinced.

"We might do a Bonding with Bond marathon," I say, even though Toby randomly walked out just as Patrice fell to his death.

Toast walks over to us. "Hey, Amelia," he drawls. On top of his flannel, he's now wearing a T-shirt with a picture of Bryan Cranston that says "Heisenberg" underneath. "This awesome shirt was eighty percent off. How great is that?"

"Pretty great," Ray says.

"We're going to split now. You want a ride home, Amelia?"

"Sure."

"I thought you were waiting for me." Ray sounds hurt.

"It's okay." I try to sound casual. "I'm more on Toast's way than yours."

"Really?" Ray gives me a don't-be-mad-at-me-just-because-I-called-you-out look.

Back in Toast's car, I feel like a bad person for leaving Ray so abruptly and for lying about my brother's whereabouts. It's one thing for me to lend him money and not blab to my parents about his increased pot habit, but it feels weird to keep stuff from Ray. One of the best things about Ray is how honest she is. She'll totally announce to a roomful of people that she needs to go take a shit or complain that the lunch burritos have made her a fart factory. I'm not that way at all, but Ray is my best friend. I'm always honest with her. Then again, why is she worrying about my brother? She's not related to him. She just likes him and wants to see him in stupid gym. Because he's awesome Toby Anderson.

My phone buzzes.

"You're not going to believe this," Epstein says.

"What?"

"I'm free."

"Huh?"

"I finished all my supplemental essay prompts on why my butt is cuter than the other applicants' butts. I have no more colleges left to visit and I won't swear on it, but I think my mom finally has run out of emails I should send to her third cousin's best friend's sister who went to Yale in 1970 or Dartmouth in 1995. I'm done."

"Really?"

"Yup! Want to visit? My parents really want to meet you. Or I can come up again. I don't mind."

I look at the back of Toast's acned neck and think about how I just made things weird between Ray and me, and how, these days, my brother is even weirder. "I'll come down," I say. "I'd love to spend a weekend in the city."

"Awesome. My parents will be psyched."

"What about you?"

"I won't think of anything else."

"I can't wait," I tell him.

8

THIS TOWN REALLY SUCKS
WITHOUT WHEELS

UNFORTUNATELY, IT SEEMS LIKE ALL THE WORLD wants me to do is wait to see Epstein. The week is endless, with days of standardized state testing, a brutal math test I know I bombed, and a fetal pig heart dissection lab. Plus, I'm stuck taking the bus every morning because Toby somehow dropped econ. I'm so ready for the week to be over that, for the second time in my so-called high school life, I cut class. This time, it's to eat at McDonald's with Ray and Muppet.

Of course, as soon as we get there, I totally regret it.

"I shouldn't have cut class," I tell them. "I don't know what got into me." It was one thing to blow off half of French and music for Toby and his peace pipe last spring, but math is another story. Without the protective bubble of cool Toby, I feel like I'll get busted. Muppet, who must be stoned, says, "Hash browns are like the world's best invention. Who invented them? Mr. Brown?"

Ray nods.

"I shouldn't have skipped class," I say. "Or gotten this McMuffin. It's just going to make me bloated."

"You're not fat, Amelia," Muppet says.

"You should talk," I tell her. Muppet is a lot thinner and taller than I am.

"You skinny bitches better not say anything about being fat," Ray says. "I'm breaking Paleo for this shit."

"You're doing that again?" At least four times a year Ray goes on some random vegan diet for a week. She isn't fat, but she's got a butt and hips and since her mom is *really* heavy, I know she worries about her weight. Plus, I'd never be able to work at CinnaYum! without eating all kinds of crap.

"My stepmom does 4-Hour Body stuff," Muppet tells her. "But I think it's basically Paleo. Except on Sundays. On Sundays she eats shit all day." She looks down at her hands like she's never seen them before. Then she looks up at me. "Are you so excited to see Epstein?"

"She better be. It's all she's been freaking talking about," Ray says.

"Sorry," I say. I never actually said sorry for leaving so abruptly in the mall, but I texted her a bunch of emoticons when I got home, which she responded to with more emoticons, so I assumed we were okay.

"I'd be so sad if my boyfriend lived far away," Muppet says sympathetically. "Sometimes I think Toast is too far and he's only a mile from my stepdad's." She giggles.

Did Toast and Muppet have a Defining the Relationship conversation? I have to have one with Epstein this weekend. "It's two hours by train," I tell her. "It could be worse."

"Ha," Ray says.

Muppet and I look at her.

She shrugs, gets up, and storms into the women's restroom. She pushes the door kind of hard, causing it to go in and out a bunch of times.

"What's with her?" Muppet asks.

"I don't know."

"Maybe she needs a boyfriend. Maybe she's jealous because we have boyfriends and she doesn't."

"Maybe," I say, although Ray isn't the type to be jealous or to want a boyfriend just to have one. And she wouldn't kiss Toast for a million bucks!

"I think she likes your brother," Muppet says.

"Oh. Yeah. I guess." I remember the conversation we had about him in the mall and feel slightly ill.

Muppet squirts ketchup on the last of her hash browns. "I guess Toby isn't interested."

"I don't know. We haven't talked about it."

"I don't think he's interested in any girl. Not that he's gay. I guess he's more into the Beatles, his poems, and *Lord of the Rings* stuff." Muppet empties an entire packet of ketchup into her mouth and swallows. "Toast says he doesn't even want to play video games that much anymore."

Ray clomps back to our table. "You guys ready? Second period is going to start." She doesn't sound pissed anymore. But when we get to school, she announces that she's going home.

"Really?" I look at her. "Why?"

"I'm PMS-y. I need a personal day."

"I'd skip, but I have lab," Muppet says in a very Muppet-like way. I wait for Ray to make fun of her, but she doesn't.

"Have fun in the city," she tells me.

"Yeah, thanks."

As I sneak past the side-door guard and slip into the locker room for gym class, I realize that without Ray I don't have a ride to the train station. My parents are at work and my grandmother is antiquing with Harry. A taxi from school will cost me almost thirty dollars and I don't want to show up for a weekend in NYC with only ten dollars.

I walk down the hall cursing myself for not driving or having a job. Toby really needs to pay me back.

Shit, shit, shit, I think as I whack a tennis ball across the court to Sonia Sanchez. We're partners only because her BFF Madi Richter is absent.

"Great serve, Amelia," Ms. Fenster, the gym teacher, calls.

"Jeez, Amelia," Sonia says. "You're making me work over here."

"Sorry."

"I don't want to sweat." Sonia makes a face. "When Madi is here our goal is, like, to *not* sweat."

I run up to the net. "Sorry. Hey, Sonia. Do you have a car?"

She looks at me strangely, which makes sense since we haven't said more than ten words to each other since seventh grade. I have nothing against Sonia, but her friends are the girls who always wear tons of makeup and go to all the boys' games to flirt. Basically the only thing Sonia and I have in common is the tennis ball between us.

"Yeah. I have a car. Why?"

"I need a ride. To the train station. To visit my, um, boyfriend. He lives in Manhattan." *I like saying boyfriend. I hope it's true.*

"I would," Sonia says, "but I have to work and the station is on the other side of town from where I need to be. I'm an aide at the nursing home by Oakes Park."

I feel like such a loser. Of course Sonia has a job. Which explains why she's wearing Under Armour and I'm in a pair of ratty Gap sweats.

"You don't have a car?"

I shake my head. "I don't even have a license."

Sonia looks at me like I have nine heads. "Why the fuck not? You're sixteen, right?"

"Almost seventeen. I don't know. I'm an idiot."

"Driver's Ed is fun. Mr. Munson is the man. This town really sucks without wheels."

"I know."

"What about Rayelle?"

"She's not here."

"That tall skinny girl? Pointy chin? She's your friend, right?"

"Muppet. Yeah, I guess. Her boyfriend drives her all over now. Toast."

"Ewww. That boy's a skeez." Sonia makes a face. "What about your cute brother?"

For some reason I'm happy that Sonia called Toby cute. "Yeah . . . I guess I'll ask him. If I can find him."

"I'm tired," Sonia whines. "I'm going to tell Ms. Fenster I'm hypoglycemic."

And just like that, Sonia Sanchez disappears and I spend the rest of PE smacking the hell out of the ball on the backboard. I tell myself that as soon as the bell rings I'm going to the office and signing up for Driver's Ed. Sonia is right. This town really sucks without wheels.

But after gym, instead of signing up for Driver's Ed, I go

to Smoker's Gate, which is behind the shed where the lawn mowers and salt stuff are kept. It's illegal to smoke anywhere on school grounds, but the rule is only enforced at Smoker's Gate about twice a year. Toast is there, blowing smoke rings for some bored-looking emo sophomores. Abdi Osman is there too with a camera.

"Hey, Toast. Hey, Abdi," I say. I nod politely to the emo kids next to them because school shootings make you think twice about making enemies. "Have you seen my brother?"

"Yeah," Toast says slowly.

I wait for him to continue but he doesn't.

"Where did you see him? When?" *Stoned people are so annoying. Do I get this stupid when I smoke pot?*

Toast looks at his phone. "Um. An hour ago?"

Abdi puts his camera down. "Toby said he was going to forage for food. Ten minutes ago."

"So he's in the cafeteria?"

Abdi shrugs. "I'm just filming. Documenting."

"He's going to make me the next Ryan Gosling," Toast says, grinning.

"Thanks," I say to Abdi.

It seems like a miracle that Toby actually is in the cafeteria, sitting in the back, with a full plate of fries that look, from the amount of ketchup on them, like they've been the victims of a murder. He's hunched over his notebook and doesn't look up when I slide across from him.

"Hey, Toby."

He looks up, startled, like he had no idea I was there. "What? What do you want?"

"A ride. At 2:45 to the train station. Please, please, *please?*"

He looks back at his notebook.

"I *really* need to make the train, Toby. Please! I haven't seen Epstein since forever."

"Okay."

"You can't flake. We have to leave right at 2:45 or I won't make the train."

"2:45," my brother says, slightly monotone.

"I owe you," I say, even though if he'd paid me back I wouldn't be in this situation. "Why are you sitting by yourself way back here?" Normally Toby sits with all the popular people.

"I'm working," he mumbles.

I can't remember a time when Toby chose school over friends, but I guess it's good. "Are you eating your fries?"

He shakes his head and I help myself to a few. They're soft, cold, and gross, but I eat them anyway.

"I can hear you chewing," he says.

"Huh? These things are so mushy there's nothing to chew. They're like baby food. What are you writing?"

He closes the notebook. "Just some things. Important things."

I try to see what's in the book, but he covers it quickly. I notice that his fingernails are stubby and bitten.

"Fine," I say, getting up. "Be that way with your secret information. I'm going to class. See you at 2:45." Toby seems not exactly stoned, but *something*. But I'm so glad he's going to drive me that I decide not to think about it. I also decide to forget about signing up for Driver's Ed. *Maybe I'll just be one of those people who never learns to drive.* I'll live in areas with good public transportation or be rich enough to have a driver.

The rest of the day creeps by. I only come up with two Cinematic Chauffeur Movies (*Driving Miss Daisy* and *The Princess Diaries*) and Mr. Norton rambles on so monotonously about integrating multiple sources of information that I can barely keep my eyes open. Finally, the bell rings and miraculously, Toby is sitting in his car when I get there.

"Thanks!" I shout over "Dear Prudence." "Have you been here awhile?"

He nods and backs out of the spot. *Did he skip all his classes today? Flunking an entire marking period isn't going to get him into college. And I can't cover for his report card. My parents can log on to the school website for that whenever they want.*

Don't be like Mom, I tell myself. It doesn't matter. Toby is Toby. He'll do what he wants, when he wants, and for a good reason.

"*Look around round. Look around round round. Look around,*" Lennon or McCartney yells.

"You're going to go deaf," I tell Toby.

"You have to listen to really hear, Amelia. Prudence is, like, prudent and that's how God is. This song is really about the Beatles trying to get us to, like, believe in God. It's about God."

"I thought the Beatles were anti-God. Didn't John Lennon get in trouble for saying that the band was more popular than Jesus?"

I thought my brother would be pleased about my Beatles trivia, but he guns it through a yellow light at a busy intersection just as two SUVs are about to turn. I will kill my brother if I die and don't get to see Epstein again.

When we get across in one piece, I say, "Jeez, Toby. Yellow doesn't mean speed up. You gave me a heart attack."

"This song is so good," Toby says. "The message is in here, too."

I look out the window at the passing houses, a Gold's Gym, two banks, a package store, and Kepler's vet.

"The message!" Toby sounds excited. "You hear it, right?"

"What are you talking about?" I look at him.

"You know. The meaning of it."

"In the song?"

He shakes his head. "Between the song. You have to listen hard for it." He turns the volume up.

I turn the volume down. "It's too loud. I don't hear any message. I just hear the words to the stupid song and it's giving me a headache."

Toby makes an unusually wide left turn onto State Street.

"What are you doing this weekend?" I ask.

"Don't know."

"I saw Toast before. He seemed pretty fucked up."

"Toast is Toast. You can't just try to control everyone, Amelia."

"What are you talking about?"

"Just because you're not in the inner circle doesn't mean you can just destroy it. I know you know what I mean."

I feel my blood boil. Why is my brother constantly trying to mess with me? "I don't know, Toby. I don't know what you mean at all. I'm not trying to control anyone. All I did was ask if you had any plans this weekend. A pretty normal question for two people trying to have a normal conversation." I look at him, but he's focused on the road. "I have no idea what you mean by the inner circle. What is it? What are you talking about?"

Toby looks at me like I'm the one who's acting like a freak. "Forget it." He turns into the parking lot. "You wouldn't understand."

"Thanks for the ride," I say sarcastically.

"Can I borrow some money?"

I stare at him. He has some nerve. "Are you kidding? For what?"

"Stuff."

"What stuff?" My heart speeds up. If Toby is on real drugs, I'll tell my parents. Heroin or Molly or meth would trump the Secret Sibling Society. "You owe me money, Toby."

"I want to get *Sgt. Pepper's*."

"A CD?" I feel a wave of relief.

"Mine's scratched."

"Download it. No one buys CDs anymore, Toby."

"It's not the same. I need to hold the actual CD in my hands. Please, Amelia. I just want to go to the mall on my way to Toast's."

I feel stupid for thinking my Beatles-obsessed brother is a heroin addict. I open my wallet and hand him a twenty. "I can't believe I'm doing this."

"*Grazie*," he says. "'In this country, you gotta make the money first.'"

"'Then when you get the money, you get the power. Then

when you get the power, then you get the women.' *Scarface*," I
say, almost happy. "But still. Toby. Pay me back. Work at Ginger's. Mom and Dad always want another busser."

He nods.

"Pick me up on Sunday. After brunch. I'll be home in the
late afternoon. I'll text from the train."

He nods.

"Don't forget. And answer your phone for a change." I
notice the bags under his eyes. Maybe it's good he has no plans
other than getting a CD and hanging out with Toast. He needs
to catch up on sleep.

I get out of the car, walk up to the platform, get my ticket,
and look up and down the track. There's no sign of the train.
It's crazy that, after all the stress of getting here, I'm early. I
glance back over the railing and notice that Prudence is still in
the lot. Why would Toby wait? I walk down the ramp to get a
closer look. Toby's eyes are closed and he's bopping his head.
I think I can hear the music all the way up here, which must
mean he's making himself completely deaf. I think he's taken
his shirt off, too, even though it's cold. *He's such a weirdo.*
But then the train comes barreling down the track, and when
the doors open, I get on, plop down on the seat, and forget all
about my bizarre, annoying older brother.

THE MOVIE VERSION

Act III: Scene 4

AMELIA is fourteen years old

TOBY is sixteen years old

DAVID and SAM are five years old

FADE IN:

INT. ANDERSON'S KITCHEN. CHRISTMASTIME.

There are decorations around the room and
holiday music is playing in the background.
AMELIA is sitting at the kitchen table
watching something on the iPad. SAM and
DAVID burst into the room, their arms
full of bags from toy stores.

DAVID
. . . And the bow-and-arrow set is so awesome.

SAM
Yeah. And that Minecraft pillow
is really cool, too.

AMELIA
Huh? Did you guys rob a toy store or something?

DAVID
No! We bought this stuff.
With our own money!

AMELIA
You're kidding.

SAM
It's not for us.
It's for . . . charity!

AMELIA
What do you guys know about charity?

TOBY walks in with more gift bags
and rolls of wrapping paper.

DAVID
We know all about it.
Toby taught us all about it.

Toby nods and smiles at Amelia.

AMELIA
I thought you were going to wash
Toby's car. How did this turn into
a charity-shopping extravaganza?

TOBY

We were washing the car and the boys
were doing a stellar job. We saw a
Toys for Tots box at the car wash
and got to talking . . .

SAM

talking very quickly

And we found ten dollars in the seat of
Toby's car. And instead of going to buy stuff
for us we bought stuff for a poor boy (or
maybe a girl but hopefully a boy) who won't
get enough at Christmas. Because Christmas is
about being thankful for what you have and
being generous. Because we're lucky.

DAVID

We have a nice house and food and we
always get a lot of presents. But lots
of kids don't have all that.

AMELIA

Wow. That's so nice. It looks like you got
more than ten dollars' worth of stuff, though.

TOBY

The twins decided that they would each give
five dollars. So I thought I'd contribute, too.

AMELIA
quietly
You must have spent over
a hundred dollars, Toby.

TOBY
shrugs
It's for charity.

DAVID
And that's not all. After we wrap the
presents, we're going to put them in the Santa
box! And then we're going to get the big jug
of change in Toby's room and we're going to
go to the grocery store and buy all kinds of
foods that poor people might want to eat!

SAM
Toby thinks he might have fifty dollars! Can
we go do that now, Toby? We're going to go to
a food bank, Amelia. It's like a bank but
instead of money they have food. We're going
to bring them bags and bags of good food.

TOBY
smiling and nodding
Sure Sam, sure David. Be careful
with that jug. It's really heavy.

The twins run upstairs.

AMELIA
looks at Toby
I don't know how you did that, Toby. Yesterday David and Sam fought over every toy in the house. And now, they're buying for other kids and excited to go to a food bank!

TOBY
It's just the Christmas Spirit. That's it.

AMELIA
really looking at Toby
No, it's not just that. It's you, too. It's definitely you.

FADE OUT.

9

COUNTRY PUMPKINS
IN THE BIG APPLE

I HAVE A MILLION EMOTIONS ON THE TRAIN TO NYC.
One second I'm insanely excited and the next I'm freaking
out. What if I get lost? What if Epstein thinks I'm a dorky
country hick? I'm wearing a Banana Republic sweater I borrowed from Ray, but my shoes and jeans aren't anything special. I look out at the train tracks and cable wires just before
we rush into the tunnel of Grand Central station. Am I going
to have sex? What if it hurts, or I'm bad at it? I come up
with Virginity Movies for Virgins (*The Fault in Our Stars,
The 40-Year-Old Virgin, Superbad,* and *The Sessions*) but it
doesn't help my anxiety.

But then, as soon as I step onto the platform, I see Epstein, and he looks really cute. His hair is tousled with gel
and covers most of his ears, and he puts his arms around me
and it feels so good that I could stand there forever in the
throngs of all the businessmen and -women talking quickly
on their cell phones. But eventually, Epstein grabs my hand
and leads me into the main area of the station.

"I'm so happy you're here," he says.

"Me too." I squeeze his hand. I realize that I haven't
been away from home since the summer, and it feels good to
be away.

"And now I'm going to kiss you," Epstein says. The kiss

is warm, slow, very movie version. When we come up for air, he leads me back upstairs, through a passageway, and onto the S train.

"We'll shuttle to Times Square," he explains. "Then we'll get on the 2 or 3 train. Our stop is Ninety-Sixth Street."

At the 72nd Street stop, a bunch of people practically trample me on their way off, but then Epstein reaches for my hand and pulls me toward an empty seat.

"Your hair got long," I tell him. "It grew really fast since the last time I saw you."

"Yeah. My mom wanted me to cut it before my interviews, but I didn't. No one ever got rejected from Dartmouth for having too-long hair."

"Dartmouth," I say. "Wow."

Epstein shrugs. "Might be too 'New Hampshire' for me."

"Long hair is the style now," I say. "My brother's hair is long, too." *Toby's hair is really long, actually.* He could probably wear it in a ponytail, which is not his style.

When we get to 96th Street, I follow Epstein off the train, up Broadway, and over to Riverside Drive to a large white building on the corner of 101st Street. The building seems old but nicely polished with marble floors and a strong, but not bad, smell of pea soup.

"My man," a doorman says, giving Epstein a handshake with one hand and holding the door for me with the other.

"Hey, Oscar. Oscar, this is my girlfriend, Amelia."

I want there to be fireworks flashing when the word "girlfriend" comes out of Epstein's mouth! I feel stupid that I wondered and worried about it for so long.

When Oscar smiles at me, I give him a dorky grin back. Girlfriend! I am a girlfriend. And I didn't even have to have the dreaded DTR! I fight the urge to text Ray that it was totally fine for me not to bring it up.

"My parents home?" Epstein asks Oscar.

Oscar nods. "They just came back from Fairway. Lots of bags."

"Oscar knows everything," Epstein says. "He could ruin the residents with the dirt he knows."

"Me? I know nothing." Oscar pretends to look shocked. "Have a nice visit, Amelia."

"He really does know everything," Epstein says as we walk through the open elevator doors. He pushes eight. "He knows who comes home drunk, who's having late-night visitors, who orders Chinese every night."

Following Epstein out of the elevator and down the hall, I get nervous. What if Epstein's parents don't like me? What if they want him to have an Ivy League girlfriend? I met his aunt and uncle over the summer, but parents seem more serious. If they don't like me, then things could be bad. I think of all the awkward Meeting the Parents movie moments: the terrible *Family Stone*, of course *Meet the Parents* and *Meet the Fockers,* and the scene in *Fever Pitch* when Jimmy Fallon freaks out about hearing the Red Sox score when he's having dinner with Drew Barrymore's parents.

I'm jolted back to real life when Epstein's mom opens the apartment door. The first thing I notice is that she looks just like him. Or rather, he looks like her. Like Epstein, she's got fine, reddish hair, although hers is a little gray. Her ears appear normal-sized but she has his almond-shaped blue eyes, long slim nose, and the same smooth-looking skin. The second thing I notice is that she's a lot thinner than my mom. I guess that's what happens when you don't have four kids or own a restaurant. She's wearing stylish black glasses, a hint of lipstick, a fitted and expensive-looking black top, dark jeans, and a chunky jade necklace that Ray would want.

"Amelia," she says warmly. "It's nice to finally meet you." She hugs me like we've met a hundred times. She smells like a combination of lavender and cinnamon.

"Hi," I say when she ends the hug. "This is for you, Mrs. . . ." I swallow and realize with a panic that I have no idea what to call Epstein's mom. Mrs. Barnes? Ms. Boffee? Mrs. Boffee-Barnes? I feel so flustered that I practically shove the present my mom gave me in her face.

"Call me Isabelle. I insist. Oh, this is lovely. Thank you so much." She looks pleased with the bottle of Meyer lemon–infused olive oil. "Geoff, honey," she calls. "Amelia is here."

"Hello," Epstein's dad says, walking down the hall. "It's nice to meet you, Amelia."

Epstein has mentioned that his dad is weird, but I'm not prepared for how short he is—and how nasally his voice sounds. Not to be shallow, but I like that Epstein is five inches taller than I am and only sounds nasally when he has a cold.

"Thank you for, uh, having me," I say.

"Our pleasure." Isabelle sounds like she means it. "It's so nice to meet the person our son talks about so often." She smiles and I feel like she likes me and that everything will be okay.

"You must want to wash up," Geoff says.

"Dad." Epstein sighs. "He's a germ freak," he explains.

"She was just on the train," Geoff says. "Do you know how—"

"Honey." Isabelle puts her arm around her husband. *What a weird couple*, I can't help but think. She's so pretty and normal and he's so weird.

"Let's show Amelia where she'll sleep," Isabelle says to Epstein.

Epstein and I glance at each other. Two of his best friends are girls and his parents have never had any rules about keeping doors open or anything. But he's never had a girlfriend spending two nights. *Girlfriend*, I think with a thud. *I'm officially 100 percent Epstein's girlfriend!*

I follow Epstein and his mom through the kitchen, which is small but nice in a hanging-fruit-basket, pans-above-the-oven kind of way.

"Help yourself to whatever you want," Isabelle says. "Our food is your food."

The kitchen leads into the living room, where there's a window the entire length of the room overlooking the river. There are a few antique chairs and couches, and a whole back wall is stacked, floor to ceiling, with books.

After the living room, I'm shown an office, which has a small bookcase, a small desk built into the wall, and a futon sofa.

"I told your mom you'd sleep well here," Isabelle says.

"Thanks."

"You should see Epstein's room. He's got the best room

in the whole apartment." I try to imagine my mom telling a boy to go see my room, but it's impossible.

I follow Epstein back down the hall. The room isn't that big, but it's practically glowing from the deep orange sunlight.

"Wow," I say.

"This is the west side of the building so it has the best light, especially in the afternoon. I think it's what photographers call 'low light' because it's, like, warm as opposed to being bright, but I could be wrong." There are concert posters for the Beastie Boys, Phish, String Cheese Incident, Vampire Weekend, and moe. There's also a framed black-and-white picture of the Rolling Stones, a signed Marc Maron poster, and, of course, a million books.

Epstein closes the door and pulls my hand, and I sit down next to him on the bed. "I love having you here. With me. Amelia."

A jolt runs through my body. Epstein saying that he loves having me here is practically him saying he loves me. I feel like I could burst. Epstein rolls over onto his side, takes his glasses off, and puts them on the table next to his bed. The table has more stacks of books, a giant pair of Bose headphones, and lots of issues of *The New Yorker*. *He's so much smarter than I am*, I think, rolling onto my side to look at him. He puts his hands in my hair, which I'm happy I took the time to blow-dry before school. "You're so pretty."

Jolt, jolt, jolt.

"Kiss me," I say, like I'm an old-timey actress.

And he does. And I kiss him back. We are kissing like

I've never kissed before. His lips move onto my lips, my tongue slides onto his tongue, then inside his mouth. My whole body feels awake and electric. I can't imagine anything feeling better than kissing Epstein. My boyfriend, Epstein! He slides his hands under my sweater and onto my bra, and then squeezes my breast.

Jolt, jolt, jolt.

I put my hand on his crotch.

He kisses my forehead and gently picks up my hand. "You don't know how bad I want to. But let's wait. My parents should leave soon."

"They're going out?"

He smiles. "A play. *And* dinner."

We lie there, just smiling at each other for about five minutes. Then I remember that I promised I'd call my mom when I got in. She's still jumpy about Toby "going to Vermont" without telling her, so I call Ginger's. Luckily a waitress answers so I get away with just leaving the message that I'm safe.

After I hang up, Epstein says, "I don't believe it."

"What?"

"I forgot to introduce you to Entirely."

"Entirely?"

He stands up, pulls his chair out from his desk, and reveals the fattest cat I have ever seen.

"Wow! That's a fat cat."

Epstein pets the mound of fur. "You're not fat, honey. You're just big-boned. He's a Maine Coon."

"He takes up the entire chair!"

"Yup." Epstein sounds proud. "Entirely Jones Boffee-Barnes, meet Amelia Jane Anderson. Despite the fact that she just insulted you, she's a pretty nice girl."

I get up to pet the cat. He opens one eye lazily, then closes it. "Sam's the cat lover in my family. My heart belongs to Kepler, but Entirely is a good name. For a cat."

Isabelle knocks on the door. "Ep?"

He opens the door. Isabelle has changed into a black sweater and a long gray skirt and heels. Ray would know all the brands and prices.

"Dad is getting the elevator. I'm really sorry we're not taking you out, Amelia, but we've had these tickets for months."

"That's okay." I hope I don't sound too happy. "Have a good time."

"There's plenty for dinner. Hummus, pita, pizzas in the freezer, chicken if you eat meat."

"We're fine," Epstein says. "You don't need to be a stereotypical Jewish mother, Mom."

I could never talk this way to my parents, but Isabelle just ignores him. "Or go out. Take Amelia to one of our favorite restaurants, Ep. Take the Visa."

In a million years, my parents would never say anything like "take the Visa."

But Toby would approve. This dialogue is totally movie version.

"All right," Isabelle says. "Have a good night. We'll be back late so we'll probably see you in the morning."

"Thanks, Mom," Epstein says impatiently. "Bye."

When we hear the door shut, Epstein scoops Entirely off the chair, puts him in the hall, closes the door, stands behind me, and takes away the Harvard Hillel pamphlet I randomly picked up from his desk. "Shalom," he says, leading me back to the bed, taking off my shirt and unhooking my bra. As soon as we're lying down, he kisses me. Then he slides down the zipper on my jeans. I slide his down. He takes his pants off, then mine. I'm wearing Ray-approved red high-cut Victoria's Secret bikini bottoms that I bought last week. Ray tried to convince me to get a thong but I can't deal with a string up my ass.

Epstein looks at me. "I love you."

"I love you, too," I whisper. I want to scream it over and over again, but then Epstein gently takes off my underwear and just like that, I'm totally naked.

Other than the shower, I can't remember the last time I was totally naked. *With three brothers you just don't spend that much time in your birthday suit*, I think.

Relax, I tell myself. *Stop thinking about your brothers!*

I concentrate on kissing Epstein, try to remember how often I dreamed of seeing him. I do okay for a little while, but then my eyes wander over to his desk and I remember all the fancy colleges he's applying to. Then I think of all the movies that take place in the Ivy League, like *Legally Blonde* and *Good Will Hunting*, and *The Social Network*.

"Amelia?" Epstein looks at me. "Are you— Do you want to?"

"Yeah," I say quickly. "I want to."

I'm sure I want to have sex with Epstein. My mind might be thinking of movies, but I love this city boyfriend of mine.

Epstein slides off me, opens his night-table drawer, and pulls out a condom. I'm relieved he puts it on himself.

Honestly, sex is kind of awkward. Not incredibly so, because I feel like it's mutually awkward, which makes it slightly better. First Epstein's penis gets a little soft when he puts the condom on. Then, after he gets hard again, we have trouble getting his penis inside me. I feel more nervous than excited and when it finally gets inside, it doesn't hurt, but it feels like this thing that's just sort of digging around. Epstein seems a little hesitant at first but then he starts moving faster. I figure I should move, too, so I do, just a bit, but then he whispers that I should slow down, which gives me a complex, so I just lie there. I'm about to get a complex about that, too, when Epstein yelps.

"Sorry," he says.

"Why are you sorry? I'm sorry."

"You have nothing to be sorry for."

"Wasn't I moving too fast?"

"No. You're great. I was just afraid I was going to, you know, come too quickly. Which I did."

"Oh," I say. "It's okay. I don't care." I feel bad saying I don't care because it might sound rude.

"We'll just have to practice," he says, trying to sound all Barry White.

"Practice makes perfect," I say, trying to make my voice even deeper.

"I love you," he says. "I love you, Amelia Jane Anderson."

"I love you, Epstein Boffee-Barnes."

We look at each other, without moving, just lying there.

I feel happy, I realize. The sex wasn't Hollywood, but while we were doing it I didn't think about a single movie or sex scene in a movie! I couldn't think of a better guy to lose my virginity to, either.

I'm amazed at how comfortable I am being totally naked with this Manhattan prep school boy who likes hippie music. *This could be in a movie*, I think. Of course, technology ruins the mood when Epstein gets a bunch of texts. After reading them and frantically texting for five minutes he says, "So, Ramona, Chloe, and Holden are currently at Ramona's apartment, making us dinner. And by 'us' they mean 'you' because they want to meet you. They're my best friends."

"I guess I should meet them."

"Ramona and Chloe are into cooking. Holden is a pain but ridiculously entertaining. You'll love him. All ladies love Holden. The food will be good. Ramona's parents are away."

"Cool. That sounds fun," I say, even though I'm not totally sure.

While we're waiting for the subway, a big man in a filthy coat comes up to us on the platform. "The devil!" he screams. He smells like ash and onion and there are bits of food in his beard. "You and the devil and the pots and pans of redemption."

Part of me wants to laugh because "the pots and pans of redemption" sounds so bizarre, but he's only about a foot away and I'm pretty sure crazy people have pushed innocent bystanders into oncoming trains.

"Samson!" the man hollers at Epstein. "Samson! The

redemption was raped out his ass. Jimi Hendrix, too. I saw Jimi Hendrix. He was raped by the fucking system of assholes."

"Let's mosey," Epstein says calmly. He leads me farther down the platform.

"Assholes!" the man yells. "The world is full of assholes. Everyone's an asshole. Don't I know it?"

"Welcome to the Big Apple," Epstein says. "A city of psychos."

"That never happens where I live."

"Because you live in the 'burbs."

"It's more country than suburbs. Before the twins we lived next to a farm. There were cows and everything."

"Country bumpkin." Epstein squeezes my hand.

"City . . . city pumpkin."

"Pumpkin?" He laughs.

"It's the only thing I could think of." And then we crack up thinking of things that rhyme with "pumpkin" and the people on the train look at us as if *we're* totally crazy.

10

EPSTEIN'S FRIENDS AND RED WINE

I'M INTIMIDATED THAT TWO OF EPSTEIN'S BEST friends are dinner-party-throwing girls, but as soon as Ramona opens the door, I feel better. It's superficial, but I'm happy that while Ramona has a very pretty face, she's short and pear-shaped. Even though I've never seen any pictures of Epstein's other girlfriends, I can tell that she's not his type. I can't take my eyes off Holden, though. I've never seen anyone quite like him. He's very tall with shaggy hair, a prominent Adam's apple, insanely tight velvety pants, and a "Free Pussy Riot!" T-shirt.

"*Finally*," he says to Epstein as Ramona hangs up our coats. "We've been waiting to meet you. For. Like. Ever." He smiles at me.

"Hi" is all I can think of to say, because even though there are LGBTQ students at Washington Lincoln, they mostly hang out with one another except on Coming Out Day, when they rainbow-sticker everything and hand out buttons. Except in movies with terrible gay stereotypes, I've never heard anyone actually talk like Holden. But there's something about Holden—not just his swishy voice, but his entire style—that's captivating.

Ramona smiles. "I'm Ramona. It's nice to meet you, Amelia." I notice that she looks me right in the eyes.

"Thanks for having me over," I say, looking around.

From what I can see Ramona's apartment is twice the size of Epstein's. My amazement must be obvious because Holden says, "Classic six," as we follow Ramona down the hall.

"Huh?"

"A classic six is a living room, dining room, kitchen, two bedrooms, two bathrooms, and a maid's room," Epstein explains. "It's a classic six apartment. Except this is a super-nice classic six."

"Mo's loaded," Holden tells me. "Because her daddy is the vice president of a soul-sucking bank with an ATM on every corner."

"Shut up, Holden," Ramona says. "It's tacky to talk about money. Besides, the soul-sucking bank lets you hang out on Martha's Vineyard every summer."

"True that," Holden says.

We follow Ramona into the kitchen, where Chloe is taking a pan out of the oven.

"Lo, this is Amelia," Epstein says, grabbing a piece of bread off the tray.

"Hey," Chloe says, fake-slapping Epstein's hand. "I'm making bruschetta. It's nice to meet you, Amelia." Chloe is as tall as Epstein with long brown hair pulled over to one side. She's thin and pale with dark brown hair and bangs that have a slight Zooey Deschanel in *(500) Days of Summer* vibe. She has a very angular face and largish feet and hands. Even though she's wearing a black dress and pearl necklace, she doesn't look that dressed up.

"I need a drink," Holden says. "I'm pathologically de-pressed. Where's the vino?"

Even though I just met Holden, I can tell he's just being dramatic.

"Nothing good, Holden," Ramona tells him as he opens a clear fridge that's actually built into the wall.

"Remember that time we drank that, like, five-hundred-dollar bottle?" Chloe laughs.

Ramona shakes her head. "It *wasn't* funny. I don't want to get in trouble."

"Is this okay?" Holden pulls out a bottle of wine. "It's from the middle shelf."

"Google it. If it's more than fifty dollars, no way."

Drinking wine on the Upper West Side with kids named Ramona, Holden, and Chloe makes me feel like I'm in a Wes Anderson movie.

I just wish I liked it. But the wine tastes like wine— bitter and kind of gross. The bruschetta is good, though, and I compliment Chloe.

"Chloe is an amazing cook," Epstein tells me.

"I'm impressed," I say. "Me and my friends never cook anything. Unless you count frozen pizza or nachos."

"Your parents have an awesome restaurant, though," Epstein says.

"Yeah, I guess." Ginger's just seems cute and country compared to wine-drinking in a classic six.

Holden puts his iPhone on the impeccable marble counter in dramatic disgust. "New York men are awful," he says. "They're so faggy."

"Try dating." Chloe sets the timer on her phone. "Instead of Grindr-ing your way through the boroughs, you slut."

"I do not do Queens," Holden says indignantly.

Everyone laughs, but since I feel like they're speaking a different language I just smile. Epstein smiles at me and I remember that about an hour ago his penis was in my vagina. And he said he loves me and that I was his girlfriend!

"It'll be different in San Francisco." Holden gets up and twirls Chloe around. When he dips her, oven mitt still on her hand, we all clap and I *really* feel like I'm in a play.

"You're going to San Francisco?" I ask.

"That's their grand plan," Epstein tells me.

"My parents made me apply to Berkeley," Chloe says. "Because that's where they met and fell in love blah blah. But I won't get in. And if I do, I'm not going."

"Chloe wants to be Alice Waters," Ramona tells me.

"I don't need to be her," Chloe says. "I just want to *learn* from her. Or Dan Barber."

I make a note to Google Alice Waters and Dan Barber.

"I'm going to royally disappoint my parents, who've spent a million dollars educating me, and take classes at the California College of Arts," Holden tells me. "I can't wait to sit around and make tie-dye and macramé all day. That and get to *know* lots of Cali boys."

"You're a junior, right, Amelia?" Ramona asks.

"Yeah." I think about my brother. He's the same age as Epstein and his friends, but he barely talks about college. Even Holden, who just wants to have sex and make tie-dye, seems to have a plan. *Don't stress about it*, I tell myself. It's typical Toby. He'll probably kill it at community college and then transfer to Harvard or somewhere amazing.

When Chloe announces that dinner is ready, we follow her into a huge dining room with incredibly high ceilings, where a long black table is set with black square plates on top of green place mats. The whole thing looks like something out of a cooking magazine, and the rest of the night passes in a delicious food-eating, Holden-making-me-laugh blur. After dinner, when Ramona and Chloe go to prepare some kind of chocolate soufflé, Holden announces to Epstein that he's stealing me.

"Come, darling," he says, touching me by my elbow.

I get up and follow him. "You should be in the movies," I tell him. "You're so funny."

"I know," he says seriously as we walk into the living room, where there's a big liquor cabinet. "I'll be the next Dwayne 'The Rock' Johnson in a summer action flick coming to theaters near you."

"You'd be a good documentary," I say randomly. "I'd just follow you around all day." I think about Abdi filming Toast and the emo kids at Smoker's Gate.

"It'll be the next *March of the Penguins*," he says dryly.

"The second-highest-grossing documentary of all time."

Holden stares at me. "Epstein did say you knew a lot about movies."

"A lot of stupid trivia about them."

"What do people drink with soufflé? Port? Brandy?"

"Sounds good to me," I say, even though I have no idea. I'm starting to feel warm so I take my sweater off and throw it onto the white couch. "In my house, a white couch would be trashed in seconds."

"You're telling me, Easter Bunny. On the Vineyard, Mo's parents had a white party and everything they served was white. You couldn't get a decent glass of red for a million bucks."

"How long have you been friends with my boyfriend?" I don't think I'll ever stop loving saying "boyfriend."

"Since we were wee threes," Holden says in a British accent.

"Really? Three?"

"We were best buds in the Rodeph Sholom School Threes class."

"Epstein must have been so cute at three."

"Adorbs. We had a good thing with the blocks and trains, but Isaac Steinberg arrived in pre-K and there was a bit of a setback with the Holden-Epstein world domination agenda."

"Wow. Isaac Steinberg, who would've thunk it?"

"It was all resolved by first grade. FYI, Isaac Steinberg moved to Westchester and, according to Fakebook, he's a BMW-driving douche who goes to Solomon Schechter."

"Thank goodness for you."

"Despite his embarrassing passion for jam bands, he's a good guy," Holden says seriously. "A great guy. He was the first person I came out to. Even before my parents. Not that the world didn't see the neon 'faggot' sign radiating on my forehead." He picks up a dark bottle of liquor. "Epstein said all the right things, of course. Equal rights, use a condom, blah blah blah. But then he went and did all this research about the history of gay men. Stonewall. Harvey Milk. Barney Frank. Tim

Cook. Anderson Cooper. The whole shebang. The kid went to an actual library!"

"Wow."

"It was sweet for a straight thirteen-year-old. To this day he knows more gay men than I do. I mean he knows the names of famous, historical gay men. A bunch of those Greek philosophers. He doesn't actually *know* gay men, Toots."

"I knew what you meant."

Holden takes two big bottles and some tiny glasses, tells me he'll go mix us up something delish, and disappears.

I sink into the white couch.

"Here you are," Epstein says, entering the living room. "You okay? You didn't reappear with Holden."

"Yeah." I smile. "I'm great."

"My friends really like you."

"I really like your friends. Holden is a movie star. But they're all great. You're great. Everyone is great."

We start kissing on the couch. It's nice but all I can think about is the white party and how sperm is white and I wonder if it would blend into the couch. But we don't get that far.

"We shouldn't do this," Epstein says.

"Yeah," I say. "It's rude."

"I think I know somewhere a little more private." Epstein stands up and I follow him down the hall to a small room at the far end.

I shouldn't advocate this, but ditching out on the party makes sex more fun. The only awkwardness is when Epstein tries to get me to move left and I roll right and his penis slides out. But then we put it back in and it feels pretty good except for a little bit of soreness.

The next thing I know I hear Holden sing from outside the door, "*Le soufflé est né, Lapins de Pâques.*"

"What is he saying?" I ask Epstein.

He smiles. "I think he's saying: 'The soufflé is born, Easter Bunnies.'"

I thought I might feel embarrassed seeing Epstein's friends after disappearing to have sex, but they treat me like I've been sitting there all night. And, right in the grand dining room, they're smoking a joint! So I guess city and country, some things are the same after all.

By the time we get back to Epstein's at 3:00 AM, I'm exhausted. Without bothering to brush our teeth or discuss it, we tiptoe into the guest room, take off our clothes, and fall asleep in a completely entwined, movie-version way.

At 6:00 AM my phone buzzes. I open one eye, then close it and fall back asleep. At 6:15 it buzzes again. I look at Epstein, whose mouth is slightly ajar. My body aches and my head hurts.

At 7:00, there's a knock on the door.

"Amelia," Isabelle says, softly.

"Yeah?" My voice sounds thick and gravelly.

"Amelia. The phone is for you." She sounds tired and worried.

I get out of bed, put on my jeans without any underwear and Epstein's Brooklyn sweatshirt, and open the door.

If Isabelle notices Epstein she doesn't say anything. She hands me the phone. "It's your grandmother."

Grandma? Calling Epstein's apartment? I take the phone. "Hello?"

"Amelia," my grandmother says quickly, "I'm sorry to bother you, honey. I left messages on your cell, but . . . Can you come home?"

"Of course, Grandma. What's wrong? What happened?" My heart is racing and I'm having trouble taking deep enough breaths.

"It's your brother. It's Toby. He's in the hospital. Something happened, honey. You should probably get home."

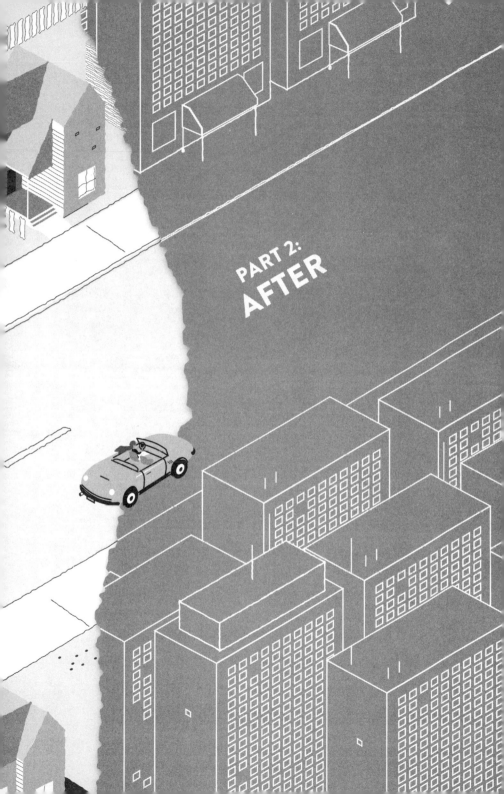

PART 2:
AFTER

11

ANOTHER HOMECOMING

RIDING THE 8:00 AM METRO-NORTH ON FOUR HOURS of sleep with the fear that your brother is going to die is probably up there on a list of horrible ways to spend a Saturday morning.

Except, Toby isn't going to die. He's not dying. My grandmother said *incident*, not accident. She said he couldn't calm down or be reasoned with. "The only choice was hospitalization," she said cryptically.

I barely remember getting on the train. All of this—waking Epstein to explain that I had to go, getting dressed, and saying goodbye to his sleepy but concerned parents in the lobby, having a doorman get me a cab—feels like a surreal dream. My thoughts feel cobwebby and heavy, but I have to work to not think about anything: not my brother, not my throbbing brain or the fact that this weekend went from amazing to beyond terrible in one two-minute phone call. I don't even want to think about movies. When I get off the train it's a bland, blah day, which is fitting. The sky is almost white and the branches on the trees look especially empty.

I know things are bad when I see my dad's truck in the parking lot.

"Meals," he says as I get into the truck, lightly touching my shoulder before peeling out of the parking lot and into a Dunkin' Donuts. He turns off the car. "I've been up all night," he says. "I need coffee. Want a donut?"

I shake my head no. After he leaves, I turn and look out the window at the dumpster, which is overflowing with boxes. How did I end up here? This is so not how the weekend was supposed to end.

I think back to the last time I saw Toby. He was annoying and weird, driving to the station with his loud music and inner-circle nonsense, but once the train came, I forgot all about him. *How could I do that? How could the good egg just abandon the fort?*

My dad comes back with three coffees. He hands me one, which makes me feel grown up. Feeling like a grown-up makes me remember that I had sex for the first time less than twenty-four hours ago. But how can I think about that when Toby is hospitalized? I take a sip of the coffee, but it's gross so I put it down in the sticky cup holder. My father gulps his coffee and shoves a jelly donut into his mouth. When he's done, he clears his throat, wipes the crumbs off his Mets sweatshirt, and says, "Something is wrong with your brother, sweetheart."

I nod.

"The doctors think Toby might be very sick, Amelia."

I bite the inside of my bottom lip.

"Last night . . ." He clears his throat. "Last night, your brother . . ." My father swallows.

Holy shit. He's trying not to cry. My dad. Mr. Tough. My entire being becomes seized with a wave of cold, because if my dad is this upset, then something is *really* wrong.

"He was hallucinating," he says. "Hearing things, seeing things, taking off his clothes. He couldn't have a conversation. He was, uh, totally, well, out of his mind. Mom and I had to take him to the hospital."

"Maybe it was drugs. Maybe someone drugged him."

He shakes his head. "I don't think so. Toast brought Toby home, Amelia. *Toast*," my father says, very slowly, letting me know that he knows Toast is a total stoner. "*Toast* was worried about Toby. He was scared. He said he hadn't taken anything. That he just showed up at his house talking about the Beatles this, *Lord of the Rings* that . . . well . . . Anyway, we're waiting for the tox screen, but I've worked in restaurants my whole life. I know what people are like when they're on all kinds of shit, pardon my French, and this did not seem like drugs."

"What did the doctors say?"

"They don't know much. They had to restrain him. He's being evaluated."

I get an image of my brother, strapped to a bed, like Lisbeth Salander in *The Girl Who Played with Fire*.

"We should know more later." He takes a deep sighing breath. "Sorry your visit got cut short."

"It's okay."

"It's a lot to handle. You want to talk about it?"

For a second I think my dad wants me to talk about New York and losing my virginity, but then I realize he means Toby and I feel stupid. I shake my head and look out the window at the pigeons on the cable wires. I imagine filming them. There's something beautiful about the way the wires bisect the gray sky and how neatly the birds are lined up. If I were a pigeon, I wonder, what kind of pigeon would I be? How nice it would be to be a bird with a brain too small to have fears or worries or any thoughts except maybe waiting for someone to sprinkle crumbs on the ground.

"I'm here. I'm not a great talker or anything, but you can ask me anything."

I look away from the birds. "I know."

"You know you're my rock, Meals."

"I know, Dad."

I thought we would go to the hospital, but my dad takes me home, since the woman who's been watching the boys needs to leave. Part of me is angry. *Why did I come home if not to see my brother? Do my parents just think of me as a babysitter?* But part of me is relieved not to have to see Toby in the hospital.

When I get into my house, the twins are lying on the couch watching TV. I scoot in between them. They seem smaller and younger in their mismatched superhero pj's.

"Toby got sick," Sam says.

I nod. "I know, Sammy." Am I supposed to say anything more to them, I wonder? But what? Luckily, they get sucked into an episode of *Adventure Time* and don't ask me any questions. For a minute I consider asking *them* questions, but I don't say anything. We sit there, the three of us sucked into the world of Ooo.

At noon Epstein texts: how r u doing?

I don't reply because I'm not sure.

An hour later my mom calls. "Amelia," she says as soon

as I answer. I can tell that she's been crying. "I'm sorry, honey. I knew you'd want to know . . ."

I get off the couch and walk into the kitchen. "It's fine, Mom. Of course I'd want to know. How's Toby?"

"We don't know. They gave him something to help him sleep. We're waiting to talk to the psychiatrist on call."

I open the fridge, then close it.

"I'll let you know when we know more," she says. "They haven't said anything definite. How are you doing?"

"Okay."

"I know it's upsetting. It seems like this just came out of nowhere."

I remember how Toby took his shirt off while I was waiting for the train.

"Are the twins okay? Have they said anything?"

"Sam said Toby was sick, but that's it."

My mom sighs. "Poor Sam was scared. Toby woke them up. They heard a lot of yelling."

"They're fine," I assure her. "Sam will be okay. I'm going to tell them to clean their room if they want more screen time."

"Thanks, Amelia. I'll call when I know more. Love you, honey."

"I love you, too." When I get back to the living room, Sam and David have put on *Despicable Me* for the millionth time, but for some reason I stay and watch it anyway.

At 5:00 PM Epstein texts: u okay? how's your bro?

Me: I'm ok. sorry i had 2 go

Epstein: totally understand. how's toby?

Me: don't know yet

Epstein: keep me posted

Me: ok

After I put my phone down, a wave of loneliness hits me like a tsunami. I know it's screwed up, but I miss Epstein so badly that I kind of hate my brother for whatever's wrong with him. But for some reason, I call Ray instead. I don't feel like answering Epstein's questions. He already thinks Toby's weird and probably not in a cool way.

"What's up?" I ask when Ray answers.

"Nothing. I just left work. Aren't you in the city?"

No. I'm not in the city. The city was a lifetime ago. "No. Toby's in the hospital. I'm home."

"The hospital? Oh my God! What happened?"

"I don't know," I say, bursting into tears. It's so weird. How did I go from not even feeling teary to a major flood?

"I'll be right there," Ray says.

I wait for Ray on the front porch even though it's cold. The air feels good, like it's cleansing the city out of me. When she pulls into the driveway and sees me, she doesn't bother to get out because she knows in the way that only a best friend can that I just want to sit in her car. Once I get in I take a cigarette out of her pack without considering what would happen if the twins wandered outside. Yesterday, I wouldn't have dreamed of smoking, but with my brother restrained in the hospital, I suck down Ray's Marlboro Light like a pro.

"What happened? What's wrong with Toby?"

I take another puff. "I don't know. The doctors haven't really said anything to my parents." I look out the window at the pile of leaves in our yard. "Toast brought him home. If Toast is worried then you know it's not good. Did Toast say anything to you?"

Ray shakes her head.

"I hope he doesn't go blabbing about it all over school. I hope he didn't put anything on Facebook . . ."

"Toast's not like that." She touches my shoulder in this weird, almost adult way. "He's gross but not gossipy."

"What if there's something like really wrong with Toby? I thought he was just slacking big time, smoking too much weed." I rub my eyes with the back of my hand. "Do you think there's something really wrong with him?"

Ray looks down.

"Well?" I look at Ray.

"Yeah," she says quietly. "I do think something is wrong. I thought that before. When he disappeared that weekend. I get him not telling your parents, like if he had a bad time on Molly or something, but why didn't he tell you? You guys were so close."

Were close? I think. *Doesn't she mean are close?* Ray's words hang like invisible icicles. Not the small pretty ones that people use for Christmas lights, but gigantic ones that hang from dark caves. The kind that kill people when they break off.

"My degree is WebMD, but yeah, I think something is wrong," Ray says. "Think about how much he's changed."

I try to think about Toby like a movie montage from the past twelve months. Last Christmas, Toby was seeing Samantha Luisenos, a very pretty freshman who was really into him and gave him a million presents for Christmas. On the twenty-sixth he drove the three of us to the mall and we hung out with Ray, just goofing off. Toby spent a ton of money on these fancy French jeans, which he told my mother he wasn't going to wash for four months because he'd read a blog all about denim care. Then he tried to explain what a blog was to Grandma, who just didn't get it, which made both of us laugh. Last Halloween, even though it's usually only the twins who still dress up, he pushed for the whole family to dress as characters from Star Wars with my dad as Darth Vader, Sam as Yoda, David as Luke Skywalker, my mom as a Stormtrooper, me as Leia, and himself as Boba Fett. Our picture was even in the local paper with the cheesy headline: "The Force of Family." So this year he didn't dress up for Halloween, and he hasn't had a girlfriend in a while. And maybe he smokes a lot of pot, but I've been drunk before and Ray smokes cigarettes and obsessively shops. Pot isn't that big a deal. Lots of people do way worse.

"He's changed a lot," Ray says again.

"People change, though," I sort of snap. "It's not a crime to change. Remember your 'wannabe black' phase? You were so into hip hop."

"That was sixth grade."

"So? Muppet's a total stoner now that she's with Toast."

"Isn't there a difference between a twelve-year-old girl listening to a lot of Jay Z and Drake and an almost eighteen-year-old guy whose personality does a one-eighty? And Muppet does smoke more pot but she kind of acted stoned before. She's not really *that* different. But when was the last time Toby played guitar? Hung out in the mall with us? How come he doesn't hang out with anyone anymore?"

I picture my brother by himself in the cafeteria writing frantically in his notebook.

"Ever since I've known him, since like the fourth grade, he's had a million friends, always been on his phone, making plans, but now he's always by himself."

"He and Toast hang out."

Ray shrugs. "Toast hangs out with *Muppet*. Toby sees Toast to get high."

All this sounds really bad coming out of Ray's mouth.

"He used to be so much fun, but now he's just high all the time. It's like he can't be himself anymore."

I close my eyes. I hate that Ray is right. When was the last time Toby and I spent time together on purpose? For fun? When was the last time he took the twins scootering in the skate park? When was the last time he pushed us to do something fun and different and a little bit wild like cutting French to get stoned under a tree?

"When Epstein was here he kept talking about things that didn't make any sense. Even after he calmed down, he was *weird-weird*, not just drunk- or high-weird."

I want to say lots of people are weird, lots of people don't make sense. But I don't. I hate thinking about that night, about how Epstein must see my brother.

"He didn't sleep all night, Meals. He kept talking about these things that God was telling him to do. Stuff like writing a manifesto. That's why I didn't come into your room. I didn't want to leave him alone, Meals. He just needed to talk and talk. All these bizarre theories. I felt like I couldn't go."

"How come you didn't say anything?"

Ray shrugs. "It didn't seem like the kind of thing to tell your parents over waffles. And eventually I got him to shower, he smoked a little pot to calm down. But he's not himself. Maybe we should've said something."

You don't get it, I think. *You're like Epstein, an only child. Toby and I are in the Secret Sibling Society.* If Ray feels bad for not telling on my brother for that one night, I should be put in jail. The list of things I let him get away with is endless. It took Toast, ridiculous druggie Toast, to clue my parents in.

I put my head in my hands and squeeze my eyes really tightly.

Ray pats my shoulder.

I take a deep breath. "I should go check on the twins."

"Do you want me to come in?"

I shake my head.

"You want to be alone?"

I nod. I just can't figure out what to tell Ray anymore. I can't think of anything to say at all.

When I get back in the house, I realize that I forgot to tell Ray I lost my virginity. I pick up my phone to text her, but then wonder, *Why bother?* My brother is restrained in a hospital. What does my virginity matter?

My mom calls in the late afternoon. "We still don't know anything," she says. "Are you okay?"

"Yeah. How's Toby? Have you seen him?" I rub Kepler's belly.

"Well, he's sedated. They gave him something called Trazodone."

The name of the medicine and the word "sedated" sound scary. It makes me think of sleeping pills and suicide. "Is Grandma still with you?"

"Yes. I'll call you when I know anything. Give the boys dinner. They'll eat fish sticks with ketchup. David likes mayo. Maybe some broccoli. Don't let them stay up late."

"I won't."

"I love you."

But would you love me if you knew how many of Toby's secrets I kept from you? "I love you, too."

I finally call Epstein at 10:00. I hope he doesn't answer, but he picks up right away. "Amelia. How are you? How's your brother?"

"Okay, I guess. I don't know. He's sedated."

"Sedated. Wow."

"Yeah."

"Are you at the hospital?"

"No. I'm home with Sam and David." I feel a thud of lameness that I just let them watch TV all day because I didn't want to deal. Toby would not approve of this non-movie version of the day.

"Do you know what happened?"

I get a lump in my throat.

"Amelia?"

"I miss you," I say. "I wish I was there."

"I miss you too. But your family needs you."

"Yeah. I just wish you got to know my brother . . . I wish you knew him before all this."

"Yeah," Epstein says, sort of absently. "From what you've said, he's a pretty terrific guy."

Terrific? That's not how to describe Toby. He's charming and brilliant and bright and shiny. Toby is the movie star in his own movie! In all our movies!

"I gotta go," I lie. "Sam just woke up. I need to get him back to bed." I hang up, fighting the urge to sob.

I wake up in the middle of the night to my mom crying. I hear my dad whispering but I can't hear what he's saying. *What if Toby died? What if he just never woke up? What if they gave him too many sedatives? He didn't die,* I tell myself. *If he died they'd wake me up. He's my brother.*

In the morning everyone but my dad is at the table. Sam and David are eating cereal, my mom is stirring her coffee, and my grandmother is looking at the newspaper.

"Toby's not home yet," Sam tells me. "He's still getting better. Daddy is making sure the doctors do a good job."

Without looking at my mom or grandmother, I pour cereal into a bowl.

"Nana, will you take me to GameStop?" David asks.

My grandma puts the newspaper down. "I don't know, honey," she says in a way that means she won't.

David goes on about some game he wants and how he has money until my mom tells him and Sam to go play upstairs. My grandmother says she's going to call Harry and pats the top of my head on her way out. My mom slowly stirs her coffee but doesn't drink it. When I can't sit there any longer, I sponge off the counters, put the cereal away, and load the dishwasher.

It's only when I come back to the table with a sponge in my hand that my mom puts her hand gently on my wrist. "We're not sure what's wrong with him yet," she says. "There was pot in his bloodstream, but they don't think that's what caused the hallucinations. They think the hallucinations were . . . *organic*. That's what one of the doctors said. But they don't know for sure."

Shit, shit, shit.

"They might not know for a while, but it could be something in his brain."

"Like bipolar disorder?" We learned about bipolar disorder in health class. About half the class was convinced they had it because the symptoms are like feeling great one day and terrible the next.

My mom nods. "They don't know yet. It's too soon. He's going to be under observation for a little while."

"How long?"

"They don't know yet. Also, unrelated to what happened Friday night, his foot is infected. I have no idea why he didn't tell us about the wound. He's on antibiotics for that."

I feel another blast of guilt remembering the cut on my brother's foot after he came home. He wasn't wearing shoes. How could I let that slide?

"Oh, Meals." My mom puts her hands on my shoulders.

"I just don't know how this happened. How could I not have noticed?"

Maybe because I kept covering for him. I must be the worst person in the world.

"Right now we'll just have to wait and see," she says.

"He's going to be okay, Mom," I say. I mean, how could he not be? There's no way Toby Anderson, my amazingly awesome big brother, can't *not* be okay.

Act IV: Scene 2

TOBY is sixteen years old.
AMELIA is fourteen years old.
SAM and DAVID are six years old.
Their parents, MEG and LOU ANDERSON,
are in their early forties. DAD is
intently reading the local paper.

FADE IN:

INT. THE ANDERSONS' KITCHEN. MORNING.

DAD
looking up from the paper
Man, that Sawyer kid over at the high
school is incredible. Do you know he
single-handedly scored twenty-seven
points over Chatham last night?

MOM
Oh. That's good?

DAD
Good? That's unbelievable, Meg. That's
incredible. That's NBA-good. This kid is
going places. Do you know him, Toby?

TOBY
Brian Sawyer? Yeah, kind of. We've been
at some of the same parties. But he's a
senior. And I think he's kind of a jerk.

DAD
not really listening to his son
Unbelievable! I'm telling you guys,
remember the name Brian Sawyer. He's
going places. We gotta go see a game.
I want to see this kid play before I
have to shell out a hundred bucks
to see him on the Knicks.
looks at Toby
Get us some tickets for the next home
game, okay? There are some twenties
on my dresser. We'll all go. It'll
be a family thing.

TOBY
I don't know, Dad. I've heard he's
kind of mean. To girls and stuff.

AMELIA
I don't want to go to a stupid basketball
game.

SAM
Me either.

DAD

But he's incredible.

TOBY

We should go see the girls' team play.

DAD

looks at Toby like he's crazy

Why would we want to do that?

DAVID

Yeah. Girls can't play sports, dude.

TOBY

points at David

Um, that's why, Dad. Girls can play
sports, David. Have you heard of Venus and
Serena Williams or Steffi Graf or Annika
Sorenstam? What you said is sexist. We
really should go see the girls, Dad.
The guys' games are packed, but no one
ever goes to see the girls.

Mom puts her arms around Toby.

MOM

My son, the feminist hero!

SAM
What's sexist? What's feminist?

TOBY
Sexist is not being fair to someone
because she's a girl. Like if I said
Amelia couldn't play Lego Star Wars
because she's a girl. Or mom can't throw
a ball because she's a lady. That's
sexist. We have to see them play and throw
before we can decide how good they are.
And being a feminist means you stand up for
girls. And women. They have to have
the same rights as dudes.

DAD
Jeez! All I want to do is go to a lousy
high school basketball game. Not get all
political.

MOM
Toby is right, Lou. We should support the
girls. It would send a good message.

FADE OUT.

CARD: TWO WEEKS LATER.
INT. Packed high school gymnasium.

During the half time, a coach climbs up
into the bleachers to where the Anderson
family is sitting.

COACH PULLMAN
I just have to tell you how
wonderful your son is.

MOM
Thanks. It's been a great game.

COACH PULLMAN
I don't know how he did it, but Toby
has single-handedly packed this place.
You're wonderful, Toby.

TOBY
blushing
It's nothing. The team is great.

COACH PULLMAN
Your son has just energized my girls.
I really can't thank you enough. If we
win State, we'll put your name on
the trophy, too.

DAD
That's my boy.

12

THE DIAGNOSIS

WE'RE LOOKING FOR RAY'S FAVORITE LIPSTICK AT
Sephora when my dad calls from his cell. It's such a rare
occurrence for my dad to actually call me that I think once
again that maybe Toby has died.

But when I answer, my dad says my mom told him I was
with Ray at the mall and do I need a ride home? He can come
and get me if I want. I know I have to say yes.

Ray stands outside Macy's with me.

"It's about Toby, right?" she asks.

I shrug. "He didn't say." It feels like so long ago that
Toby parked outside here and made that cop crack up.

"Maybe he's coming home."

"Maybe." He's been under observation for ten days now.
In the movie version, the sister would go to the hospital. You
would know she doesn't want to—you could tell from the
tense background piano music that she's dreading it—but she
would show up. In the real-life version scaredy-cat Amelia
Anderson starts texts, but never sends them. What are you
supposed to write to someone who's been hospitalized for
hallucinating? "Get well soon" just doesn't seem right. In
the unfortunate real-life version Amelia Anderson never hits
SEND. She just stays home watching her younger brothers
watch TV.

When my dad drives up, I jump in, barely saying bye

to Ray. But instead of taking me somewhere, he drives be-hind the mall to the service area where all the trucks unload and turns off the engine. There aren't any trucks here now, and it's so big and empty that even I could drive all around and not worry about hitting anything. My dad takes a deep breath and says, "Amelia, there's something wrong with Toby's brain. It's not working the way it should."

This is not a memory I want to file, but I can't help it: it's December and everything seems to have a touch of pink to it because it's probably going to snow, and my father's truck smells like coffee and cough drops. I'm wearing my fa-vorite jeans and a puffy red jacket I got at the Gap last year. It was on sale, I remember, and Ray wanted one, too, but they didn't have her size.

"Amelia," my dad says in a choke.

Don't cry. Don't cry, don't cry, don't cry. I turn away from him and lean my forehead against the window. It's cold and feels good.

"Honey, Toby is sick. And it's serious. It's not his fault and it's good that we found out before he hurt himself."

"What is it?" I take my forehead off the window and look at my dad.

"Schizophrenia. Toby has been diagnosed with schizo-phrenia. He hears things and sees things that aren't really there."

My brother is crazy? *My brother is crazy!*

"He had what they call, um, a psychotic break that night. But there were probably signs that we've missed. I missed a lot." He sighs. "It's not a one-hundred-percent diagnosis . . .

they'll wait a little while for that, but the doctors are pretty sure that's what's going on." He rubs his eyes with the sides of his knuckles.

"Can they get rid of it? Is there medicine?"

"Well . . . he'll take medicine. They're figuring that stuff out now. But it's more complicated than that. The medicines won't cure it. I have, uh, these books." He leans around to the back of the truck and picks up two books from the floor. "Your mom bought these today." He lays the books gently in his lap. The one on top would make me laugh if it wasn't so tragic. It's called *Schizophrenia for Dummies*.

Schizophrenia. The word seems angry and neon and rubbery in my head.

"They seem good. Straightforward." He takes the other book from underneath *Schizophrenia for Dummies* and puts it on top. This one is smaller and green—and the title, which is in big red letters, says *Surviving Schizophrenia: A Family Manual.*

"A psychiatrist at the hospital recommended this one."

"Oh," I say. I wish I could make this unreal feeling go away, but I can't. This all just seems so crazy.

Crazy, I think again. *Your brother is crazy.* All those weird conversations and the freak-out around Epstein and the conversation in the car about the Beatles and God and *Lord of the Rings* were because he was going crazy!

I lightly close my eyes the way I do when there's a violent scene in a movie.

"These are for you," my dad says, putting the books on my lap. "Your mother and I have our own copies. But we thought it would be good for you to read them, too. The twins are too young, but . . ." He clears his throat.

I open my eyes. It's strange, but my impulse is to get the books off me, so I put them on the floor by my feet.

"I usually have a lot of homework," I say idiotically. "Plus, I, uh, just signed up for Driver's Ed. The class is after school, you know." I cross my fingers. *You'll sign up to-morrow*, I tell myself. *It's not a total lie if you sign up for it tomorrow.*

"You did? You're going to get your license?"

I nod.

"That's great, Meals. I'm so proud of you. You tell Mom?"

I shake my head. "Not yet."

"She's going to be thrilled." My dad sighs. "So I know you're busy, but the books might help."

I nod and look out the window at all the empty parking spaces. I imagine a time-lapse scene like in *Breaking Bad* when they show time passing by using fast shots in different colors. *How does that work?* I wonder. Do they copy a shot and change the color effects? Or do they speed up the film?

"Schizophrenia *can* be treated. Not cured, but there are a lot more medicines available now." My dad sounds like David or Sam when they're practicing spelling words. Just rote, get-it-over-with memorization.

S-C-H-I, I think, closing my eyes.

Z-O. I open them again.

"It's not his fault," my dad whispers. "It's not anybody's fault, Meals. That's what all the doctors have said."

"Okay," I say, thinking it's actually kind of my fault. If I had said something months ago maybe it wouldn't have gotten so bad. "It just really sucks."

My dad nods. When he squeezes my hand, tears start rolling down my cheek.

"Oh, sweetheart," he says. "It's terrible."

I take a deep breath, but I have no clue as to what I should say.

"Your mom and I are going to do our best to be honest even if we don't know the answers. While making things age appropriate for seven-year-olds."

"That sounds good." *How are the twins going to get any of this?*

My dad leans over me, opens the glove compartment, and fishes around for a pack of ancient-looking vitamin C drops and puts three in his mouth. "Want one?"

I shake my head.

"Your mom and I want you to feel comfortable asking us questions, but there are other people who can help you, too, Meals."

"Okay." I wish I could get past all these one-word answers, but I can't.

"Toby's sick, Amelia."

Why does he keep saying that? Does he think I forgot the last three minutes?

"I know I keep saying it," my dad says, like he's reading my mind, "but I have to remind myself of it. I thought he was just screwing around, smoking too much dope, worrying his mother, but he's been a real sick, very scared kid."

"Can he ever come home?"

My dad nods. "They want to keep him there for another five days or so. I guess two weeks is the norm to figure out the meds. And he'll need to see a psychiatrist once he's released."

"But he'll be home. He'll live at home?" I don't know why, but I was pretty convinced that someone with schizophrenia had to live in some kind of institution.

"Yes." My dad turns the key in the ignition and puts his truck in drive. "He'll be home for Christmas."

13

AMELIA ANDERSON RIDING IN CARS TELLING PEOPLE HER BROTHER IS SCHIZOPHRENIC

AFTER TALKING TO A BUNCH OF DOCTORS AND THE hospital social worker, my parents decide not to tell the twins that Toby most likely has schizophrenia. They don't think they need that information right now, because there's no need to scare them.

And it's scary because there's no cure for the disease.

Just like that, my awesome older brother is mentally ill. Toby has a mental illness.

Just like that, he's really sick.

For the next few days, I walk around feeling that nothing is real. With Toby hospitalized it feels like I shouldn't be able to keep eating cereal next to a slurping Sam or asking my mom to put more money on my lunch account. How can I just watch random movies off my Netflix queue with Kepler when my brother is cut off from the outside world? But nobody stops Sam from slurping or tells me to turn off the TV. The world keeps going: the twins fight over Legos, telemarketers call during dinner, Kepler moves from spot to spot. My parents and grandmother seem sad and slow. But they still wash the dishes, answer the phone, and lock the doors at night. My parents go to work and my grandmother tries to stop the twins from fighting. The only difference is that Toby's diagnosis limits my movie viewing since I no longer want to watch movies with brothers and sisters, hospitals, illnesses of any kind, or any music by or reference to the Beatles or any other British band.

I watch a lot of movies off Kepler's Netflix queue, because movies about dogs, especially the G-rated ones, tend to be safe viewing. I don't even come up with a clever theme for the movies I watch. Half the time I'm not even sure I really watch them. I just see dogs on the screen.

I wonder if telling Ray, three days after my dad tells me, will feel real, but walking to her car after school, I still feel like I'm outside myself. I wonder if crying would help get rid of the unreal daze I'm in. I haven't cried since I came back from NYC. I haven't shed a single tear since my dad said *schizophrenia.*

Pretty much as soon as we drive out of the school parking lot, I come out and say it. "So, um. They know what's wrong. With Toby."

Ray looks at me expectantly.

I imagine saying *he needs a liver* or *they're removing a brain tumor. It's risky but he should be fine.* I look down at my hands and wonder if I'll ever want to bother to paint my nails again. It seems like the most insignificant thing in the world right now.

"Meals?" Ray says softly.

I feel like I'm going to throw up, but I have to tell Ray. I have to tell someone. "He has. Um. Toby has schizophrenia."

"What?"

"I guess you were right after all. He is really sick. He did change a lot." My voice sounds flat and monotone.

"Jesus. Oh God." Ray drives to this small little pond, not far from the senior center, where old people feed the ducks, and parks the car. Of course, now the pond is frozen so the ducks and old people are gone.

"He has schizophrenia? Like that guy in the movie . . ."

"I don't want to talk about movies," I snap.

Ray unbuckles her seat belt and gives me an awkward driver's seat hug. "Oh, Meals. I'm so sorry. This is horrible." She starts crying, like really crying.

"It sucks." I think about how my dad told me about my brother in his truck and now I'm telling Ray in her car. Toby and I used to like watching Jerry Seinfeld's *Comedians in Cars Getting Coffee*, and I wonder for a split second whether I could make my own web series: *Amelia Anderson Riding in Cars Telling People Her Brother Is Schizophrenic.*

Probably wouldn't be as popular as Jerry's.

"Should we visit him?" Ray blows her nose. "Can we do that? I don't know anything about schizophrenia."

"We don't need to visit him. He'll be home soon. Can I bum a smoke?" I take one out of the pack before she says yes.

"I don't believe this. I'm in shock. How are your parents?"

"Shitty. Don't say anything to the twins. Things have to be PG."

"I won't."

"Don't say anything to anybody."

"I won't. Not even my mom."

"Thanks. Can you take me home?" I don't feel bad mooching rides or smoking anymore. I wonder if feeling bad about my brother has stopped me from feeling bad about anything else. *Am I suddenly capable of doing horrible, terrible things?* I wonder.

"Are you sure? We could go somewhere. 'I got a full tank of gas, half a pack of cigarettes . . .' I don't remember the rest of it but I'm happy to drive anywhere you want. I really do have a full tank of gas."

The quote Ray wants is: "It's 106 miles to Chicago, we got a full tank of gas, half a pack of cigarettes, it's dark . . . and we're wearing sunglasses." But Toby loved that quote—for a while he annoyingly said it whenever we got into his car, and I'd always have to say *"Hit it"* before he'd drive—so I push it out of my brain and just say, "I'm sure. I want to go home."

We drive to my house in silence, which is a first. Ray always has music on. *Music while driving is a must for movie versions,* Toby would say. Nobody would pay ten dollars to watch sad teenagers silently drive. *At least play the classical radio station Grandma likes,* I imagine him saying. *Y'all need some violins up in here.*

I close my eyes and hold onto the handrest as Ray guns it up my steep driveway.

"Should I come up?" Ray asks. "We could watch a movie or something."

I think about how tired my mom looks and how sad my grandmother and dad are and how, although it seems impossible, Sam and David are fighting even more.

"It's probably not the best time. You won't tell anyone about Toby?"

She shakes her head and then stops. "What about Toast?"

"Definitely not Toast!"

"But Meals, he was with Toby. He brought him to your house. That night. He got him help."

Unlike me. I gave him twenty bucks, left the fort, and jumped on the train.

"He's been worried. That night kind of fucked him up."

"Toast is always fucked up," I snap.

"You know what I mean. Toast did the right thing. A lot of people might have freaked. And who knows what would have happened then."

"I don't want Toast to know. I don't want anyone to know. Washington Lincoln is gossip central. It'll be on Facebook and tweeted in like three seconds. I can't do that to Toby." I open the car door. "Thanks for the ride."

After I tell Ray, I decide to tell Epstein. It's just too weird texting and talking like everything is fine. I can't keep it a secret from my boyfriend, from the person I lost my virginity to. In the end, I write him an email, which is random but seems better than a text or Snapchat.

I write:

Hi Epstein,

I know it's weird that I'm emailing, but I don't want to do it

over the phone/text. So anyway. My brother has schizophrenia.
Life stinks right now. Email me back if you want to.
I miss you.

xo, Amelia.

Epstein writes me back right away.

Dear Amelia,

I'm SO sorry to hear about Toby. I love you.
I am here for you.

Love, Epstein

I feel worse after I read Epstein's response. It's the perfect email, the perfect response to what I wrote, and I shouldn't be surprised because Epstein is the perfect boyfriend. But with Toby in the hospital, nothing is right. Not even Epstein.

14

DOING DRIVER'S ED

I DON'T KNOW IF IT'S FUNNY, PATHETIC, OR IRONIC, but ultimately, it's my brother's illness that makes me finally sign up for Driver's Ed. My dad told my mom all about it after our Big Schizophrenia Talk, and my mom was so happy about it that I couldn't disappoint her.

Besides, after I hand over the check to the school registrar, I realize that even though I'm taking the class, I probably won't pass the road test. And even if, by some miracle, I do actually get my license, I'm in no position to buy a car since I have no money and no job.

On Monday afternoon, I go to my first Driver's Ed class, which is taught by Mr. Munson, who has a long walrus mustache and a hoop earring in each ear. The class is all sophomores except for me and Abdi Osman, the two juniors.

I sit down next to him.

"Have you taken this class before?" he asks.

"No. I don't have my driver's license yet."

"You don't? Oh. I have mine. I'm a great driver, but the insurance company has no record so I'm stuck here. Again. You get a lot off insurance when you have Driver's Ed."

"Oh." I take out a pen and notebook.

"The first two weeks suck. It's endless statistics. How many people die a year driving. How many people die a year driving while texting. How many people die driving and texting drunk. The tests are moronic if you show up."

"I'm kind of scared of driving."

"Yeah?" Abdi looks at me. "There's nothing to be afraid of. Unless you really listen to Mr. Munson's stats." He smiles.

Mr. Munson comes in and writes "3,000" on the blackboard. "Does anyone know what this number represents?"

Abdi raises his hand and Mr. Munson nods at him. "The number of teens who die in car crashes every year."

I feel sick. Three thousand is a lot of people. What if I kill myself driving? What if I kill someone else? *You don't have to drive.* Just take the class.

While Mr. Munson drones on citing endless statistics about the terrible things that happen when teenagers drive, I write a list of Road Movies with <u>No</u> Crashes: *Nebraska, Little Miss Sunshine, The Puffy Chair, Borat, About Schmidt,* and the horrible *Due Date.*

When Driver's Ed is over, Abdi says, "You left out a few."

"Were you reading over my shoulder?"

He shrugs and gives me a small smile. "I took the class already. What am I supposed to do?"

"It's okay," I say, because I honestly don't care. "What did you come up with?"

"*Sideways* is a road trip. *The Puffy Chair* was a great movie. I'm impressed you know it."

"I love the Duplass brothers. *Safety Not Guaranteed* is seriously underrated. *Sideways* can't count. There's a crash."

"Really? Don't they just drink wine and drive a convertible?"

"To explain his broken nose, Thomas Haden Church crashes Paul Giamatti's convertible into a tree."

Abdi nods. "*Thelma & Louise*. They don't crash in that."

"They *land* in the Grand Canyon. They both die in the end."

"You don't know that for sure."

"You can't drive from one side of the Grand Canyon to the other. Besides, there's no *Thelma & Louise* sequel."

"You have a point. What about *Easy Rider*?" We both turn to walk down Hall D.

"That's motorcycles. My list was cars."

Abdi nods. "Well, you still left off the best road trip movie. It's a documentary called *Sherman's March*."

I flip through the movie files of my brain. "I've never heard of it."

"It's crazy old school. 1980s. But it's awesome. It made me want to make documentaries. Well, that and Morgan Spurlock—the guy who did *Supersize Me*."

"You want to make movies?"

He nods. "I want to go to either Duke because they have an awesome Center for Documentary Studies or Michigan State because they have documentary programs that under-grads can take. A lot of programs are just for graduate students."

"Wow." I'm totally surprised to hear the random camera kid sound so together. Taking the SATs in May is barely on my radar. I haven't thought about what or where I want to study.

"I'll lend you *Sherman's March*," Abdi says.

"I have Netflix," I say. "I'll just stream it."

"Not on Netflix. I'll bring my DVD tomorrow."

"If you want," I tell him, leaving the building.

Waiting to get picked up, I realize that sitting in Driver's Ed and talking movies with Abdi Osman is the longest I've gone without thinking about my brother or his diagnosis in an entire week.

15

A CRAZY KIND OF CHRISTMAS

WHEN I GO DOWNSTAIRS ON DECEMBER 24TH, I discover that decorations have taken over the house: There's a garland and a crèche on the mantle, a big plastic snowman in the front yard, and white lights strung everywhere. It's way more decorations than we usually have.

"Did you stay up all night doing this?" I ask my mom while she hangs mistletoe between the living room and the kitchen. "The house is drowning with holiday spirit."

"It's Christmas, Meals. We should try to have a nice holiday." She blinks her eyes and I know she's trying not to cry. "The twins having been looking forward to Christmas since July."

I keep it to myself that the holiday overload makes Toby's diagnosis seem sadder and walk around the pine-scented house in a daze. Everything feels different, wrong, and unreal. Even Kepler is off. She can't get comfortable in her usual spots and has no interest in her peanut butter Kong.

After lunch, when my parents have left to do last-minute shopping before picking up Toby and I've cajoled Sam and Kepler to watch *A Christmas Story* with me, Ray calls.

"Hey," I say. I feel happy to talk to someone who isn't related to me. "What's going on?"

"Work is horrendous. This is like the first time all day that I've had time for a break. What's going on?"

"Toby's coming home."

"Really? Awesome. When?"

"Today."

"So he's okay? Better?"

"I guess. I guess he's okay enough to come home."

"I can't wait to see him," she says. "Do you think it will be weird?"

I close my eyes. Is it going to be weird to see my brother for the first time in eighteen days? Is it going to be weird to see my brother, the schizophrenic? My brother, the mentally ill person? My brother, who sees and hears things that don't exist?

"Meals? You there?"

"I'm here. What are you doing tonight? CinnaYum! closes early, right?"

I know Ray knows that I totally blew off her question, but because she's Ray she just goes with it. "I'm here till four. My mom is going to her sister's, but there's no way I'm spending Christmas there."

"Yeah." Part of me wants to invite her over. Thinking about her alone in her house, smoking, watching bad TV, and looking for eBay deals makes me feel bad. But the other part of me, the bigger part, is scared that it will be weird with Toby back.

"My break is way over. I should go sell more cancer-causing sugary shit to the drones."

That's what Toby said, I think with a start. That's a Tobyism! "Okay. We'll do something soon."

"For sure. Tell Toby I can't wait to see him."

"Merry Christmas."

"You too."

After *A Christmas Story* ends, I go up to my room and dig out the documentary Abdi lent me. He actually drove past me waiting for the bus, parked his car, and ran out to give it to me. It was weird and a little embarrassing, but I guess kind of nice, too. I remember when his family moved here, because the elementary school made huge banners welcoming Abdi and his siblings and there was a big article in the paper about their journey from Somalia to life in a small upstate town. It seems random that I just started talking to him this year. "All right, *Sherman's March*," I say to Kepler. "Let's see how awesome you are." Honestly, I just want to be distracted from looking at the time every five seconds.

Although it starts slowly, I start to get into it. It begins with this Southern filmmaker Ross McElwee talking about how he's going to make a movie about General Sherman's march through the South, but then it turns into this film mostly about him meeting women and traveling to the places Sherman went. It's not like reality TV at all; he's really thoughtful. What he says doesn't sound at all scripted or rehearsed—it just sounds truthful. I also like how he has the camera linger on seemingly random shots, or moves it to something unexpected, like a bunch of little kids pressed against a screen door, when the action is someplace else. It's kind of weird, but honest and smart. It's interesting that a white girl from upstate New York and a guy from Somalia could both like it. I learn from Wikipedia that the filmmaker is an old guy from North Carolina who teaches at Harvard. After it's over, even though it's long, I kind of want to watch it again, but Sam yells, "Toby's home! Toby's home! Toby's home!"

I take a deep breath and walk downstairs, where my brother is standing in the middle of the living room, holding his backpack. He looks a little pale and more unshaven than I've ever seen him, but pretty much the same. Sam and David stare at him like he's just landed from outer space.

My grandmother comes out from the kitchen and gives Toby a huge hug, but I lamely just pat him on the arm.

"I'm so glad you're home," I tell him. "I totally missed you."

He nods.

I wonder what would happen if I gave him a movie quote, but I don't.

"Do you want something to eat?" my mom asks.

"How about something to drink?" my grandmother adds quickly. "I bought you Coke."

Toby sits down on the couch and starts bouncing his knees up and down. "Coke is good."

"Can I have a Coke?" David asks. I have to give him credit that he never stops trying to get in on the action.

"No," my mom says.

My grandmother comes back with Toby's soda.

"We're having pulled pork and garlic mashed potatoes for dinner tonight," Sam tells Toby. "We chose it because it's your favorite."

"Thanks."

I wonder if he remembers that, other than the year my dad got the flu, we haven't had a single Christmas Eve when we didn't have Lobster Newberg.

"Are you tired?" my mom asks.

"A little."

"Do you want to take a nap? We won't eat for an hour or so."

Toby stands up. "Yeah. Maybe I will take a nap."

"Okay," my mom tells him. "Have a good rest, honey."

How can Toby Anderson be practically speechless? I want to do something, I want him to do something, but instead I silently watch him leave. Then I drag Kepler on a walk she doesn't want to go on.

Two hours later, Toby still hasn't emerged from his room. Sam and David are delirious with hunger and my dad looks like he might punch someone. He keeps wanting to wake Toby, but my grandmother and mother tell him not to. I walk past Toby's door about ten times, wondering if I should knock, but I don't.

When he finally comes downstairs, he seems clueless that he's made the rest of us wait for so long. He picks at his food, says very little, and then, instead of joining the rest of us to watch *A Charlie Brown Christmas,* he goes up to his room.

"It's been a long day," my grandmother tells my parents. I think she means it's been a long day for Toby so they shouldn't blame him for not wanting to hang out.

My dad nods in agreement. "I'll say." I think he means

that *he's* had a long day since he picked up his oldest child from the psychiatric ward of the hospital.

My mom doesn't say anything, and for a minute, I feel the sorriest for her.

My parents are not dumb enough to make Sam and David wait for Toby to open their Christmas presents. The four of us watch them tear into their gifts, leaving a sea of wrapping paper under the tree.

By noon, when the twins are already bored with their new games and the dishwasher is humming with breakfast and lunch dishes, I notice that my mom keeps looking upstairs.

I pause *Die Hard*. "I could go knock on his door."

"I don't know," she says. "The books I've been reading say it's important that . . . that he have his own space. I don't want to bother him. But he should take his meds."

"I'll knock," I say to her. *In the movie version*, I tell myself as I walk upstairs, *the sister knocks on her brother's door and reminds him to come down for Christmas.*

There's music coming from Toby's room so I force myself to knock.

"What?" He sounds annoyed.

"It's me. Can I come in?"

There's a pause and a softer, "Okay."

I open the door. Toby still hasn't shaved and is wearing ratty blue sweatpants and a baggy white T-shirt. His room has an artificial orange smell since my mom cleaned it last weekend. She didn't throw anything away except the obvious garbage, but she put all the papers into folders and stacked them neatly on his desk on top of all his notebooks. She also washed, folded, and hung up all his clothes. I wonder if he noticed or thanked her.

"What are you doing?"

"Writing," Toby says.

"Yeah?"

"I'm writing a book."

"Really? That's cool." I feel like Toby is the same old Toby. He's so the kind of guy who would just write a book. The same way he taught himself to juggle, do cartwheels, and play guitar.

He shrugs. "It's okay. I have a lot of work to do."

"Well, I'm sure you can do it. So, Sam and David opened their presents ages ago."

"Today's Christmas, right?"

"All day."

"I didn't buy anyone any presents."

"'I know how you feel about all this Christmas business, getting depressed and all that. It happens to me every year. I never get what I really want.'"

Toby looks at me blankly.

"It's what Lucy says to Charlie Brown in *A Charlie Brown Christmas*." *Why did I say "depressed"?! He just came home from the hospital! Why would you go bombarding him with random quotes? You weren't going to do that!* "Sorry. Totally random."

He shrugs.

"I did horribly with the present-giving this year, too. No one cares. We all understand . . . You've been away."

"To the loony bin. The fifth floor. The psych ward." He puts air quotes around "psych ward."

I'm not sure how to respond. "Did Mom and Dad tell you I'm finally taking Driver's Ed?"

"That's nice. I'm not supposed to drive Prudence till they get my meds right." He rolls his eyes.

Thinking of Prudence just sitting in the garage nearly brings me to tears. But I'm not about to start crying in front of my brother. I take a deep breath. "I just started *Die Hard* aka Best Christmas Movie Ever. Want to watch it?"

Last year Toby would have said something like, "Yippee-ki-yay, motherfucker. Do I want to watch it?" But this year he just shakes his head no. "I'm kind of busy."

"I saw this random documentary yesterday. *Sherman's March*. You'd like it. That guy Abdi Osman lent it to me. Want to watch that?"

He shakes his head.

We don't say anything for a few minutes. Toby turns up the volume on a song I've never heard.

"I'm so happy to have my music back," he says. "It sucked not having any music. It helps me, you know, to have music to listen to."

"Yeah." *Am I supposed to ask him about his illness? What do I say?*

"Do you want to come downstairs? Dad made bacon."

He shrugs. "I guess." He turns to follow me out of his room. I'm a little surprised that he's not changing out of the sweats, but I guess nothing should surprise me anymore.

» » · « «

The rest of the day drags, which I remind myself happens every year, not just this one. I get the usual Christmas presents: money, gift cards, three movies that were on my Amazon wish list, a bag that I sort of like from my grandmother, and SmartWool socks. Toby doesn't seem that interested in his presents, and after everything is unwrapped he excuses himself.

My mom looks at him. "Where are you going?"

"My room."

My grandma shakes her head. "But you just came down, honey."

"It's Christmas, Toby," my mom says.

Toby shrugs. "Do I have to stay?"

My mom tears up. "Well, you don't have to. But we'd like you to."

Toby ignores her and heads upstairs. After we hear his bedroom door close, my mom covers her face with her hands.

"What's wrong, Mommy?" Sam asks.

"Do you boys want to go skating?" Harry asks. "We'll have the Huguenot pond to ourselves."

"I hate ice skating," David says. "My feet always freeze and I don't have hockey skates. Can't I play Xbox hockey?"

My dad shakes his head. "Wear extra socks. You're *going* skating, boys. Thanks, Harry."

"My pleasure," Harry says.

"I'll get my things," my grandmother says. "Want to join us, Amelia?"

"No thanks, Grandma."

After the skating contingency leaves, I throw Kepler's

new squirrel toy to her out in the yard. After a few minutes she refuses to give it back and plops herself down on a mound of snow to chew it alone. I go back inside and up to my room. Feeling very Sam-like, I hang my face over the edge of the bed. There are a few dust bunnies next to the schizophrenia books my dad gave me. I imagine picking them up and reading something, but my phone rings.

"Happy birthday, little baby Jesus," Epstein croons in a bad Elvis impersonation.

I laugh. "Yeah. Happy birthday, baby Jesus."

"How's it going? Good loot?"

"Money, gift cards."

"Me too. And a new and improved iPad mini."

"That's pretty good for someone who's half-Jewish." I feel like I'm going to cry all of a sudden.

"Are you okay, Amelia? You sound funny."

"Yeah." It comes out in a snort.

"Sure? You sound upset."

I take a deep breath. "No, I'm okay. Toby came home. Yesterday."

"He did? That's great." It's weird how much Epstein sounds like Ray. *Because they don't get it*, I think. Normally if someone had a broken leg or pneumonia it would be great for them to get out of the hospital, because they'd be recovered. I think about how everyone in my family is totally miserable right now. Except maybe Toby. He seems clueless.

"It's terrific," I say miserably.

"I just read a very interesting book," Epstein says cheerfully. "It's called *Henry's Demons*. And it's written by a father and son—they alternate chapters. The son, Henry, is schizophrenic. Like Toby."

A whoosh of cold air swirls from my heart into my stomach.

"It was really insightful," Epstein says.

Why is Epstein reading books about schizophrenia? And why is he using words like insightful?

Impulsively, I hit end. I can't believe I just hung up on my boyfriend. Because he read a book? What's wrong with me?

I call him back. "Sorry," I lie. "I lost you for a second."

"That's okay. I was babbling. Do you want to come down for New Year's Eve? Holden wants to organize a party, but it'll probably be the usual crew hanging out."

I think of the walls of books in Epstein's apartment and the way the sun looks in his room at five o'clock. Even though it's in the middle of a city, it seems especially peaceful right now. "That would be fun," I say. "But I'm not sure I can. You know, with everything. I'll ask my mom."

To my surprise, my mom says it's totally fine for me to spend New Year's Eve in the city with Epstein. She and my dad will be at Ginger's for a prix-fixe dinner, and the twins are spending the night at Ryan's, because my grandmother and Harry have dinner plans with friends. But my mom is planning to leave Ginger's before ten, and my grandmother won't be out that late either, so Toby won't be alone for too long. Not that it would really matter, as he's barely left his room all week.

I feel like the kid in *The Sixth Sense* and my brother's

the ghost. Or maybe he's the kid and we're all ghosts to him. Either way, I feel like someone has died.

"You really think it's okay?" I ask my mom.

She's sitting in front of the big mirror on her dresser, tweezing her eyebrows. "Staying home won't do anything. Go see Epstein. Your last visit got cut short. You can have a life, Meals. It's good for you to go out and do things."

I swallow hard. I know that I didn't cause Toby's schizophrenia, but I also don't feel good about going and doing things. "Epstein's friends are having a party. Maybe Toby would like . . ." But I don't finish the thought. If this was last year and Toby was still Toby, I'd offer to bring him with me, which he'd never agree to anyway, because he would have had plans. Last New Year's he had three or four parties he needed to "make an appearance" at. But, if for some reason he did go with me, everyone would have loved him. Ramona, Chloe, and Holden would all get big crushes on him and Epstein would finally know what I meant when I said my brother was so cool. Last year Toby would have been the life of any party in any city, but this year I can't imagine him going anywhere at all.

16

NEW YEAR'S, SHMOO YEAR'S

NEW YEAR'S EVE AFTERNOON, I RUN INTO TOBY COM-
ing upstairs with a laundry basket.

"Hey," I say. "How's it going?" I sound loud and awkward, but I'm excited to see him out of his room doing something, even if it's just laundry. "What's going on?"

"Nothing. I don't know. I don't talk to anyone anymore."

That's for sure. "Well, people want to talk to you, Toby.
Didn't Ray text you?"

He shrugs. "I'm not using my phone."

"Why not? How will people call or message you?"

"That phone wasn't good."

"Is it broken?"

"I guess."

"I'm sure Grandma or Mom will take you to get a new
one."

"Nah. I'm too busy. I'm washing my clothes. They're
really dirty."

I nod, even though this doesn't make any sense since
Toby is still wearing the same clothes from Christmas.

"They've poisoned my clothes," he whispers.

"Who?"

"You know . . . Mom and Dad. Grandma. David. Sam."

"No, they didn't. That's crazy, Toby." *Crazy. How could*

I use that word? What's wrong with me? I wonder if I should apologize but my tongue feels stuck.

"Are you in on it?"

"In on what?"

"The poisoning."

How can he think that? "No! No one is trying to poison you, Toby. I promise." I wish I had at least looked at the books my dad gave me.

Toby looks at me suspiciously.

"I swear. We're really happy that you're home. No one is poisoning you. I was just coming to see if you have any plans tonight," I say without thinking. "It's New Year's Eve."

"So?"

"I'm going to see Epstein. Do you want to come?"

Why did I just say that? *Please, God, don't let him want to come.* What if he has another episode? What if I don't know if he's having an episode? And where's he supposed to stay? In Epstein's guest room?

Toby yawns. "I don't think so. I'm tired."

"Yeah . . . It will probably be pretty lame." I hope my relief isn't obvious.

"I need to do more laundry."

"Alright. Well, have a good night."

My grandmother drives me to the train on her way to Harry's. With her maroon coat and freshly coiffed hair, she looks nice. On our way, we drop the twins off at Ryan's. Sam and David are their usual selves on the ride over, calling each other names, accusing one another of farting, and punching each other. My grandmother keeps saying, "Boys, boys," which does nothing. Eventually, I tell them to shut up, which makes me feel like the movie version of the mean teenage big sister. I don't want to be so edgy, but I'm anxious.

After the twins are safely ushered inside their friend's house, my grandmother sighs with relief. "I love those boys, but they wear me out."

"I hear you, Grandma."

"When you and Toby were that age, you weren't like that. You weren't always *at* each other."

"It's hard being a twin. Toby and I fought sometimes."

She shakes her head. "Very rarely. I remember *you* wanting to play with him *all the time*. When he went to kindergarten, you'd look out the window just waiting for the school bus."

"Pretty pathetic. Like Kepler waiting for me."

"It was sweet. You just loved him so much."

"I still love him."

"Of course! We all do. Of course! But it's good you're doing things for you, too. Pretty soon you won't need me to drive you around. You'll have your license."

"I guess." Two weeks of Mr. Munson's endless statistics of teen deaths due to poor decisions while driving has not made me any less scared. I make a mental note to bring Abdi's DVD back when school starts.

When we get to the station I say, "Thanks, Grandma. I know this is out of your way."

"Nonsense, honey. Do you need money?"

"I'm good."

"Keep it close to you. You don't want to get pickpocketed."

"I'll be fine. Have a good night with Harry. Happy New Year."

"You too. Happy New Year. I'll pick you up."

"Thanks. I'll be back on Sunday."

"Well, that's a nice long visit."

"Yeah." I feel awkward. *Is my trip too long? Should I stay home? Should Toby be alone for the next three hours?*

I get out of the car. "I think I hear the train," I lie.

I can't relax on the train at all. When I close my eyes I keep seeing a movie montage of Toby and me as kids—playing on the beach, laughing, chasing each other, watching movies in our pajamas—with a Morgan Freemanesque narrator saying, "This was twelve years before Toby Anderson would be diagnosed as a schizophrenic."

Five guys wearing baseball caps—probably in their early twenties—get on in New Rochelle. They're loud, slightly obnoxious, and excited, and watching them makes me realize just how unexcited I am. I keep imagining all the trouble Toby could get in all by himself at home. The last time I went to New York City, Toby ended up in the hospital. What will happen this time?

By the time we pull into Grand Central, I feel like I might throw up. For a minute, I think about staying on the train and going back home. I could get a taxi at the station. Maybe when I got back home, Toby would be just starting a movie. He'd be so psyched I came back that he'd make "nasty" nachos and we'd go back and forth in a legendary movie quote battle and we wouldn't even notice that it was already the New Year.

Too cheesy for even Hollywood, I think, standing up and shuffling out behind the loud guys.

"Happy Shmoo Year," one of them croons to his friend. "It's the year of the shmoo!"

"Amelia!" Epstein says when he sees me.

"Hi." I want to sound more enthusiastic, but I can't.

Luckily Epstein has enough enthusiasm for both of us. As we walk through the station, he tells me all the ideas he has for what to do while I'm in the city.

On the subway, half-listening to Epstein, I take in the other passengers like I'm watching a movie. The camera lands first on an older black woman carrying two bags from Bloomingdale's, then it pans to a young white guy with really big headphones reading *The Economist*. From there the camera pans to an Asian man with three yellow plastic shopping bags. I watch a mom wipe snot off her kid's nose and then move the invisible camera to two young boys, probably not much older than the twins, who keep punching each other. I wonder how all these random people are going to celebrate the New Year. Do any of them have a brother they can't stop thinking about?

My mom didn't give me anything for Epstein's parents, but Isabelle doesn't seem to notice.

"Amelia!" She envelops me in a huge hug. "We're so happy you were able to come down again! How are you?"

"Fine. I'm fine."

"Wonderful." She finally stops hugging me and looks me right in the eyes. "We're *so* sorry for your troubles."

"My troubles?" I look at Epstein but he's texting.

"Toby's illness," Isabelle says. "My heart just breaks for everyone, honey."

I don't know why I didn't get that Epstein would tell his parents about my brother—they obviously knew something was wrong—but hearing Isabelle talk about my brother's illness makes me feel like I've been hit in the chest.

"It's devastating. Your whole family has been in my thoughts. I'm planning on writing your parents—"

"I'm okay," I spit out. "We're okay."

Isabelle gives me a smile that says *I know you're not really okay, but it's fine if you want to pretend.*

"We're just dropping off Amelia's stuff," Epstein tells his mom. "We're headed out."

"Okay," Isabelle says. "Have fun. Be careful. Avoid Times Square. And please let me know if there's anything you need, Amelia."

I know she's offering me more than an extra pillow or towel, but I ignore it and follow Epstein into his room, where he puts my borrowed-from-Ray Herschel duffle on his bed and gives me a hug. I hug him back, but my mind wanders. *Is Toby really going to just wash clothes all night? Is that healthy?*

"You ready?" Epstein asks.

"Yeah," I say, willing my brain to stop thinking about Toby.

» » · « «

After we leave Epstein's, we meet Ramona, Chloe, and three other girls, Jane, Olive, and Avery, for sushi. I'm not crazy about sushi and I don't know if it's because there are people I don't really know or if I'm just in a bad mood, but as the night goes on I just keep feeling different from everyone. Unlike me, all Epstein's friends have been to Europe. Unlike me, they all go to private schools. Olive's older sister is spending New Year's with Lena freaking Dunham! Unlike me, none of them has a schizophrenic older brother who thinks his clothes have been poisoned. I wonder what will happen if he decides to go for a drive somewhere or wants to sneak a bottle of liquor from my parents' locked liquor cabinet.

By the time we get the check, I'm miserable and hungry. Raw fish isn't filling.

After dinner, we cram into an Uber and head downtown to some girl named Sky's loft. I'm only half-listening to the conversation Epstein is having with Olive and Avery, but I think they said Noah Baumbach once filmed in Sky's apartment. Normally, I'd ask a million questions, but right now I don't care.

Sky and I are the same height, but that's where the similarities end. She has butt-length blond hair that's pulled to one side and is wearing a see-through knit sweater with nothing underneath, not even a bra, silver leggings, a lot of silver bracelets on her arms, and knee-length black boots that look impossible to even stand in. It's hard to believe she's in high school. She looks like she comes from another planet. The apartment is a loft that's bigger than my house.

Epstein keeps introducing me to people, but it's awkward and I can't remember anyone's name. There are at least eleven Emmas, five Avas, and six Charlottes. A guy named Steel, with two huge earlobe-stretching tapers, spins actual records.

I am happy to see Holden, who shrieks when he sees me.

"Hi, Holden," I say, looking up at him.

"It's been too long, *mon chérie*."

"It has. How are you?"

"De-pressed," he says in a bad Texan drawl. "There is nothing for me to love on. I'm a sad, sad urban cowboy."

"No, you're not."

"Oh, but I am a depressed cowboy, Amelia Jane."

"Holden."

"Ok, but imagine how hot I'd be if I was one."

"But you're not *really* depressed."

"Oh no, that's true. I really am depressed. I'm just totally miserable." He winks at me. "My chances of getting laid are depressingly miserable. It's vagina central here. Look at all these *girls*."

Suddenly I feel miserable. Holden's probably one of the happiest, funniest guys I've ever met.

"Oh. Sorry, Amelia." He puts his arm around me.

"Why?" I look at him.

"I shouldn't have said that. Sorry. I forgot about your brother. My bad. I shouldn't be so cavalier about depression." He gives me a shy smile, but suddenly I'm furious. At Holden, at Epstein, at everyone.

"My brother's not depressed," I spit out.

"Righto," he says cheerfully. "Well, I'm going to get us an effervescent beverage." He saunters away.

Who does Holden think he is? I see him radiating laughter as he talks to Sky. I'm so angry that I hope he wakes up suicidal tomorrow.

I regret my thought instantly. I don't want Holden to feel suicidal. I don't want anyone to feel that way. More than anything, I don't want to feel the way I feel right now. I'm not suicidal, but I feel like Sky's loft is an ocean with waves of people I don't know how to talk to. I don't see Epstein anywhere.

To do something, I go find the bathroom, which is bigger than my bedroom. I can't believe Epstein told his mom and Holden about Toby. If Holden knows, then Ramona and Chloe probably do, too. Everyone at the party probably thinks of me as "Epstein's girlfriend with the schizophrenic brother."

I stand up and wash my hands, wondering how long I can spend in the bathroom. But I don't want to hide in some fancy New York City bathroom. I should have stayed home. I could have helped at Ginger's or stayed home with Sam, since he hates sleepovers. Or I could have watched a movie on my couch instead of having to hide from a loft full of rich city kids.

Someone knocks on the door.

"Just a second," I call. I look in the mirror. I'm still me: Amelia Anderson, Toby Anderson's little sister. Schizophrenic Toby Anderson's sister. *Happy Shmoo Year's. The year of the shmoo.*

I walk out of the bathroom. The music is loud, the loft is hot, and I don't feel remotely social. I don't want to see Isabelle and Geoff over bagels in the morning. I can't imagine being relaxed enough to have sex with Epstein.

I could go home, I think with a jolt. There's nothing stopping me. Even if Toby spends the whole night doing laundry, I can leave and go home to Kepler, my couch, and a movie.

So I do probably the craziest thing I've ever done.

I leave.

Without a word, I slip out of Sky's loft, run down seven flights of stairs, and onto 16th Street; after checking my phone to make sure I know exactly where Grand Central is, I walk all the way to 42nd Street, weaving myself through the throngs of happy drunk people who are spilling out of restaurants and bars, who are holding hands and smiling, excited for the New Year to begin.

Amazingly, I make it onto the 9:25 PM train.

I leave without my stuff—Ray's bag is still on Epstein's bed.

I leave without saying "thank you" or "goodbye" or "see ya later" to my boyfriend.

I just go.

Miraculously, there's a cab at the station and the roads are empty so I get home before midnight.

The house is quiet but normal. Only appropriate lights are on, Kepler is sleeping on the couch, all the burners are off, Prudence is still in the garage, and my parents' liquor cabinet is closed. Even though I'm relieved, I can't help but feel a tiny bit disappointed.

"Hey, Toby," I call as I walk up the stairs. "You here?"

"Yeah?" he calls from behind his closed door.

"Hey." I open his door. "How's it going?"

He's lying on his bed, *The Lord of the Rings* next to him. "Aren't you supposed to be out?"

"I came back early. The city was lame. I thought it would be fun to hang out. With you."

"I'm busy. I've got to work on my book. And my letter to Peter Jackson."

"What letter?"

"I'm telling him all the places he got wrong in the movies." Toby holds up a yellow legal pad.

Is he really going to send Peter Jackson a letter about movies that he made more than ten years ago? I think about my response. "You can't take a break? For one night? We could watch a movie . . ."

He shakes his head. "Got any pot?"

"No. Where's Mom?"

"Stuck at the restaurant. Grandma is coming home."

"Oh. You wanna watch a movie? We could make sundaes. I know where Mom stashed the sprinkles."

"I don't feel like hanging out."

I came home for this! I completely bailed on my boyfriend on New Year's Eve for this. I pulse with rage as I walk downstairs, hang up my coat, and turn on my phone. *Don't blame Toby. He didn't tell you to come back.* I have seven texts, five missed calls, and three new voicemails, but I can't handle hearing Epstein's voice so I just delete them. Tomorrow I'll call Epstein. Tomorrow everything will be better. But I have to let him know I wasn't murdered. I try fifty variations and finally send this incredibly lame text:

Me: sorry. had to leave. something came up. @home. safe.

Epstein: what? you're gone? left???

Me: sorry. @ home.

Epstein: Wtf??? what happened? r u okay? toby? I'm freaking out!!

Me: i'm fine. toby is fine 2. i needed to get home. ttyl

Epstein: ttyl?! wtf? call me!!!

But instead of calling Epstein and trying to find the words to explain what I've done, I turn off my phone again. I can't believe I snuck out of a party. How is Epstein going to explain my absence to Isabelle and Geoff? What am I going to tell Ray about her bag?

Ten minutes before midnight, my grandmother and Harry burst into the house, flushed and happy.

"Hi," I say.

"Oh, Amelia. You scared me! What happened? Why are you here?" My grandmother looks up toward Toby's room.

"Things are fine, but Epstein got the flu," I tell her.

"Poor thing. Toby's okay?" She glances upstairs again. "Your mom said she's running late."

I nod. "Toby told me."

"Come watch the countdown with us."

"If I can stay awake," Harry says through a yawn.

"Don't be an old fuddy-duddy," my grandmother says.

"I *am* an old fuddy-duddy," Harry says.

I can't remember ever feeling so lonely. "Thanks," I say. "But I'm tired. You guys have fun."

"I hope *you're* not getting sick," my grandmother says as she and Harry walk down to her apartment.

After they're gone, I open the fridge but nothing looks appealing. I stare at the holiday cards that cover the entire fridge. There are dozens of smiling kids, some of them on sleds or Santa's lap, on tropical beaches, holding new brothers and sisters, smiling toothless smiles under words like "merry" and "happy" and "bright." I hate the words "merry" and "happy" and "bright" and I don't know half these kids. They don't have any idea who I am either. *Who am I?* There has to be more to me and to my life than just being a sister to a schizophrenic. I can't spend the rest of my life not going to parties because I'm scared of what my brother might do.

At 11:55 PM I call Kepler and step out onto the deck. The sky is bright with stars and it feels like it might snow. I walk down to my dad's truck, open the door, and get in. I put my hands on the steering wheel, close my eyes, and imagine turning the ignition, putting the gear into drive. I think how great it would be to drive to school or to Ray's, to drive to the train station, and help my parents by chauffeuring the twins around. *I could get a job.* I could get an after-school job and make money. I could do so many things if I had my driver's license. Then I think about *The Sweet Hereafter, Casino Royale, Gone in 60 Seconds, Premonition,* and *The Fast and the Furious,* and imagine crashing into a fence, a tree, a semi, or a bus full of children.

I open my eyes and turn the keys that are, as always, in

the ignition. I look at the time. It's 11:59 PM. I turn the engine off, open the passenger door, and call Kepler, who jumps in, barking happily.

"Sorry," I say. "No ride, Keps. We're counting down the New Year."

I pet the back of her head and she lies down. "Do you have a New Year's resolution, Kep? More naps? That seems good. I haven't made a resolution in forever. I think they're silly." I rub her belly. "So, it's not a resolution . . . It's a pledge, Keppie. I'm going to drive this year," I whisper into her head. "I'm tired of being in the passenger's seat. I really need to drive."

I go back in the house and stand outside my brother's room. "Happy New Year," I tell the door. "I hope this year is better than last year." I know it's silly, but I cross my fingers anyway.

Act V: Scene 2

TOBY is seventeen years old.
AMELIA is fifteen years old.

INT. AMELIA and TOBY are in Toby's car,
which looks like a typical teen's. There
are a few empty soda bottles and chip bags
on the backseat next to two backpacks.

TOBY
We need to stop by the Salvation Army
before we go home, 'kay?

AMELIA
Why?

TOBY
We're looking for an acoustic guitar.

AMELIA
Why?

TOBY
So I can learn to play it and then find some
other people to play with me so we can play
at the Battle of the Bands.

AMELIA
You want to start a band?

TOBY
How's the name "Cheeky Monkey"?
Cheesy? What about "Rainbow Unicorns"?
"Have A Nice Day"? "The Ex-Boyfriends"?
Oooh, that's good. The Ex-Boyfriends.
That sounds cool, right?

AMELIA
I guess. But you don't know how to play
anything.

TOBY
I know. That's why we have to find
me a guitar, like, right now.

AMELIA
But you can't just learn it in,
like, a week. And who's going to be
in your band anyway?

TOBY
I don't know. But I'll find people. The
Ex-Boyfriends are going to rock!

AMELIA
Isn't the Battle of the Bands in, like, two

weeks? How are you going to learn guitar, write songs, form a band, and practice enough to play in front of people?

TOBY
We're not just going to play—we're going to win! First prize is two hundred dollars.

Amelia shakes her head doubtfully.

TOBY
Trust me.

FADE OUT.

CARD: TWO WEEKS LATER

INT: The high school auditorium, which is so packed that students have even crowded the hallway outside.

RAY and AMELIA are in the crowd.

RAY
yelling
Your brother is amazing. I had no idea he could play guitar and sing.

AMELIA

Me neither. It seems like just yesterday he was buying that crappy guitar for twenty bucks.

RAY

The Ex-Boyfriends are the most random group of people, but they're really awesome.

AMELIA

I know. I don't know how he does it. I think they'll probably win, too.

RAY

Definitely. They're the best band here.

Camera moves away from them and onto the stage, where Toby looks like a rock star.

FADE OUT.

17

WINTER BLAHS AND BLUES

FOR THE FIRST TIME EVER, I'M READY TO GO BACK TO school *before* vacation ends. Although nothing bad has happened, nothing good seems to be happening either. My brother comes downstairs for meals and answers questions if you ask him, but he doesn't seem interested in anything except listening to music in his room. My mom stops going into Ginger's so she can take him to various doctors' appointments. Ray's filling in as assistant manager of CinnaYum!, and since my parents need even more babysitting, I spend a lot of time watching the twins, who get to watch a lot of TV.

I swear my dad calls me "good egg" more than my name. I don't say anything but I don't feel good about anything at all.

I start a hundred texts and fifty emails to Epstein, but I don't send a single one. I don't know how to explain why I left.

One morning my parents spend hours on a conference call with the high school principal and Toby's guidance counselor. I don't know what they talk about, but my mom looks even more miserable when the call ends.

I watch *Sherman's March* again, and even though I really like it, I wonder if I spend too much time watching movies and if I should try to do something more meaningful with my time.

» » · « «

The night before school starts I call Ray to confess that I lost her bag.

"Really?"

"I left it on the train," I say. "They're looking for it, but it doesn't look good. I'm really sorry. I'll pay you back."

"Oh. That's okay. No biggie. I made mad cash this week. How was New Year's in the big city?"

"Okay."

"Just okay? I thought you'd be out till dawn, walking home across the Brooklyn Bridge."

"Did you binge-watch *Sex and the City* with your mom again?"

"Sadly it was my best New Year's option." Ray sighs. "That or hanging out with Muppet and Toast. Should we call them Moast from now on?"

"It wasn't like *Sex and the City*." *But it kind of was*, I think, picturing the trendy sushi place and Sky's loft. There was a time when I would've loved describing the details of my night in New York to Ray, but now I can't bring myself to tell her anything.

"So how's Toby? He hasn't texted me back."

"Um . . . pretty good. His phone isn't on."

"Oh."

I want to say something more, something about how not okay Toby is, but I can't.

"Do you guys want a ride to school tomorrow?"

"Yeah. If you don't mind. That would be great." If he

can't drive Prudence, it will be better for Toby to go to school with a friend rather than our parents or the bus.

"I'll pick you guys up at 7:15. I can't believe I haven't seen Toby since he's been home!"

"You'll see him tomorrow."

Before I go to bed, I knock on Toby's door. He's wearing a green hooded sweatshirt over his baggy white T-shirt, which I try to see as an improvement.

"Hey," I say. "Ray said she'll drive us to school tomorrow."

I wonder if he'll say something about Prudence, but he just says, "I can't go back to school."

"It won't be so bad." My heart starts thumping. *What is school going to be like for my brother? If he can barely have a conversation with our family, how's he going to deal with classes? What are his friends going to think when they see his clothes and beard?*

"It's going to be hell," he tells me matter-of-factly.

"You'll be okay. I'll be there."

He shakes his head.

"Ray's coming at 7:15," I say lamely.

He shrugs, then turns around and closes his door. I look at my phone, but I think Epstein has officially stopped communication. I don't feel exactly ready to talk to him, but what if I never talk to him again?

The next morning, after I shower and dress, I knock on my brother's door, but he doesn't answer. I don't know what to do. At 7:10, when he still doesn't respond, I take a deep breath and open the door. To my surprise, he's sitting at his desk, still wearing the green sweatshirt.

"Ray's going to be here soon."

"I already told you, I'm not going to school." He sounds annoyed.

"Really? Can you do that?"

"Of course I can do that," he says confidently. For a second I get a glimpse of the old Toby, the healthy Toby, who would give me a look like: *Of course you can skip French to smoke a joint with me.*

"Mom and Dad are okay with that?" I feel like a goody-two-shoes, but I can't help it. He's missed *a lot* of school. I wonder if that's why Mom was so upset after the call to the principal.

He nods. I look at him. Despite the stubble and acrid rankness that seems to emanate from him, he's tall and thin, his eyes are a piercing blue, his eyelashes thick and long and dark. I would love to see him shave off his stubbly beard thing and get a haircut, but I would never suggest it. "See ya," he says, getting up and closing his door.

Only my grandmother is home, but she's so busy hustling David and Sam that I don't tell her that Toby's not going to school. *The Secret Sibling Society lives*, I think. But what's Toby going to do at home all day? Does schizophrenia mean he'll spend his life in his room?

Ray is visibly disappointed when I get into her car alone. "Where's Toby?"

"He needs another day."

"Another day?" She sounds shocked.

"It's not that big a deal."

"But he's missed a shitload of classes. Do you think he'll be able to graduate?"

"I don't know! But we're going to be late. Can we go?" I sound harsher than I mean to. Ray backs down my driveway fast and I clutch my seat as we narrowly avoid hitting the icy shrubbery.

I watch the frozen, gray landscape slip by through the window. The whole world seems jagged, heavy, and awkward. *I am going to school without my brother*, I think. *The New Year is not starting off any better than it ended.*

"Do you notice something different about me?" Ray asks.

I look at her. Her long hair looks the same. She's wearing her standard big silver hoop earrings, a little more mascara than usual, her furry Sorel boots, and Via Spiga faux-fur bomber jacket. "You look thin," I say, even though it's hard to tell when someone is sitting down.

"Bullshit. I ate mall crap all week."

I look at her again, but she looks like Ray.

"Maybe think about something I'm *not doing*." Ray stares at me.

"Not doing," I mumble to myself. "Ummmm . . . You're not bidding on eBay . . . Smoking! You're not smoking!" I can't remember the last time I was in Ray's car when she wasn't smoking. Smoking while driving and listening to loud music is Ray's favorite activity.

"I quit. Well, I'm trying to quit. One day at a time, like AA would say."

"That's great."

"Everyone says you gain like ten pounds."

"Better than cancer."

"Yeah, I know." She turns into the student parking lot. "I don't think I've ever made an actual New Year's resolution. So we'll see how it goes."

Resolutions make me think of telling Kepler I would drive this year. But with my brother in his room, not going to school, not shaving, not talking to anyone, it seems impossible that I will actually keep my pledge. "It's good that you stopped," I tell Ray.

"When I want one, which I do, I just try to think about how much money I'm going to save. Would a Chanel bag be totally insane? I found one on Bluefly for eight hundred dollars."

"It's a lot . . ." I think of what movies I would show in a cigarette-themed film fest: *The Insider, Thank You for Smoking, Coffee and Cigarettes.*

"Yeah, but I spend more than that on cigarettes in a year."

As Ray deftly backs into a tight spot, I watch a bunch of seniors piling out of their cars. *Toby should be here.* He shouldn't need one more day. He should be joking around and throwing snowballs with the other senior guys. Suddenly, I feel angry that Toby spent Christmas break in his room, wearing awful clothes, not talking. *This was the worst vacation ever,* I realize. Even suckier than the Christmas I had pneumonia. At least then Toby tried to get me to laugh by teaching the twins, who were toddlers, to say things like "Leave the gun. Take the cannoli," and "You are a smelly pirate hooker." *Toby used to do things. He wanted people to do things like they do things in movies, but now he won't even watch a movie with me.*

"Want a pack of gum?" Ray says, bringing me back to reality. She grabs a small box of Trident from her backseat and hands me a pack. "I got like fifty packs at BJ's."

"Thanks," I say, hearing the flatness in my voice. I hate myself for sounding this way. *This isn't Ray's fault*, I tell myself. *It isn't anybody's.*

In Driver's Ed, Mr. Munson says we're ready for the simulators, so we make our way to the back of the room and sit behind semi-enclosed desks with screens and steering wheels.

"This is the best part of the class," Abdi says. "Don't kill any deer. They'll fuck up your car."

"Ugh," I say, putting my hands on three o'clock and nine o'clock.

But simulator driving is nothing like real driving. Once I figure out that I'm taking the right turns too wide, I do fine and don't get any police sirens or anything.

After class, Abdi says, "Wasn't that kind of awesome? I hit the dog this time!"

"I love dogs! It was kind of like playing video games with my brothers."

"Yeah. It beats listening to statistics and rules for thirty-five minutes. How is Toby? I haven't seen him around lately. I mean, I didn't back before vacation."

Abdi sounds totally nice, totally genuine, but I don't know what to say.

"Um . . ." I cough a little. "He should be in school to-morrow. You can talk to him then. I didn't know you were friends."

"I wouldn't say we were friends. But I filmed a lot at Smoker's Gate this fall and he was always there. With Toast and them, even though he didn't smoke. Well, not cigarettes."

"Oh." I wonder what Abdi thinks of my brother. Cool senior? Stoner? Freak?

"I have footage of him if you ever want to watch it. He's pretty funny."

"Maybe," I say, even though I know I'll never want to see it. "What's the movie about anyway?"

"That's the million-dollar question." He shakes his head. "It's kind of about the emo kids. And Toast. Toast's not emo. He's just Toast. They're actually kind of interesting."

"Really? I thought emo kids just felt sorry for them-selves, got high, and listened to shitty music."

Abdi laughs. "One on one, some of them said some in-teresting stuff, but right now it's fifteen hours of mostly bor-ing kids who feel sorry for themselves, get high, and listen to shitty music. I need to edit it. It's all about the editing, really. Hey! You should come to film club sometime."

"Washington Lincoln has a film club?"

"Who do you think sponsors the monthly movie series?"

"We have a monthly movie series?"

"You've never been? I don't believe that." Abdi sounds shocked.

"Sorry. I don't really do any extracurricular—"

"I'm kidding. I mean, we do show monthly movies, but

the only people who come are us, the film geeks, and a few random people from town."

"Oh," I say, feeling better.

"We do try to show decent movies, though. I always want to show documentaries, but I'm often vetoed."

"Oh! I totally forgot. Your movie!" I open my backpack and hand him *Sherman's March*. "Sorry I had it for so long. I watched it twice."

Abdi grins. "Isn't it awesome? I'm psyched you actually watched it. My friends always nod off after like ten minutes."

"At first I thought it was slow, but it was good. Different."

"I know. I totally want to make movies like that. To me, he's a lot more honest a director than Michael Moore. You should check out film club. Officially we meet Wednesdays, but someone is usually down in the room—it's B5—just hanging out, watching something. I'm usually watching my footage. I'm going there now, actually. There's only three of us."

"I'll think about it." I want to be polite, but I can't see myself going to film club. Three people isn't exactly a club, and I'm not really an extracurricular kind of girl.

But when I walk into the cafeteria after talking to Abdi, I wish I had followed him to film club because Toast, Muppet, and Ray all get quiet when I sit down.

"What?" I ask.

Ray gives me a look that I can't interpret.

"Is your brother okay?" Toast asks.

"Did he have a breakdown?" Muppet asks.

I glare at Ray, who shakes her head.

Toast rubs his red eyes. "All I know is that your brother was not having a good night. I drove him home, because driving didn't seem like a wise thing for him to do. I took him home. That's *all*. I'd like to know how he's doing, Amelia. I haven't heard anything from him at all."

I feel six eyes bearing into my soul. *What happened to Toby? What's wrong with your brother?*

I wish I knew. One minute I had a cool older brother, an amazing boyfriend, I lost my virginity, drank red wine, and everything was great—and the next minute my grandmother called and everything changed. I don't know how it went from so good to so bad so quickly, how my life became this never-ending tsunami, pushing me under, not allowing me to breathe.

I open my mouth to say something because I want to get it over with, get it out in the open. I want to say, "Toby's schizophrenic," but my brain and tongue can't figure out how to say it, so I close my mouth and look at the splattered ketchup on the mushy, uneaten fries on the plate next to me.

"Amelia? Are you okay?" Muppet asks gently.

I force myself to move my head up and down, but I don't look away from the bloody fries. I remember when Toby told me I was chewing so loud. *He was sick then.* He was sick and all I did was beg him for rides.

I look up at my friends: Toast with his bloodshot eyes, skinny Muppet with her oblong chin and braids, and Ray,

my best friend in the world. I know they just want to understand what went wrong, but all I can do is wonder: *Why isn't
it one of them?*

Of all the people—of the three hundred and fifty students in Washington Lincoln High School—why Toby? Why
my brother?

"Amelia . . . ," Ray says. "We're here for you."

But I can't talk about it. I can't tell these people who
used to think my brother was so cool how awful vacation
was, how weird it is to see my mom put out gigantic pills
next to my brother's cereal bowl each morning. I still can't
tattle on Toby.

"I have to go," I say, getting up from the table and bolting for the doors. I go to the library, which is empty except
for the librarian, who doesn't look up. Social networking
sites are blocked, but I still try to check Facebook. When I
can't get on, I check my email, but there's nothing.

I haven't communicated with Epstein in five days.

Without thinking about it, I type *schizophrenia* into the
Google search bar. I'm not even sure I spelled it right but
more than 23 million pages of links come up. I click on Wikipedia and read how its root comes from a Greek word that
means to split and how it's characterized by abnormalities
in the perception or expression of reality. I learn how dis-
tortions in perception may affect all five senses and that it
typically occurs in young adulthood. I read that schizophrenia is a chronic condition that requires lifelong care. Then
I get paranoid that someone will come in and see what I'm

reading and know that it's about my brother so I close the site and sit there just staring at the screensaver, which says "Washington Lincoln" in this bouncing text, until the bell rings and I get up and go to my next class.

18

SCHOOL DAZED AND CONFUSED

TOBY DOESN'T GO TO SCHOOL ON TUESDAY, EITHER. My grandmother has a doctor's appointment so I get the twins on their bus and avoid potential Toby talk by spending lunch in the library reading movie reviews on Rotten Tomatoes.

Things are different on Wednesday. When I come downstairs, my dad is home *and* awake and Toby is downstairs spooning sugar into a cup of coffee. My mom is unloading dishes from the dishwasher even though that's technically my job. The air feels electric and tense.

"I'll drive you and Toby to school today," my dad says like it's perfectly normal, even though he's probably taken me twice in the last ten years since he likes to be at Ginger's by 5:00 AM.

"Beats the bus." I smile at Toby, but he looks away.

"*I* can drive," Toby says. "I have a license. *And* a car."

"I'm driving," my dad tells him. "And I'm picking you up at 2:40."

"For my appointment." Toby puts air quotes around "appointment."

"Oh, Toby," my mom says. "We want to help you. We want you to get better."

"There's nothing wrong with me. Except you're treating me like a prisoner." Toby scowls angrily at her, which makes me furious. Doesn't he see how sad she is?

I offer Toby the front seat, but he gets in the back and

slumps against the door. It's no surprise that the only conversation that happens is on the radio. Two guys keep yelling at each other about some game. When we get to school, my dad reminds Toby to be outside, because he's leaving work early to get him. Then he peels off like there's nowhere he'd less like to be.

I look at Toby. He's still wearing the green sweatshirt, but has, thank God, taken off the sweatpants and is wearing khakis. They're dorky, but at least it's not sweatpants.

"Well, I guess we should go in," I say. I start walking through the doors and, to my relief, so does Toby. "You'll be okay," I tell him. "It won't be so bad."

When we get inside I realize that he doesn't have a backpack, which means he has no books or pens.

When we get to my homeroom, I stop. "Well this is me."

"Alright," he says.

"See you later."

He nods. I watch him shuffle down the hall and make a left. Where's he going? His homeroom isn't there. *Don't think about it*, I tell myself. *At least he's here.*

I don't see Toby for the rest of the day. Twice there are announcements over the loudspeaker and I panic, but it's only about cancelled club meetings and room changes. One of the cancelled clubs is film club and I wonder if Abdi is bummed. Ray has work, so after school I go to Starbucks with Abdi, Muppet, and Toast because I can't think of any reason not to. It's not like my dad is picking *me* up to take me to my therapist. *Unlike Toby, I'm free to do what I want,* I think, *so I might as well enjoy it.*

Even though Toast and Muppet don't say anything

about my brother, it's hard to have fun. A bunch of seniors are there and I can't help but watch them and imagine what it'd be like if Toby was there, too. Abdi spends a lot of time filming Toast, and Muppet spends most of the time eating sugar packets and beaming at her boyfriend.

But when I get home, I'm thrilled to see that Toby is in the living room, watching TV.

"Hey! What's up?"

He shrugs.

"Where is everyone?" I wonder if I should sit next to him. Then I realize how sad that is and plunk myself down.

"Out." His voice is monotone.

"What are you watching?"

"It was a show about this guy who blew stuff up, but then this lady came and . . . I don't know. It doesn't make sense."

I feel like I'm sitting next to a stranger. I want to ask Toby all these questions: *Did he go to class? Were people weird? And what about his psychiatrist and the pills he takes? Does anything help?* I have all these questions for my brother, but I feel like I'm sitting next to this guy who used to be my brother, and I'm not sure where my real brother has gone.

Thursday is like Wednesday. My dad takes us to school and I don't see Toby till I come home, which is late, because now that we've supposedly mastered simulated driving, Mr. Munson is having us drive an actual car after school. Because there's only one car and eleven students, there's a lot of waiting around. I spend it talking movies with Abdi, who's seen every documentary ever made. While we're waiting, he keeps adding more and more movies to my Netflix queue. He's pretty funny about it. He'll think of one movie to add, which will make him think of two other ones. When it's my group's turn, I tell Mr. Munson that I'm nauseous, so he lets me sit in the backseat with the window rolled down and doesn't make me drive. When I finally get home, Toby is watching cartoons with Sam and David, my mom is making dinner, and my grandmother is setting the table. For a glorious few minutes everything feels back to normal.

On Friday my dad says he has to be at Ginger's early, so Toby and I take the bus to school. I imagine being able to drive so Toby wouldn't have to be the only senior on the bus, but he doesn't seem to mind. He sits right behind the driver, takes out his notebook, and proceeds to write the entire ride there. After we get off the bus, I don't see Toby for the rest of the day, but by now that's not much of a surprise.

19

SO NOT WHAT HAPPENS

A FEW DAYS INTO TOBY'S SECOND WEEK BACK IN
school, I relax. A little. Sure, he still spends most of his time
at home either in his room or mutely watching TV, but after
a long phone call my mom had with a new therapist, he's
begun to set the table and sit down to dinner with us. My
mom barely seems to work at Ginger's anymore and my dad
is there more than ever.

Instead of worrying about Toby, I worry about Driver's
Ed and Epstein. Between fake cramps and pretend migraines,
and a wonderful snowstorm that canceled all after-school
activities, Mr. Munson has totally figured out that I've never
driven the student-mobile and I know I'm going to have to.

I haven't heard from Epstein. During lunch on Wednesday, I tell myself I have to email him, that I can't leave the
library until I do. But I just sit at the ancient wood table
staring at the blank Gmail Compose screen. I don't have the
words to describe how I felt in that fancy NYC bathroom,
while everyone else was so happy and free, so I leave the library and go down to the basement just to see where exactly
the film club meets.

I'm planning on just peeking in, but as soon as I walk by,
Abdi sees me. "Amelia!" He sounds excited.

"I'm just, uh . . ."

"Come in, come in. You won't regret it."

When I walk in I see a row of computers on one side, a huge monitor, a tripod, a bunch of wires, and a microphone. Other than Abdi, there's a Chinese skater guy named Tony who's a senior, and Jessie Eaves, the Hello Kitty freak.

Jessie smiles. "Yay, another girl!" She sounds so nice and happy that I feel bad for thinking of her as a freak.

"We're trying to decide our February movie," Abdi says. "Maybe you can help."

"I think we should show romantic movies, but the guys want to go all anti-romance," Jessie tells me. She's wearing a pink, hooded Hello Kitty sweatshirt and two Hello Kitty wristbands.

"You want to show *The Conjuring*, right?" Tony asks.

"That's too scary," Jessie says. "We can't show that."

"You've never seen it," Tony says.

"Because it's too scary."

I can't help but laugh.

"What about *Love Actually*?" Jessie asks.

Abdi and Tony both groan.

"My mom loves that movie," I say. "She loves Hugh Grant."

"Hugh Grant is a dipshit," Tony says.

"But maybe Amelia's mom would come to the film series. That would practically double our attendance," Jessie says.

"We had six people for the January showing of *Boyhood*," Tony says. "And that includes me, Jessie, Abdi, and Ms. Fisher, the adviser."

"I loved *Boyhood*," I say. "That was so cool how Richard Linklater used all the same actors."

"You should watch the *Up* series," Abdi tells me.

"Here we go," Tony says, shaking his head.

"We need more people to come to the monthly movie," Jessie says. "So we need to show movies that people actually want to see."

"I don't care how many people come," Abdi says. "I want to show *good* movies. I want to show art. People can watch Chris Pratt at home."

"Art, shmart," Jessie says. "I love Chris Pratt. And I want people to come."

I look at Abdi. "What do you want to show?"

"*Blue Valentine*," he says. "It gets the valentine in, but it's still a great movie. And it's not a documentary."

"It's *so* depressing," Jessie says. "People don't want to watch people fighting. Not on Valentine's Day."

"It is pretty sad, dude," Tony says. "But Michelle Williams is hot."

Abdi looks at me. "Amelia? Have you seen it?"

"Yeah, I've seen it. It is sad, but it's a good, real-sad, not a cheesy-sad like *Marley & Me* or *Old Fashioned*. But there's a dead dog in it and I hate movies with dead dogs. And more than dead dogs I hate movies that have kids looking for dead dogs. So I'm going to have to go with Jessie's choice."

"Do you have a list of Movies with Kids Looking for Dead Dogs?" Abdi looks impressed.

"No," I say. "But that could be a good one. Except, of course, I don't think I could watch it again."

"Yes!" Jessie says. "I'm so happy you're in film club, Amelia."

"I'm not exactly . . ." I notice the huge collection of DVDs on the back wall. "Do all these movies belong to the school?"

Abdi nods. "And you can totally borrow them. There are a lot of good documentaries. I help Ms. Fisher do the ordering."

"You order all the movies," Tony jokes. "Ms. Fisher just authorizes the purchase card."

Abdi shrugs. "I have excellent taste."

I'm about to check out all the DVDs when Toast comes running in. "Amelia!" he says.

My brain switches to high alert. "What? What's wrong?"

"Cafeteria. Toby," he says.

In slow motion, we follow Toast out of the room, down the hall, and up the stairs. I notice a lot of students spilling out of the cafeteria even though the bell hasn't rung, but I don't see my brother.

I hear Toby before I see him. For one thing, he must have a megaphone—and for another, there are about fifty students watching him.

"YOU NEED TO GET OUT!" he bellows from the table he's standing on. "YOUR SOULS ARE SICK. DEMONS ARE POISONING THEM. YOU'RE SURROUNDED BY DEMONS AND THE BLACK RIDERS, YOU DON'T EVEN KNOW IT!"

I push Jake Sweeney out of the way. "Hey!" he yells. When he sees who I am he says, "Oh—sorry, Amelia."

My brother *is* on a bullhorn. *Where did he get that?* I wonder before I remember that it's completely unimportant.

"Toby!" I scream when I get to the front of the crowd.

He looks at me for a second. He's dripping with sweat and very flushed. "You're all assholes," he says. "You have no idea what The Eye can do."

"Maybe 'cause we're not crazy!" Justin Carroll taunts. "You've read too much *Lord of the Rings*, you wacko."

"Shut the fuck up, Justin," I hear Ray say from somewhere. *Ray*, I think. *Where is Ray? She can help.*

"YOU'RE ALL FUCKING NUTS!" Toby screams. "I'M THE ONLY ONE WHO WILL TELL YOU THE TRUTH, MOTHERFUCKERS. YOU'RE ALL GOING TO DIE, YOU STUPID ASSHOLES." He pulls his shirt off, and I notice that he's not wearing any shoes.

"Do you think he has a gun?" I hear Jessie whisper.

"Please don't let this be a Newtown," someone else says.

"YOU'RE ALL GOING TO DIE. THE BLACK RIDERS HAVE BEEN RELEASED FROM MORDOR, MY FRIENDS. LORD SAURON IS STAYING FOR BREAKFAST, LUNCH, AND DINNER, MY FRIENDS. AND YOU JUST SMILE AND WAIT FOR THE END OF THE WORLD LIKE LAMBS TO SLAUGHTER!" Toby clutches his notebook to his bare chest.

Do something! I tell myself. *You have to do something or this is going to get much worse.*

I hear someone behind me saying the Lord's Prayer.

"Toby!" I try to sound forceful. "Please get down!"

Toby takes a step back on the table and looks at me. "AMELIA," he says over the bullhorn. Hearing my name amplified embarrasses me even more.

"Get off the table. We can talk about this. You're feeling confused," I say, trying to remember anything that I read on Wikipedia.

"OH, AMELIA," he says. "OH, MY NAIVE LITTLE SISTER."

"Come on, Toby," Ray says. Thank God, she's made her way to the front, right next to me. "You should get down."

"Ray and Amelia are right, Toby," Abdi says. "Get off the table before you get in serious trouble."

"HI, FILM BOY," my brother says sarcastically. "WHERE'S YOUR CAMERA? YOU SHOULD BE FILM-ING THIS. THIS IS YOUR MILLION-DOLLAR MOVIE!"

I glance at Abdi, but he doesn't have a camera.

"Toby!" I plead. "I'll help you."

"YOU CAN'T HELP ME!" Toby screams. "NO ONE CAN HELP ME. I'M JUST TRYING TO WARN YOU! THE NECROMANCER IS COMING!" Pools of sweat stream down my brother's forehead, and it seems like he's having trouble swallowing.

"Toby!" Tears are running down my face, but I don't care. I am desperate for him to get down from the table. If he gets down, I'll take him by the elbow and lead him through the crowd. Everyone will make a path for us, and we'll get into Ray's car, and she'll drive us wherever we want to go.

Of course, this is so not what happens.

Three seconds later, four security guards, a cop, and two vice principals come bursting in, barking at everyone to get out of the way. Toby rambles on about Sauron and the im-pending darkness until the cop and the biggest security guard lift him off the table, wrestle the bullhorn out of his hands, and carry him out of the cafeteria.

I watch all this, just standing there, numb. Muppet hands me a bottle of water. "Oh, Amelia!" She puts her hand on my shoulder. "You're shaking."

Ray gently leads me to the table and I sit down. "What are they going to do with him?" I ask. "Where are they going to take him?" *Please don't let him go back to the hospital.*

"The nurse?" Muppet says.

I look at her. "The nurse?" I think about the nurse, a woman so ancient that she was here when my dad went here, and who asks if you're having your "monthlies" if you complain about a stomachache. I think about this woman, and I think about my brother, who seems to think that the end of the world has a date, and who has talked more in a ranting, frightening, crazy way over a bullhorn in the cafeteria than I've heard him say the entire five weeks he's been at home.

I look at Ray, Muppet, Toast, Jessie, and Abdi. And then I start laughing. I crack up, imagining the little old nurse offering my delusional brother a Dixie cup of water and an aspirin. I laugh until Ray starts laughing, and Toast, and then Abdi, and then Muppet, and finally Jessie. We sit there laughing until, after all these long weeks, I start crying, the tears flooding out of me, an ocean of tears so intense that I have no choice but to put my head down, between my arms, on the disgustingly sticky table.

"Amelia?" I don't look up, but I'm pretty sure it's Madame Lapelle, my old French teacher. I feel gentle hands on my shoulders. "Are you okay, honey?"

I shake my head because nothing makes any sense right now. It seems like it was just yesterday when I left her class to go to the bathroom and ran into Toby in the hall. I can practically taste the M&M's we shared that glorious day on the grassy spot above the school. I want that brother back. I want the movie quotes and the prom dates and the cartwheels all wrapped up in a big red bow.

"Amelia?" Madame Lapelle says again.

"She's okay," Ray tells her as she pats my head. "She's okay." I love Ray because she stays with me, patting my head long after everyone else but Abdi has left the cafeteria. Ray stays next to me until I feel like I can bring my face off the table and then she and Abdi walk with me, silently, to the principal's office so we can find out what's happened to Toby.

20

MEALS ON WHEELS

RAY AND ABDI AND I WAIT FOREVER FOR THE PRINCIPAL who, when he finally comes out of his office, is annoyed that we're there.

"Where's my brother?" I ask Mr. Hayes.

"The proper authorities have been called," he says.

"Is he home?" I ask. "In the hospital?"

"I'm not at liberty to discuss it," Mr. Hayes says. "We are handling this in accordance with school policy. Now, Miss Anderson, if you'd like to talk to someone, I'll give you a pass to see Dr. Kellerman."

"The guidance counselor? You're not going to tell me where my brother is?"

"I'm not at liberty to discuss it. Mr. Osman and Miss Guerra, I suggest you get to class."

"Seriously?" Ray says.

"Very," Mr. Hayes says, giving us a look before he walks back into his office.

"That's a load of crap," Abdi says, loud enough for the principal's secretary to hear. I know he's my random movie/Driver's Ed friend, but it's sort of nice that he's here, too.

"I'm not going to class," I say as we walk down the hall.

"No shit," Ray says. "Let's blow this Popsicle stand."

The three of us silently walk to the farthest end of the farthest student parking lot. People call it North Dakota and dread having to park here, especially on a freezing day like today. But I don't really notice the cold. I just keep putting one foot in front of the other. When we get to Ray's car, I get that nothing-is-real feeling, look at Ray, and say, "Can I drive?"

"Driver's Ed is in thirty minutes," Abdi says.

"I don't want to go to Driver's Ed. I just want to drive. Can I?" I look at Ray.

She hesitates for less than a second before she gives me her keys.

"Do you want to come?" I ask Abdi. I'm not sure why he's still hanging around, but I ask him anyway.

"Absolutely," he says gamely, which is weird since he knows I've used every excuse not to drive. I wonder if Mr. Munson would accept "schizophrenic brother" as an excuse today as I slide into the driver's seat. Ray sits shotgun, and Abdi hops in the back.

I put the keys into the ignition and turn on the car. I put my hands on the steering wheel and close my eyes. I see images of Toby screaming.

"Amelia?" Ray says.

I open my eyes.

"You can do it," Abdi tells me. "It's exactly like the simulator except it's real. And there aren't any deer." He takes his camera out of his bag. "Do I have permission to film?"

"Permission granted. If I kill us, there'll be evidence."

"You're not going to kill us," Ray says.

I take a deep breath, put the car into drive, put my foot on the gas, and go.

I pull out of Ray's parking spot, into the one right in front of her, and then make a left and a right, pull into another spot, slam on the brakes, and put the car in park.

"Awesome," Abdi says. I look at him in the mirror, to see if he's joking, but he smiles from behind the camera.

"Do it again," Ray says calmly. "Keep driving, Amelia Jane."

So I do. I drive to all the spots in the lot. In and out. Out and in. My phone buzzes and buzzes inside my bag, and I know it's my parents calling to talk about my brother, to let me know where he is and what's happened, but I ignore it and drive until I have driven from one side of the parking lot to the other. By myself.

"Meals on wheels," Ray says, turning around to face Abdi's camera. "Finally!"

I pull into the last spot, put the car in park, and turn off the engine. Neither Ray nor Abdi say anything. The vibrations from my ringing phone seem especially loud, but I still don't answer. Abdi might be filming, but I don't know. I just sit in the driver's seat for a very long time and then turn to Ray and say, "Can you drive me home now? I'm done driving for today."

21

LIKE SOME KIND OF ACCIDENT

"OH, AMELIA, HONEY," MY MOM SAYS WHEN I GET home. From the way she says my name, I know that Toby is back in the hospital. "He had to go back in, Meals. Dr. Perry, his psychiatrist, said he was having a break. This can happen when the medicine isn't working." She swallows.

"Can they give him new medicine?"

She nods. "Yes. They're going to try something else at a different dose. It's upsetting that it happened so soon after he got out, but we're going to get through this." She sounds more resolved than I would have thought. She reaches her arms around me.

"It must have been awful, honey. Dad is at the hospital. I'll go later. Grandma took the twins to Harry's for the night."

"Oh. Okay."

"Let's talk, honey. I know you're going through an awful lot."

I nod, but I feel incredibly exhausted, so I tell her I'll be in my room. I call Kepler, and she comes in right away and curls up on my bed. I lie next to her, my hand rubbing her belly, staring up at the ceiling. And then, in the same out-of-body way that I drove a car for the first time, I take out my phone and finally call Epstein.

"Hello?" His voice pierces through me. "Amelia?"

My tongue moves inside my mouth like it's an alien worm.

"Amelia, I know it's you. My smart phone is smart."

"I know."

"Hey," he says. "You talk."

"Yeah," I say. "I guess."

After a long silence he says, "So, why are you calling?"

I'm doing a lot of new things today, I think. *I went to film club. I drove about a quarter of a mile. I witnessed my brother having a schizophrenic break in a cafeteria full of people and thought maybe I should call you, since that's kind of new, too.* "Do you hate me?" I ask.

"No."

"I hate me," I say. "I hate everybody."

"Amelia," Epstein says gently.

What if it were me? I wonder. *What if I was the one with the mental illness? What would Toby do?*

"Amelia?" Epstein says again. "What's going on? Where have you been? What have you been doing?"

"Well . . ." How can I possibly explain to Epstein what I've been doing?

"I know mental illness can devastate a family," he says.

This is not what I expected to hear. I don't know what I thought he'd say, but definitely not mental illness devastating a family. "How do you know?" I ask, kind of harshly.

"Well, I . . ."

"Did you read intriguing books about it? Go online? Research it in the library?"

"Amelia."

"Is there someone in your family who writes letters to

Peter Jackson about the mistakes in the *Lord of the Rings* trilogy? Did *your* brother ever ask if you'd poisoned his clothes?"

"No," Epstein says. "I've never experienced that stuff firsthand."

"Okay, then."

"I didn't mean . . ."

"It's fine," I say. "It's not your fault that you've never experienced schizophrenia firsthand."

"I did read some books about it," Epstein says seriously. "I read this one called *Me, Myself, and Them*, which was written by a guy who actually has schizophrenia. And I just started *Challenger Deep*. The author's son is schizophrenic and his drawings are in it."

"Oh."

"I've been reading these books because I want to know what you're going through, Amelia."

Figures. It figures that you would go and be the one to read the books about it. That's probably why you're going to Dartmouth or Brown or Harvard. But, no matter how many books you read, you can't know what I'm going through! "I never asked you to read books about it."

"I know. Do you know *This American Life*?"

"The podcast? Yeah. I had an English teacher who played it a lot."

"I can't remember what the theme was, but there's one about a woman with schizoaffective disorder. She started this coffee shop that serves toast and fresh-squeezed grapefruit juice . . . You should listen to it. It's very interesting."

"Interesting?"

"Well, yeah."

"I don't want interesting," I say. And then, totally surprising myself, I throw my phone as hard as I can across the room, where it hits the wall and shatters. "Piece of crap," I say to a very startled Kepler, like it was some kind of accident.

22

"GUIDANCE" WITH DR. K

THE NEXT DAY, THURSDAY, MY MOM TELLS ME IT'S okay to skip school. She says I shouldn't spend the whole day just watching movies, though, so while random animated dog movies play in the background, I clean my closet and organize my dresser. It feels good to spend most of the day going through all my clothes, and matching socks, and folding underwear, and avoiding people. I keep thinking of all the people who saw my brother yesterday and how they'll never be able to unsee him ranting again. Jake Sweeney used to be on my Enemy List because of what he did to Ray last year, but now I'll always think of him as one of the first people I saw during Toby's rant and how he said my name so apologetically. It's almost funny that I used to think Jessie was a freak because she had Hello Kitty laces in her Hello Kitty shoes. I wonder what she thinks of my brother.

But on Friday, I'm back at school. Toby is still in the hospital.

"Why aren't you taking my calls, Anderson?" Ray asks when I sit down to eat lunch.

I focus on spooning chocolate pudding from the container into my mouth. I keep my eyes on the spoon so I don't inadvertently see the table Toby stood on.

"You didn't text me back either," Muppet says.

"It broke," I say.

"What broke?" Ray looks at me, but I concentrate on trying to chew the pudding.

"I feel really bad for Toby," Muppet says. "I feel really bad for your whole family."

"Don't feel bad for me," I say. "Everything is awesome-sauce."

"Amelia," Ray says. "We know what happened."

"We were all here," Toast reminds me.

"Then why do we need to keep talking about it?" I snap. "You're free to do what you want. It's a free country. Tweet it; put a link about breakdowns on your Facebook page. What do you want from me?"

"Nothing," Ray says. "We don't want anything from you." I'm surprised that she sounds so surprised.

"Sorry, Amelia," Muppet says softly.

"We're here for you," Ray says. "No one wants to blog about it."

"I want . . ." I want to stop picturing Toby's rant. Wednesday's scene could have been in a movie, I realize. I want all this to be a very long movie that Toby and I are watching. And after it was over we'd just be like, *Ugh, schizophrenia is a horrible disease. I feel really bad for people who have it, and their families.* And then we'd put the DVD back on the shelf and go about our non–movie version lives.

"You know we love you, Amelia," Ray says.

I know that my friends care about me, but it just feels like too much to try and thank them, so I look at my pudding and wish for something—not too awful, maybe just a fire drill—to happen.

And then, out of a freaking movie, my name is called over the loudspeaker. "Amelia Anderson, report to Dr. Kellerman's office. Amelia Anderson, please report to Dr. Kellerman's."

"Gotta go," I say, practically bolting through the cafeteria doors.

I'm so relieved about escaping the cafeteria that it's not until I'm standing outside Dr. Kellerman's office that it hits me: I've been called to the guidance counselor because someone thinks I'm in need of some guidance.

Dr. Kellerman is short with graying hair and a gray suit. The office is nondescript except for three plants on the windowsill and a framed photograph of the Eiffel Tower.

When I walk in he says, "Hello, Amelia."

"Hi."

"So we haven't talked much this year."

Are you kidding? Who is this guy? I don't think I've even seen him since freshman orientation.

"I've been busy," I tell him.

"I can imagine. Junior year can keep you on your toes. So catch me up on what you're thinking about for future college plans." He opens a folder on his computer. "Your grades have slipped a bit."

Yeah, well, my life has slipped a bit, I think.

"But your GPA is still a solid B. B-ish, I would say. And if you apply yourself for the next two quarters you could bring it up. Do you have any schools in mind?"

Dr. Kellerman wants to talk about college? "I don't know," I say. "I haven't really thought about it."

"You're taking the SATs soon?"

"May." I remember the scene in *Remember the Titans* when Denzel Washington asks the big football player if he's going to college. I remember Toby chose the movie one random Friday night. At first Ray and I weren't interested because we don't like football, but it turned out to be great.

"I strongly suggest that you take them. Take them as many times as you want."

"Okay." I try to think of more "Are you going to college?" movie scenes, but I'm stuck. I come up with a Football Movies for People Who Don't Like Football list instead: *Jerry Maguire*, *We Are Marshall*, *Friday Night Lights*, and *The Blind Side*, which I liked despite my feeling that Sandra Bullock isn't that great of an actor.

"You're an excellent candidate for a state school," Dr. Kellerman says. "The SUNY system is excellent."

Excellent, I think. *What a terrible word.*

Dr. Kellerman clears his throat. "And how are things at home, Amelia?"

Well, let's see. My schizophrenic brother had a breakdown in front of everyone at school. All my friends are mad at me. Or maybe I'm mad at them. I'm not sure. And I haven't had a normal conversation with my boyfriend—if he still is my boyfriend—in weeks. School has been such a blur that I couldn't tell you what I got on my last test and, oh, I smashed my phone to bits.

I look at this fifty-year-old man and can't imagine he'd understand a word. "Excellent," I say.

"I understand that Tobias has been having some trouble lately. That must be difficult."

Part of me wants to laugh because no one, not even my dad when he's furious, ever calls him Tobias. The other part of me wants to punch Dr. Kellerman for being such a terrible movie-version cliché of a high school guidance counselor.

"You know, there's a support group here at school for those affected by mental illness. They meet the first Tuesday of the month. Mr. Lorenzo is the adviser."

"Oh."

"You might find it helpful. They always need help for their events. National Mental Illness Awareness Week is in October."

October is more than half a year away, I think. It seems totally impossible getting to October from where I am now. "I'm kind of busy right now. I'm taking Driver's Ed and I'm in the film club."

"Film club?" Dr. Kellerman says.

"They show monthly movies," I say, like I know what I'm talking about. "And they have Final Cut Pro X for editing footage."

There's a knock on the door.

"Just a second," Dr. Kellerman calls. "My next victim is here," he says, smiling.

Not funny, I think, standing up just as the bell rings.

"Well, think about it," Dr. Kellerman says. "Film club sounds intriguing. Keep those state schools in mind, Amelia. And start your SAT practice. You can practice a lot online."

Yeah right, I think, stepping out into the sea of students in the hall. I'm really going to keep a list of colleges in mind since I have so much free time between my schizophrenic brother, my possible ex-boyfriend, my stressed-out parents, my worrying grandmother, and the fact that I don't seem to have a single person to talk to right now. And even if I miraculously did find a person to talk to, I don't have a phone to do it on.

23

DEVASTATING EFFECTS

MY MOM PICKS UP TOBY FROM THE HOSPITAL ON Saturday morning, but as soon as they get back she has to rush out again because the twins have a birthday party. Since my dad is at Ginger's, it's only my grandmother and me at home with Toby. My brother looks pale with dark bags under his eyes and a full-on major beard. Predictably my grandmother runs to get him a Coke, but I feel like I should stay for a minute.

Say something, I tell myself. *Talk to him.*

"How you feeling?" I finally spit out.

"Tired. I have a headache."

What does he think about his rant the other day? Should I mention it? "That stinks."

"They gave me a lot of pills. I couldn't sleep for like forty-eight hours even on a bunch of stuff. They had to give me quadruple doses of everything." He yawns without bothering to cover his mouth.

I try to picture the Toby who would come bouncing into the house with the idea of flying a kite while ice-skating or passionately explaining why the mono version of *Sgt. Pepper's* is truly the greatest album of all time and I feel a deep, longing ache.

"You want to do something?" I ask him.

"Like what?"

"I don't know. We could go to a movie. There's a new one with James Franco. Or we could just go to the mall? I need to get a phone . . ." I wonder if this is such a good idea. We can't get to the mall or movies since neither of us can drive. And if we got a ride, we'd have to wait to get picked up, and what if he gets weird?

"I need to sleep," Toby tells me. "I can't do anything now."

I feel relieved and guilty and miserable all at the same time.

Toby holes up in his room for the rest of the day. In the afternoon, after dropping David off at Ryan's, my grandmother takes Sam and me to the mall so I can get a new phone. When I get back home, I look at my new phone and start (but don't send) three hundred emails to Epstein. In a weak attempt to be a nice big sister, I play Uno with Sam before I begin my Football Movies for People Who Don't Like Football list by watching *Radio* with Cuba Gooding Jr. and a documentary called *4th & Goal* about college students who want to play in the NFL.

On Sunday, my parents skip brunch and leave at the crack of dawn to buy a new chest freezer for Ginger's. When my brother comes downstairs at noon, he grunts one word answers to my grandmother, eats two peanut butter and jelly sandwiches, and goes back to his room. When my parents get back Sunday night, they both seem cranky and tired. My mom spends forever on her phone while my dad makes an enormous lasagna. When Toby comes downstairs for dinner, he barely speaks.

My brother doesn't go to school Monday, or Tuesday, or Wednesday. Wednesday night, after the twins are already asleep and Toby is listening to loud music in his room, my dad knocks on my door and tells me to come downstairs. My heart starts beating especially fast as I walk into the living room and sit next to my grandmother.

"Well," my dad says. He looks at my mom.

"I'm just going to say it," she says through a scratchy croak. "Mom, Amelia, we've decided that, for a little while at least, Toby should go and live in a residential treatment center."

"A what?" I ask.

"A treatment center," my dad says. "A place where he can live with doctors and a staff to help him."

"We drove up there on Sunday."

"I thought you were buying a freezer," I say.

My dad shakes his head.

"We think a treatment center is the best option right now," my mom adds. "We've talked to a lot of people. Therapists and social workers and many, many doctors."

"We didn't make this decision lightly."

"I know you didn't," my grandmother says softly.

"What?" I say. "You're sending him away?" My voice comes out so squawky that Kepler bolts off the couch.

"It's not sending him away, Meals." My mom gives me a pained look. "It's temporary. Toby needs treatment available to him day and night."

I feel like I might throw up.

My dad takes a deep breath. "The thing is, Meals,

Dr. Perry says that Toby is exhausting the, uh, community resources here. He needs more than we, than the hospital, can give him. He needs a place where they can care for him properly."

"Toby needs so much help that he can't live here?"

"It's not forever," my mom says. "He needs to learn how to live with his diagnosis. The center will help him—and us—do that."

"How long? And where?"

"Most likely six months," she says. "Not too far. Massachusetts. We're lucky Two Moons has an available bed."

I don't think we're lucky, but I keep this to myself.

"What about the twins?" I ask. "What are you going to tell them?"

"The truth," my dad says. "Modified truth."

My mom nods. "The truth is, Amelia, we can't give Toby what he needs here. At least not now. Washington Lincoln can't. Beth Israel can't. But Two Moons can. You need to trust us that this is the right decision."

"It'll be good for him," my grandmother says, blinking back tears. "It'll be good for everyone."

I want to believe them, I really do. But Toby Anderson in a mental institution? That is totally, off-the-wall crazy!

"And . . . We need to ask you to do something for us." My mom sniffs loudly. "For him. Although it might not seem that way."

I look up. "What? What do you want me to do?"

"I know this will be hard on you, Amelia," my mom

says. "It's been hard on everyone, but you and Toby have always been so close."

My mom looks at my dad, who clears his throat. "This will be difficult, but uh, we need you to not tell Toby."

I don't believe it. "He doesn't know? You're not going to tell him?" I can't believe my parents. He's upstairs in his room listening to "Hey Jude" and has no idea that my parents are plotting to send him to Massachusetts.

"We're going to tell him," my mom says. "We just don't want him to know beforehand." She wipes her eyes. "We're afraid that if he knows, he'll run away. And that could have devastating effects. He needs real help, honey."

Epstein said "devastating," too. He said mental illness could devastate a whole family. Am I devastated? Because mostly I'm speechless. How can I keep a secret this big from Toby? I don't think I've ever actually lied to him. But how can I say no to my suffering parents? And I know, deep, deep down, that they wouldn't ask me to betray my brother like this if it wasn't absolutely necessary. It would be much worse if Toby ran away.

"Okay," I say. "I won't tell him."

And with that, I kill the Secret Sibling Society.

24

VALENTINE'S, SHMALENTINE'S

HE DOESN'T KNOW IT, BUT TOBY'S LAST MEAL AT HOME is beautiful heart-shaped pancakes with warmed syrup, powdered sugar, and strawberries, because it happens to be Valentine's Day. The twins get amped on maple syrup, but the rest of us don't eat much.

I've kept Two Moons a secret for sixty hours, but it feels like sixty years.

When my mom tells Toby to go get ready for a doctor's appointment, part of me wants to rush upstairs and tell him the truth, tell him I'll help him escape, that I'm sorry I lied to him. Instead I get Kepler's leash and call her.

I'm about to open the door when my mom stops me.

"Where are you going, Meals?"

"Out to walk Kepler."

"We're going soon. What about Toby? Aren't you going to say goodbye to your brother?"

"He doesn't know it's goodbye." It sounds snippier than I mean it to and I feel bad.

"He's going to know soon enough. I know it's hard, but . . ." She takes Kepler's leash out of my hand.

I know my mom is right, so I run upstairs and knock on Toby's door. The Beatles are playing loudly.

"Toby!" I yell over the music. "Can you open your door? For a second."

He opens the door. "I can't find my green sweatshirt."

"Haven't seen it."

"It was here. I don't want the gray one."

"I'm sure you'll find it." I try to sound calm, but my heart races. I bet my mom packed it in the duffel that's in the car.

"I don't know why I have to go to a doctor on a Saturday."

"Want to borrow a book?" I ask lamely. "*Game of Thrones*? It's taking me forever to read it."

"I already read that whole series. Reading makes me nauseous anyway."

"That stinks. Is it the medication?"

"I guess. It makes me so tired. All I want to do is sleep. Ari would never go out with me now. She'd think I was disgusting."

"No, she wouldn't," I say, even though Toby's hair looks especially greasy today and his skin looks almost gray.

"Toby!" my dad calls. "We need to go, buddy."

"See you later," I say, rushing down the stairs and calling for Kepler, who's still hooked to her leash.

"Meals?" my mom says.

"Kepler needs a walk," I say.

"Honey." My mom tries to hug me, but I wiggle out. "I know this is terribly hard."

"I've got to go."

"We'll be back tomorrow morning," my mom calls. "Grandma's taking the boys to karate and then out to lunch to tell them the plan."

"You already told me."

"They'll be back this afternoon. I love you, Amelia."

I don't say anything because I'm too busy dragging Kepler out of the house, down the icy driveway, and onto the road as quickly as possible. I need to get out of here; I can't be here when my brother is driven away. *I can't believe he doesn't know where he's going! I hate my parents for not telling him. Why did I have to know? They could have waited until today like they did for the twins.* It's cold and I need to move faster than walking, so out of nowhere I start running. Kepler looks up, like she's making sure it's still me, but then she starts running and before I know it, we're jogging down Parkhurst and onto Main Street, past the little deli, the gas station, and the post office. *I should write Toby*, I decide. Since I won't visit him, the least I can do is write. I don't know if they'll let him email, and I think there's a group phone, but they have to give him actual mail. As I run past the hardware store it strikes me that I know absolutely nothing about where my brother is going.

I run even faster, trying not to think about the fact that my brother is schizophrenic and being driven far away, that it's Valentine's Day and that Epstein probably hates me. I can't help but wonder what today would be like if I hadn't freaked out. In the movie version—

Stop. It's not about the movie version, you idiot. There's no point thinking about stuff like this. You can't do any-thing to change what's happened, so just move on. Move! My brain commands my legs. *Move, move, move! Stop thinking about movies!*

Then I'm moving. Me! Amelia Jane Anderson almost whizzing past the elementary school on the north side of town, then past the YMCA where Toby taught me how to swim, the fire station where we'd get Halloween candy, the bigger grocery store. I'm running past huge piles of snow all around town until sweat—actual sweat—drips off me and I can barely breathe. I'm going to have intense blisters tomorrow, and by the time I run past the Carters' house again, I'm practically gasping for air.

And then when I finally turn the corner and run up my mountainous driveway, who do I see on the front porch?

Epstein.

Kepler barks and he looks down at me.

I look up at him.

We don't say anything. I have no idea what I'm supposed to do next because my brain is flooded with movie scenes where estranged couples see each other again for the big climactic scene like in *The Notebook* and *Titanic* and *Gone with the Wind*. *No movies*, I yell at myself as I walk up the driveway where the Honda Fit is parked. *Say something!*

I look at him, then down at my feet.

He looks at his hands. "You were running?"

"Yeah."

"I didn't know you ran. I thought you didn't run."

"Very random," I say. *Does running make Epstein appear?* The last time I ran—or tried to run—was out in Montauk. I wish I could go back to that hot July day when everything wonderful was just about to happen. Without all the terrible stuff that came after.

Epstein walks down the porch and into the driveway, where he opens the trunk of the Fit and takes out Ray's bag. "I brought this back."

"Oh. Yeah. Thanks." I try to breathe through my racing heart. "Ray will be happy." I take the bag and walk up to the porch. Epstein follows.

"You want something to eat?" I ask. There's a stack of pancakes on the counter.

He shakes his head.

"I can't believe you're here." Instead of looking at him, I fill Kepler's water bowl and put it on the floor.

"I don't like how weird things got. You disappeared on New Year's Eve."

"I'm sorry," I finally say.

"I was really worried. My *parents* were worried. I had to beg them not to call your parents. It was really bad, Amelia. And then you break the radio silence just to hang up on me?"

"My phone broke," I say.

He gives me a look.

"I just got a new one last weekend. My number is the same."

"I would've left that party if you wanted to go. I wouldn't have cared. I wanted to hang out with you. Sneaking out was shitty."

"I know."

"It's about your brother, right?"

I shrug-nod. I can't explain to Epstein what it felt like to be at that party, to have Holden be so cavalier about mental illness, to have his mom know all about Toby. I know Epstein has a right to tell his parents and friends about my brother. I know that his book and podcast recommendations came from a good place, but it makes me feel even more terrible.

"Where is everyone?" he asks after a few moments. "It's quiet."

"Out," I say quickly. If he knows where my parents are taking my brother, he'll never understand how cool Toby used to be. "How's Holden and those guys?"

"Chloe is panicking that she might actually get into Berkeley. I don't think she's stopped baking in a month. Holden went on a date last weekend. Without an app."

"Really?"

"Dinner and a movie. How crazy is that?"

"Pretty weird," I say, trying not to think about Toby. "Holden has a boyfriend?"

"It's a little early to call it that, but maybe."

"Wow."

"Was having a boyfriend that bad?"

I take a deep breath. "No, it wasn't bad." I swallow. "It was actually very nice."

Epstein smiles at me. "I *liked* having a girlfriend."

"You did?" I pretend to sound shocked.

"Yup. She was real pretty and nice and smart," he replies in an exaggerated Southern drawl.

"I should shower," I say. "I'm sweaty."

Epstein stands up, comes over to me, and sniffs. "You smell great."

"Liar."

"I'm not," he says, leaning toward me.

And then we have an amazing, Hollywood, chased-bad-guys-all-over-seven-continents-blew-up-a-hundred-buildings-and-rescued-a-dog kind of kiss. It is Valentine's Day, after all.

We kiss and kiss and after about thirty seconds I stop freaking out about how sweaty I am. I don't know how we get up the stairs because we're holding each other the whole time and then we're in my room and on my bed and my shirt and pants are off and he takes a condom out of his wallet, and puts it on in record time.

"Okay?" he asks.

I nod because now that Epstein is here things do feel okay. He puts his penis inside me, which is awkward because I feel so terrible about how terrible I've been to him. But it also feels not awkward because it's Epstein. Smart and curious and kind Epstein who will keep me safe because he's strong and sane and can protect me from everything bad that might happen. Epstein reads books about gay men for Holden and schizophrenics for me! Epstein does everything right, so how can that be wrong?

"Are you okay?" Epstein whispers.

"Yeah. Why?"

"You're crying."

I touch my face. How can I be crying without even knowing it? "I'm okay," I tell him just as my cell phone rings.

It's my brother. Without looking at my phone I absolutely know it's Toby. He's calling because he knows. My parents told him. He's calling me because that's what we do. Amelia calls Toby and Toby calls Amelia.

"Ignore it," Epstein pants. "They'll call back."

"It might be . . . ," I say. "I really need to get it."

Epstein stops. Just like that, the miraculous thing between us is gone. I pick up the phone.

"Help!"

"Toby?"

"They're taking me away, Amelia! We're not going to a doctor. It's like Tuskegee. Instead of syphilis, everyone gets AIDS."

"That's not true. Where are you? You can't be . . ." I look at Epstein and then down at the floor.

"We're at McDonald's," he whispers. "We're not even in New York anymore. They're getting me a Big Mac. Dad's watching me."

I feel sick. "I'm not sure what I can do," I say. "It might not be so bad."

"You're just like they are. They're listening to everything I say, you know."

"I don't . . ."

"There are spies here. Spies are everywhere. They're all in on it."

"Toby."

"You're not going to help, are you?" he yells and hangs up.

I close my phone and lie back on the bed. *I am just like they are*, I think. I knew about this for nearly three days. After a few minutes Epstein takes the condom off, gets off my bed, and puts it in the garbage can. Then he comes over and strokes my cheek and kisses my shoulder. I roll away from him, pick up my underwear and sweaty T-shirt from the floor, and put them back on. Then I roll over onto my side, look at the dust on my windowsill, and listen to Epstein breathe.

"Amelia?" Epstein touches my shoulder.

"Yeah."

"You can talk about it. You can tell me about Toby."

"He's sick," I say. "He's very sick."

"I'm really sorry about that. Did I tell you that my mom's cousin is severely bipolar—"

"He's not bipolar."

"I know you've said how cool he is—"

"I don't want to talk about it." I curl myself even tighter into the fetal position.

"There are a lot of really smart, really talented people with schizophrenia, you know. John Nash, the math guy. You've probably seen *A Beautiful Mind*. And Syd Barrett of Pink Floyd and Peter Green, the guitarist for Fleetwood Mac. And Vaslav Nijinsky was a very famous Russian dancer." Epstein sounds sort of excited by his knowledge.

"Stop," I tell him.

"Abraham Lincoln's wife probably had it too," he says. "And Albert Einstein's son."

"I don't give a shit about Albert Einstein's son," I snap. I've never talked like this to Epstein, but I don't want to listen to his stupid list. "I don't want to hear about the informative books you've read or the helpful podcasts you've listened to. It doesn't help." I sound angry, but I don't do anything about it.

We sit or, rather, he sits and I lie curled up, not touching, not talking. How is it possible that just a few minutes ago Epstein was this great, safe thing and now, after one phone call from Toby, that feeling is gone? I can't see it coming back, either. What will happen if Toby calls again? What will happen if he comes back home? It seems impossible to hang out with Epstein normally ever again.

All these thoughts and images feel like they're reeling around on a never-ending cinematic loop in my brain, so after a while I unfurl myself and look at Epstein and say, "I think you should go."

He looks surprised. "You want me to leave?"

"Yeah."

"You want me to drive back to the city?"

I nod.

"Now?"

I nod.

"But Amelia—"

"I know," I say before he can. "We're broken up."

Wordlessly, Epstein puts on his clothes, opens the door, and walks down the hall to the stairs and through the foyer. I hear him open the front door and then he's gone.

"You are so stupid!" I say out loud. "You are the stupidest person in the world." I want to run after Epstein but I just lie on my bed, crying, until my phone rings.

I'm not going to answer if it's another unknown number, because I can't deal with hearing Toby again, but it's Ray. "'My uncle Roger said that he once saw an albino polar bear,'" she says.

"I don't want movies quotes," I tell her. "I want to get drunk."

"On my way," she says.

25

GEEKY LITTLE DENNIS McGREEVY

THE ONE POSITIVE ABOUT THIS SPECTACULARLY SHITTY day is that Ray's mom is at a casino in Connecticut with her sister for the night so we have the place to ourselves.

"You sure you don't want to go out?" Ray asks when I walk out of her kitchen with a Pepsi-vodka cocktail. "We could go to the mall? The movies? Let's go see *all* the movies at the mall. Back to back to back. That's like the dream Amelia Anderson day. I'll spring for unlimited popcorn."

"Movies suck. The mall sucks."

"You're talking about my place of employment, dude. And you're drinking fast. That's vodka."

I take a smaller gulp.

"Explain what happened again. Epstein shows up at your house . . . with my bag. Which I'm still confused about."

"It's complicated."

"And things were good?"

"Kind of weird. But kind of good."

"And you have sex! Amelia Anderson's not a virgin!" She grins.

"It wasn't the first time," I say quietly. "It was the third."

Ray's eyes grow big.

"We did it in New York. Twice. I was going to tell you, but. It was the night. The night I had to come home early."

Ray nods. "So why did you break up?"

"His ears were kind of humongous."

"What are you talking about?"

Is it possible that Epstein's ears are normal? "It just didn't seem like we should go out anymore. I don't want to talk about it. I want to get drunk about it. Ha! Isn't that funny?"

"Puke in the toilet," she says. "I don't want to clean up after you."

"I'm not going to puke. I barely feel anything."

"Oh, you're going to feel something."

"I'm going to message Muppet. Can we have people over? Just to hang out?" Suddenly hanging out with friends seems like the best idea in the world. I can't remember the last time I really hung out! Just thinking about it makes me feel more normal. I'm going to have a normal Saturday night!

Ray shrugs. "Sure. I don't want a ton of people here, but Muppet is fine."

"And Toast," I say. "If we message Muppet it's Toast, too. They're probably together. It is Valentine's Day, you know." It strikes me as insanely funny all of a sudden that Ray and I have friends named Muppet and Toast and that it's Valentine's Day and that when I finally had the opportunity to make things okay with Epstein, I went and made them absolutely, irrevocably worse.

The next thing I know I'm in the bathroom trying to figure out if my white camisole is too see-through to wear in public. Ray must have cranked up the heat because I'm really hot.

Someone pounds on the door. "Are you okay?"

"Yeah," I say. I look at myself in the mirror.

"Amelia? Hey, Amelia, I gotta take a piss."

Toast. Of course. I open the bathroom door and there's Toast, beer in one hand, his other hand on the doorknob. He grins, revealing his stained and crooked teeth.

"CanIwearthisshirtout?" In my brain my words aren't slurred but when my mouth says them they come out that way.

"I don't know what you're talking about, Anderson. But wait. Don't go. I want to talk to you." He slides in as I walk out.

"Hey! Do you have any pot?" I ask the closed bathroom door. Smoking pot seems like a really good, really fun idea. I'm feeling like a million times better about the whole Epstein/Toby situation because it doesn't matter. Nothing matters. I walk into Ray's room to make way for some senior girls. I don't know how or when this turned into a party. I thought we were just having a few people over.

I look at a squirrel pillow on Ray's bed and wonder how much she paid for it.

Toast comes into Ray's room, sits on her bed, takes a baggie of pot out of his front pocket and a packet of rolling papers from his back pocket, and spreads everything out on Ray's nightstand.

Abdi peeks in. "Hey," he says. "When did you guys get here?"

"I've been here for years," I say. "I'm the brainchild of the whole operation." I pick up the squirrel pillow. "Me and Squirrel Nutkin."

"Amelia's drunk," Toast says.

"I see that," Abdi says. "You're not driving, are you?"

"No, Mr. Munson, I'm not driving. I don't have my license yet, remember?"

He nods. "I saw an amazing documentary today."

"I'm done with movies," I say. "Frankly, my dear, they're just too sad."

"Don't let her near a car," Abdi says to Toast.

"Never. You want to get stoned, Film Boy?" Toast asks.

Abdi shakes his head. "Nah. It's bad for my religion and worse for my art." He smiles. "Whenever I've done it, I film boiling water or something pretentiously boring."

"Do you film the water in black and white?" I ask. "I think that would look better than in color."

Abdi smiles. "See ya later, guys."

"Shut the door, man. I don't want a million people seeing my stash."

Abdi closes the door.

"What a weirdo," I tell Toast. "Why would you film drunk stoners?"

Toast holds up a very neatly rolled joint and grins.

"But worse than filming would be editing," I say to the squirrel pillow. "Having to watch a bunch of drunk people . . ."

"I keep telling you he's going to get an Oscar one day," Toast says, lighting the joint. He takes a hit and passes it to me. "So where's Toby at?" he asks, just like that.

Toby, Toby, Toby. "Not here," I tell him, taking an enormous inhalation.

"I know. I called your house. A twin said he moved to Massachusetts to get better. What's up?"

Stupid Sam and his big mouth. I exhale.

Toast looks at me for a minute, and then takes another hit of pot. Watching him is hypnotic. It's amazing how long he's able to suck in the smoke. He passes me the joint and smiles for at least two minutes before he exhales.

"You should run track," I say. "You have amazing lungs."

Toast cracks up. At first I don't get it, but then I try to picture Toast running and realize that I haven't even seen him walk fast and that he's always smoking something. I start laughing and smoke comes out of me, which makes me laugh even more, and then because I can't stop laughing I take a swig of his beer even though he has the most awful look on his face, and it turns out that I shouldn't have done that because the beer isn't beer, but Toast's walking 'n' talking ashtray, full of ash and cigarette butts, and it goes down my throat and it takes everything in me not to puke, but I actually find this sort of funny, too, so I keep laughing even though my throat is burning, and I feel tears running down my cheeks, which must also mean that I'm crying.

Oh, God. I'm crying again. Tears are streaming down my cheeks and my nose is running and I must look so gross. More than anything I want to stop crying, get off Ray's bed, and go hang out and laugh and joke with my friends. I want to do all the other normal things normal people do at parties, but I can't move. All I can do is put my arms around Toast and cry buckets onto his shoulder. Buckets. On Toast. It should not be Toast. It should be Epstein—perfect, sweet, wonderful Epstein with his big ears, which were actually perfect because he wanted me to cry on his shoulder, he wanted me to talk to him. The Right Guy I told to leave, so now I'm crying on weird, stoned, gross Toast. *Toast shouldn't be at this party,* I think. Toby should be at this party, making everyone laugh and feel special, but instead I'm here with his friend who feels so strong all of a sudden, who smells good, and then I'm kissing Toast.

Amelia kissing Toast. I actually watch myself look at Toast *in that way* and lean my mouth toward his mouth. When he leans in, I can see myself kissing him, like I'm behind Abdi's camera or something. I'm zooming in to run my tongue over Toast's teeth and my hand over his crotch and feel powerful and strong. *Forget Epstein,* I think. It'll be Amelia and Toast from now on.

But then he pulls away. He jerks his head back and closes his lips. Wordlessly, he takes my hand off his crotch and takes a deep breath.

"What's going on in there?" someone calls out.

"No fucking on my bed!" Ray yells. "This is a sex-free house, people. Who's in there anyway?"

"Toast and Emily?" someone says.

"Do not have sex on my bed," Ray yells. "Those are Egyptian cotton sheets. I spent a whole paycheck on them."

"Egyptian cotton is the best," someone who sounds like Jessie Eaves says. But how could Jessie Eaves be here? She's probably in her Hello Kitty pajamas under her Hello Kitty covers.

"Where's Amelia?" Ray asks.

"I think she went to smoke a cigarette," Owen Stevens tells her.

"Outside? Shit. She's drunk." I hear her clomp down the hall.

"I'll go with you," Owen says. "Did you hear that her brother is getting shock treatments? That's what Kelsey heard. They're like going to intentionally . . ." They must go outside to look for me because I can't hear what else Owen says.

"Amelia," Toast says quietly.

Shit, shit, shit. I can't believe I hooked up with Toast. *Toast!*

"Are you okay?"

If I open my mouth I'll puke, so I just nod even though I'm definitely not okay. Toast!

"We'll pretend this never happened, okay?"

I nod again. I want to say I'm sorry, that I didn't mean to make him cheat on his girlfriend, that I wasn't thinking.

"I think . . ."

"Don't talk about it," I tell him. I swallow a wave of puke. "It was a big mistake. Sorry."

"Me too. But do you think maybe we could talk sometime? We never talk."

"We talk. I see you in school. Lunch."

"Yeah but we've never talked about. You know, stuff."

And then I get it. Toast wants to talk about Toby. Everyone wants to talk about Toby! My mother and grandmother and Epstein's mother and my dad in his awkward way and Dr. Kellerman and Epstein and Ray and Muppet and everyone else in school. The whole world wants to talk about Toby. Except me.

"There's nothing to say," I say. I move back on the bed and lean against the squirrel pillow. I get under the covers and close my eyes. I wish my shoes weren't on but I'm too tired to take them off.

"He's got schizophrenia, right?" Toast says. "I'm like ninety percent sure that's what's wrong with him. I Wikipedia-ed it. It makes sense if that's what it is. All the hallucinations, the obsessions . . ."

I can't listen to Toast anymore so I imagine an island in the middle of blue-green water. It's one perfect little island just for me with white sand and a blue sky that's shiny and clear. What movies take place on islands, I wonder? *Cast Away. Six Days Seven Nights. Shutter Island.* Oh no. I don't want to think about that one. It's about the mental hospital. *50 First Dates.* But Drew Barrymore has amnesia, which might also be a mental problem . . .

"Amelia?" I hear Toast say. "You're okay, aren't you?" I can tell he's trying to calculate how much I've drunk and smoked to make sure I'm not going to end up a headline. I want to tell him that I'm okay, that I'm not going to die, but I can't get the words out.

Sometime later white lights pierce though my eyeballs and into my pounding brain. I open one eye. I'm in Ray's room, in Ray's bed. The room smells like smoke and I have vague memories of a singing squirrel.

I close my eyes.

I wake up again to the vacuum. I roll over and look at the clock. It's 7:25 AM. *Much too early to be up*, I think, rolling back over and swallowing back vomit that's slunk up my throat.

I wake up again when I hear a door slam. It's 9:15. I sit up slowly and try to stop the pounding behind my eyes. I look at the picture on Ray's night table. It's us in sixth grade wearing huge white sunglasses, neon bracelets, and awful pink lipstick. We look so young. *Too young to have a hangover*, I think. *Too young to know Toby would be schizophrenic. Too young to hook up with Toast. Toast wasn't even Toast back in sixth grade. He was still geeky little Dennis McGreevy.*

Hook up with Toast, I think with a thud.

I. Hooked. Up. With Toast.

On purpose.

I jump out of bed, run down the hall and into the bathroom just as a violent explosion of vomit erupts into the sink. I'm worried that it's going to clog it, but I can't do anything to stop the wave that is pouring out of my mouth.

"Are you alive?" Ray calls.

"*Bleck blech bleeeck!*" I respond.

I puke until there's absolutely nothing but blood and organs in my body. Then I blast the faucet and pray everything goes down the sink. I lie on the floor, which feels nice and cool.

Ray knocks on the door. "You conscious?"

"Maybe?"

"Want a beer?"

I dry heave at the thought of a beer. "Not funny," I tell

her after it passes. "I'm never drinking again." I stand up and turn off the faucet. There are a few gnarly chunks left in the sink but it's not clogged. I brace myself against the towel rack and open the door.

Ray hands me a Diet Coke, which I sip slowly as I follow her down the hall at a snail's pace. I plop down on the La-Z-Boy. Ray takes the couch.

"I feel like shit," I say. My head is pounding in my skull and it hurts to keep my eyes open.

"My *house* looked like shit, but then I just cleaned the shit out of it at like 6:30 in the morning. So my mom wouldn't give me shit when she gets home." She turns on the TV. "I had to sneak tons of beer cans into my neighbor's recycling so my mom wouldn't know." She changes the channel.

With a thud I realize how awful I am. Ray picked me up and took me to her house, where I got drunk and threw a party that trashed her house until I passed out in her bed.

"Um. Sorry?" I say, feeling pathetic. Sorry doesn't do justice to an apology of this magnitude.

Ray stares at me.

"I mean, sorry. It's not a question. I'm really, really sorry."

Ray nods. "I know."

"When's your mom getting back?"

"In a few hours."

"I'll help you clean up. Just give me a few minutes. My head is killing me."

"Take some Advil."

"Yeah. And I should call home. My mom is probably freaking out."

"I talked to your mom."

"You did? When?"

"She texted me to call her a few hours ago."

"Did they sound mad? I left a note."

"She didn't sound mad. She sounded sad. She said you haven't called her back." Ray goes up, up, up the mountain of channels, eventually stopping on a Dakota Fanning movie. I'm pretty sure I've seen it but my brain is too fried to remember.

"I'm a shitty friend."

Ray looks at me. "You're not a shitty friend. I understand why you wanted to get drunk, I really do. But you should have told me." She turns off the TV.

"I told you Epstein and I broke up."

She nods.

"And I told you I'm not a virgin."

"Yeah. You did. But you didn't tell me that your parents took Toby to Massachusetts yesterday. You didn't tell me that, Amelia."

So she knows. *Well, good*, I think. *Now it's out.* Toast Wiki-fucking-pedia-ed it, and Ray knows, and knowing this town, it's probably already been messaged to half the students at Washington Lincoln.

"You said things were weird with Epstein, but you didn't mention that seeing him on the same day that your brother went to live in an institution might not have been the best timing."

Why didn't I say that to Epstein? That makes so much sense. He probably would've been okay with that. But to tell him that, I would've had to tell him where Toby was going, and about his rant in the cafeteria, and how horrendously shitty things have been. I don't want him to list books and blogs and podcasts about schizophrenia. I just want him to listen and say, "I'm sorry, Amelia. That fucking sucks."

"How long is Toby going to be . . . away?"

"Six months."

"Wow. That's a long time."

"It feels like forever. It's a rehabilitation center. Not a mental institution."

She nods. "You'll visit."

No, I won't. Ray would be able to go visit my brother because she can handle stuff like that. And she could drive, but it would be too hard for me. "Also, I left your bag at Epstein's apartment, not on the train. I completely freaked out at this party. I kept worrying about Toby and I couldn't have a conversation with anyone so I split. Sorry."

"It's not a big deal. I have a lot of bags. You could've told me the truth, you know."

"I know. Did you like Toby back . . . back before he got sick?"

She sighs, shrugs, and nods.

"I didn't like that you liked him." It feels good to say it even if it's a moot point. "I don't know why it bothered me. I hate that I was like, I don't know, jealous or something weird." I look at Ray. "I'm really sorry. It's not like I thought you weren't good enough for him. I should have gotten over it."

"If something were meant to happen with us, it would have. We could have done something if we'd really wanted to."

Is it possible that they didn't get together because of me? Or was it because of Toby's illness?

"How come you didn't tell me Toby was leaving? I haven't told anyone about his diagnosis."

"I didn't tell anyone. I couldn't. My parents were afraid he'd run away if they told him, which I get, but I feel like I betrayed him by not telling him. I just . . . I don't know. I don't think I've ever lied to him before. Not even a tiny one, which is crazy. Siblings lie to each other; they're mean to each other. You've seen the twins."

Ray nods.

"Since I couldn't tell Toby about Massachusetts, I couldn't tell anyone. I still feel like I shouldn't tell anyone. Telling Epstein about his illness just made me feel worse even though he was totally great about it. I know Muppet would be fine. And I know Toast isn't the enemy. I don't know why I can't tell them, why I'm so scared. Nothing makes sense."

"It does make sense," Ray says.

"I think my mom might be right: I watch too many movies. Because I keep waiting for this to end. To be over."

Ray nods.

"Toby used to say you should do things like it was the movie version of your life. Like, would people pay to watch it? But lately I think the movie version isn't right. Not everything has to be full of action. You can appreciate all the regular, non-exciting times, too. Remember that kooky sub who tried to get us to be present all the time?"

"She was weird," Ray says. "I remember a lot of deep breathing."

"Part of me thinks that kooky sub was right. Regular, boring old life is what's good. Why try to imagine it in a movie? Movies are full of car crashes and police chases. Who wants that?"

Ray shrugs.

"But the other part of me thinks about Toby before he was sick, and I think: *No, he's right.* The movie version made things so much fun. He used to have such good ideas and be so funny."

Ray nods. "You have good ideas, too. Excluding last night."

"I guess. I don't know. Now I feel like all the movie quotes was us not really talking. Not really talking, not saying anything original."

"Don't think of it that way, Meals. You and Toby had something—*have* something—special. Your love of movies was just one part. Not everything."

"It was a lot of it."

"But not a bad part. Remember that one time in the cafeteria freshman year when you and Toby only spoke in movie quotes? That was amazing. I don't think you said one word to each other that wasn't from a movie."

"We didn't." I smile. I had totally forgotten about that.

"Just so you know, I care about Toby. And not because I liked him. I care about him as a friend. But *you're* my best friend, Amelia. You don't have to be alone with all this."

We're quiet for a little while. I feel better because things are finally out in the open, but my head is still pounding and there's something else I need to share. "Can I tell you a secret?

This one you really can't tell anyone. Ever. I will eventually tell people about Toby's illness and rehab, but never this."

Ray sits up straight. "Okay."

I take a deep breath and whisper, "IkissedToast."

"You kissed Toast?"

I nod.

"*Toast*-Toast?"

I nod.

Ray squinches her forehead. "Toast?!"

"Stop saying his name!"

"Gross! Last night?"

"Yeah."

"Does Muppet know?"

"I hope not. I don't think so. You didn't know."

"No, not a clue. Ugh. Dude, what were you thinking?"

"I wasn't. I was drunk. And stoned. And I'd just broken up with my boyfriend because my amazing brother was going to a rehab center. Toby called me from a McDonald's after my parents told him." I swallow. "It was awful."

Ray nods.

"I feel like shit."

"No one has to know."

"I feel bad for Muppet."

"Because she *chooses* to kiss him all the time."

I almost laugh. "Swear you'll take it to the grave?"

"Swear," she says. "'Best Fucking Friends Forever.'"

"Thank you, *Pineapple Express.*"

I spend the rest of the day at Ray's. I clean her bathroom sink, eat a few potato chips without throwing up, and spend the afternoon watching wonderfully terrible back-to-back-to-back Jennifer Aniston rom-coms. When she gets home, Ray's mom is in a really good mood because she won over two hundred dollars, and she doesn't seem at all suspicious. When she says she'll order Chinese for dinner, I realize I haven't been home in more than twenty-four hours. I look at my phone and see I've missed four Home calls and three texts. Shit. "I should probably go home."

"You're welcome to eat here," Ray's mom says. "I'm ordering from Mr. Wu's."

I picture dinner at my house: Sam and David will bicker, Sam will say random sweet-sad stuff about Toby, which will make my mom cry. My dad will grumble and eat too much. My grandmother will look old and tired. Greasy Chinese and bad TV with Ray and her mom seems like the much better option, so I tell Ray's mom that I'd love to stay.

When Ray drops me off a little before 8:00 PM, my mom meets me at the door. She's wearing her glasses instead of contacts and an I-mean-business look.

"First, you didn't check in. At all."

"I left Grandma a note."

"That you were spending the night at Ray's. Not that you were going to be gone all day."

"Ray said you called."

"*This morning.* What's the point of a phone if you don't respond?"

"Sorry."

"You missed dinner."

"I ate at Ray's."

She looks at me.

"Chinese," I say lamely.

"We need to make an effort to be a family," she says. I see the dark circles under her eyes. "We need to support each other. We talked to your brothers about Toby going to Massachusetts."

"I know. What are they doing now?"

"Screen time."

"They won't want to talk to me then."

"Don't you want to know about Toby? About Two Moons?"

Not really. "I guess."

"He has a small view of the ocean from his room." She gives me a sad, tired smile. "It doesn't feel like a hospital. There's a lot of structure, with very devoted and knowledgeable staff. We're sad, but Dad and I feel good about our decision."

"I guess that's good." I sound cold, but I can't help it.

"Amelia," she says. "Honey." She puts her arms around me.

"I just don't want to talk about it," I say, wiggling out. I feel so drained. All I want to do is lie down with Kepler on my bed and not think about Toby for five minutes.

"It might help to talk about it."

"I don't need help," I say. "I'm perfectly fine."

Act VI: Scene 5

AMELIA is seventeen years old.

INT. Crowded high school hallway.
Students opening and closing lockers.
A lot of chatting and noise.

A group of four students—two girls
and two boys—walk down the hall
and gather outside of a classroom.

AMELIA is sitting in the classroom
near the door. She can hear the
students, but they can't see her.

STUDENT ONE
I heard he dropped out because he's
going on tour with Paul McCartney!

STUDENT TWO
incredulously
Paul McCartney? Of the Beatles?

STUDENT ONE
Yeah. How awesome is that?

STUDENT TWO
Really?

STUDENT ONE
Yeah. I heard Paul wanted to change
things up. Play with someone new. Somehow
he got a hold of some album Toby recorded
and the next thing you know, Toby's getting
a call from Paul McCartney himself.

STUDENT THREE
Toby recorded an album?

STUDENT ONE
Yeah! With that cool band he got
together. I heard that Paul said, "Hey,
Toby, it's Paul. Paul McCartney."

STUDENT TWO
Toby Anderson went to play on tour
with Paul McCartney! That's amazing.
I'd drop out for that.

STUDENT FOUR
shaking her head
You guys are wrong. I heard that he went
to help refugees in Syria or Iran or someplace. He just stood up in global studies
and was like, "I just can't sit here and

listen to this. I need to do something! We
need to really help people." Mr. Jacobson
was like, "Yes, Toby, that's a great idea.
Let's have a car wash or bake sale." And
Toby was like, "No, I'm not talking about a
bake sale or car wash. I don't want to send
a hundred and thirty dollars to an organi-
zation in Washington, D.C. I actually want
to help. I want to give a hungry child a
meal or put a tourniquet on a wounded
soldier. I want to be out in the world!"

A blue-haired boy skates down the hallway
on a skateboard.

BLUE-HAIRED SKATER
You guys talking about Toby? Man, that guy
is so rad. He just joined Doctors Without
Borders. He was like, "Peace out, y'all,
I'm going to Afghanistan!" In the middle
of class. He just up and left to get on a
plane. He's doing amazing stuff.

STUDENT FOUR
to the group
Told ya.

STUDENT TWO
Don't you have to be a doctor to do that?

BLUE-HAIRED SKATER
shrugs
Just what I heard. Wouldn't put it past
Toby, though. He's an awesome dude. And not
bad on the board.

Blue-Haired Skater skates down the hall.

STUDENT ONE
Now that I think about it, I think maybe
Toby and Paul McCartney were going to play
for the troops somewhere scary. And maybe when he's not on tour, he's helping out
with the refugees or something.

STUDENT THREE
That makes sense.

STUDENT TWO
That totally sounds like Toby Anderson.

CAMERA PANS INTO CLASSROOM.
AMELIA IS SMILING.

FADE OUT.

26

DOG GONE IT

I SPEND THE NEXT FEW WEEKS TRYING TO AVOID Toast, Muppet, and Dr. Kellerman and thinking about Toby, Epstein, schizophrenia, and How Things Used to Be.

I do drive the student-mobile and don't kill anyone or wreck the car! The first time I drove, Mr. Munson had to keep reminding me that the speed limit meant I *had to* go fifty miles an hour, not thirty-five, but who knew that all I needed to get up the courage to drive was a schizophrenic brother in a rehab center in Massachusetts?

I end up going to two film club "meetings." They're not so much meetings as the four of us talking about movies and watching a lot of random things on YouTube. Abdi shows us a short documentary called *Bankrupt by Beanies*, which, even though it's less than nine minutes long, really gets in the whole story of this dad's obsession with Beanie Babies and how he can't sell them. Abdi goes on about how concise and well edited it is. I like how you get to know the family, and Jessie likes that it's short. Somehow this leads Jessie and Abdi to start arguing about *Sherman's March*. Jessie's never seen it because she says she's not into history or old movies.

"Let's show Amelia the movie you made of me," she says to Abdi.

"You're in a movie? I haven't seen any of Abdi's movies."

Before I know it, the lights have been turned off, a white

screen has been pulled down, and Abdi fiddles on the computer screen. He clicks the mouse a few times, and all of a sudden there's an actual movie by Abdi on the screen.

Hello looks good—not like how I'd imagined a student film. The title and credits look very professional. It starts off with a long shot of all the Hello Kitty stuff in Jessie's room. There's Hello Kitty everything: posters, hairbrushes, mugs, a hamper, an alarm clock, and a million stuffed animals. It's kind of scary and amazing. Slowly the camera starts to focus on Jessie, who's just sitting on her bed (Hello Kitty comforter, of course). At first she talks about all the stuff she has, and what cool Hello Kitty stuff there is out there, and how she once woke up at 4:00 AM to bid on something in Japan. But then she starts talking about her mom getting sick when she was nine. There are a few family photographs of Jessie and her mom, then we see Jessie back on her bed talking about how cancer treatment made her mom so skinny that she ended up wearing Jessie's clothes, and she was wearing Jessie's Hello Kitty pajamas when she died. It's super sad, but feels real, not cheesy or overdone. I love that the last line is Jessie saying "bye" in this very low-key, not staged, way.

"That totally explains the Hello Kitty thing," I blurt out. I feel embarrassed but Jessie smiles. "I can't believe that was only eleven minutes."

"What's really cool is that he had like thirty hours to start with," Tony says. "To go from all that footage to eleven minutes is pretty amazing."

"Totally amazing," Jessie says.

"My problem," Tony tells us, "is that my stuff is always

too short. I couldn't get eleven minutes of anything. My Pop-Tarts and kick flips never last more than a second."

"That ramp fall you showed me was more than a second," Jessie says.

Tony shrugs and then smiles. "I should make another top ten crash loop one of these days. My last one got mad hits on YouTube."

"Speaking of crashes," Jessie says. "I have to go to work."

I must give her a confused look because she says, "I work at an after-school program with a lot of boys." She looks at Tony. "Do you want a ride?"

He nods and we all say bye. After they leave, I turn to Abdi. "I can't believe you turned thirty hours into eleven minutes!"

"It only took me a year."

"A year? Really?"

He nods. "I shot way too much, and then I had to watch it and decide what to keep. It was my first one, so I had to learn the editing software as I went. It took forever because I didn't log my footage." He shakes his head in disgust. "Now that I know to log I edit way faster."

"What kind of camera do you use?"

"I use a 5D Mark III. It was my birthday gift for the rest of my life. It was crazy expensive. But I used to use the school's Canon Rebel. It's old, but not bad. You want to try it out?"

"I don't make movies. I just watch them."

Abdi ignores me and goes into a big file cabinet and gets out the camera. "The battery needs to be charged."

I look at the camera and try to imagine what in the world I'd film. "I'd probably just film my dog," I say.

"It's a start. There are some decent dog movies."

"*Milo and Otis.*"

"*Gates of Heaven. Madonna of the Mills.* Which, based on your dead dog thing, I don't recommend for you."

"*My Dog Tulip, Lady and the Tramp, Bolt.*"

"There should be a manual . . ." Abdi opens up the black camera bag and pulls out a small, thick booklet. "You don't really have to read it. Basically you just need to know that this is an SLR—you know, a single-lens reflex camera. You need to make sure to put it in Live View and Movie Mode.

"What language are you speaking? I just thought of another three dog movies."

"You don't have to use it. But here's a big memory card—it's thirty-two gigs."

I know it's way more likely that I'll spend the weekend watching a Dog Gone It movie marathon than actually reading the manual and remembering anything Abdi said, let alone using the camera, but for some reason I take it home anyway.

27

NOT MAKING MOVIES

WITHOUT TOBY AT HOME, MY MOM ISN'T ON THE phone with doctors all the time, so we have dinner together every night. My dad helps the twins with their Great Wall of China Lego project, and my grandmother volunteers at the Friends of the Library book sale. The house feels more relaxed, which makes me feel guilty, so I yell at David for lying on Toby's bed reading a comic book. Then I feel bad. What does it matter? Toby is David's brother, too—not just mine. I feel like I'm alone a lot because Epstein and I are over, Ray is assistant managing again, and I can't face Muppet.

I try to email Toby, but after "Hey, Toby," I don't have anything else to say. I save the email in my drafts and take the camera out of its bag. And since I have nothing else to do, I spend most of the weekend filming my dog.

On Wednesday, after the regular film club meeting, Abdi attempts to show me Final Cut Pro X to help me edit twenty majorly boring minutes into three minorly boring ones in which Kepler sleeps, barks twice, fetches a ball once, and eats.

"It's not going to Sundance."

Abdi nods. "No, not Sundance. But it's not bad. For your first movie."

I laugh. "It's not a movie!"

"Well, you shot some interesting stuff."

"Really?"

He nods. "The close up of her guzzling the water is great. You can practically feel her tongue."

"I'm a big fan of dogs drinking water."

"So what's your next three-minute movie going to be about?"

"Doesn't film club want the camera back?"

He shakes his head. "One of the perks of being a completely unknown student club is no one is going to want it. Until there's a Hello Kitty SLR, Jessie won't film anything. Joking. Sort of." He smiles. "And Tony likes his GoPro."

"What exactly does he film? I didn't really know what he was talking about the other day."

"Skateboarding, snowboarding, dirt biking." Abdi freezes Kepler chasing her tail on the monitor. "Sporty stuff."

"Is it good?"

"It's cool, but a little one-note."

"Oh."

"Do you know Jonathan Caouette's movies?"

"I never know the movies you know. Especially the documentaries."

He nods. "You might find them interesting. *Tarnation* got a lot of hype. *Walk Away Renee* streams on Netflix. They're different. Honest."

"Maybe I'll check them out."

"I should give you a trigger warning that they're about his mother. She's mentally ill."

I don't know what to say. I hate the words "mental illness." They sound so cold and final. They make me think of "mental patient" and "mental institution."

"Sorry," Abdi says.

"It's okay." I think about the books under my bed. Am I ever going to be able to look at them? If Toby had cancer or a brain tumor, I'd be reading everything in sight about it. I'd have started a Kickstarter, organized a parade in his honor, and been at the hospital 24/7. So why is his mental illness making me not do anything?

"I'm sure you'll think of something interesting to shoot."

"I doubt it. I should probably just leave the camera here."

Despite what I said to Abdi, I take the camera back home, but I can't think of anything else to film. I know she's a dog, but Kepler really doesn't like being filmed. I try to interview my grandmother, figuring that since she's older she might have things to say, but she keeps fiddling with her bracelets and telling me she's not interesting. I wonder how Abdi got Jessie to talk so freely.

Out of boredom, on the following Saturday afternoon I follow Sam around. Unlike the dog and Grandma, my brother talks a mile a minute about Harry Potter Lego Star Wars Ninja Monster Truck Batman versus Spiderman. When my parents come home from their weekly grocery shopping, my brother is doing a headstand and babbling about Death Eaters.

"What are you doing?" my mom asks.

"I'm going to be in a movie!" Sam says.

"No, you're not," I tell him. "I told you I'm just practicing. I need footage to use Final Cut."

"What's this for?" My dad sounds suspicious.

"Where's the camera from?" my mom asks. "No more headstands, Sammy. It's not good to be up like that."

"School." I turn the camera off. "It's not *for* anything."

"Why do you have it? It looks expensive."

"Why are you grilling me?" I feel annoyed. "I just borrowed it from film club. I'm shooting footage to practice editing."

"Are you in the film club?" my mom asks.

"Yeah, I guess I am."

"That's so great, Meals! I'm so happy you're doing something extracurricular." My mom beams. "All those movies you've watched can do you some good."

"Not really."

"What exactly does film club do?" my dad asks.

"We . . . Well, the president guy, Abdi, he's an amazing filmmaker. He's totally going to get an Oscar one day." I remember Toast saying this and cringe. "But mostly we just talk about movies, watch random things on YouTube. They have a pretty great DVD collection."

"This is what my taxes pay for?"

"Lou!" My mom pokes him with her elbow.

"Film club does a monthly movie series, too, Dad. That's for the community. You could go. Last month they showed *Love Actually* and *Punch-Drunk Love*."

"I love *Love Actually*," my mom says. "That Hugh Grant . . ."

"I know. We're trying to figure out what to show next month. That takes up a lot of meeting time."

"Well, I'm thrilled," my mom says. "I'm so happy that

you're getting out there more, Meals. You have a lot to offer the world."

"Mom . . ." I doubt I have a lot to offer the world since I have yet to write to Toby or talk to him on the phone. He calls home once a week—it's a set time for Sunday afternoons—but I've been too scared or embarrassed to talk to him. And I've still got the unwritten email in my drafts folder.

Sam leaps from the recliner onto the couch. "Did you get that?"

"Sorry, dude. I turned the camera off."

"No furniture jumping," my dad says, but he doesn't sound mad.

"Sam, honey, can you go play by yourself for a minute?" my mom says.

"I'm going to put on my Batman costume," he tells me. "I think it'll be a great movie if I'm dressed like Batman."

After he's gone upstairs, my mom says, "So." It's weird, with just one word, the air becomes very serious. I turn the camera back on, but keep the lens at my parents' feet so they don't know I'm filming.

"Meals, we think you should talk to someone," my mom says.

"I talk to plenty of people."

"A psychiatrist. Or some kind of counselor."

"There's nothing wrong with it," my dad says. "There's nothing to be ashamed of." He looks at my mom, who nods. "We've been through a lot these past few months. We need to support each other. And, uh, *get* support."

"I talked to Dr. Kellerman."

"That's great, honey," my mom says. "But isn't he a guidance counselor? Isn't it mostly about college and SATs with him?"

"I don't need to talk to anyone."

"It's not that we don't believe you," my mom says, "except I don't because *I'm* not okay, Amelia. Every day I wake up and I think: *My beautiful son is a schizophrenic!* Some mornings, it's very hard to get out of bed."

I turn the camera off. I don't want this conversation preserved.

My dad clears his throat. My mom pats my arm. "Listen, Meals, we talk to Toby's doctors at Two Moons, but your father and I have also started seeing Dr. Koenig. He's a local psychiatrist. He told us about a NAMI chapter—that's National Alliance on Mental Illness—that meets in the city. It's a support group. There's a meeting next week. Your father and I are going. The twins are too young, but we'd like you to come."

"Oh."

"I—*we*—want to know what other people, other family members do, Amelia," she says. "We can't do it alone."

"You're not alone," I remind her. "You have me and Dad and Grandma . . ."

"I know, sweetie. But you and Grandma are going through this, too. We need professional people, too. There's a group for adolescents, which I think would be good for you. We chose to have Toby live at Two Moons because they can support his needs, but we need support, too."

Last year at this time, phrases like "support his needs" would never have come out of my mother's mouth and my father would never have agreed to therapy. Last year at this time, Toby and I would probably still be sleeping. Although I still haven't signed up for my road test, I probably wouldn't have completed Driver's Ed or been filming random things all weekend.

"It could help," she says. "You've always been so giving to Toby. I really think an adolescent support group could help *you*. Please."

After everything my parents have been through these past few months, I can't say no, so I say yes.

28

THE GROUP

THE FOLLOWING SATURDAY, AS SOON AS MY DAD crosses the George Washington Bridge, my heart starts pounding. I know that there are ten million people in New York, but in less than an hour, I'll be closer to Epstein than I've been in weeks. The whole rest of the drive, I keep thinking about him. He must hate me. Does he know where he's going to college yet? Does he have a new girlfriend? What would happen if I saw him?

You're being ridiculous, I think as I get out of the car and follow my parents. *This is a huge city. There's no way you'll run into him.*

The meeting takes place in an elementary school. According to the schedule, we've made it for the last ten minutes of coffee and donuts in the cafeteria. After that there's a panel discussion about consent and an adolescent meeting on the third floor. There are about twenty-five people, and everyone except my parents and me seems to know everybody else. An older Asian woman hugs a fat white man while a skinny bald man shakes hands with a very old woman. I empty a packet of instant hot chocolate into a Styrofoam cup of hot water and make my way to the far corner of the room. My parents talk to a lady holding a clipboard. I sip my hot chocolate and watch my dad shovel donuts into his mouth. My mom catches my attention and indicates that I should come over.

"This is our daughter, Amelia," my mom says. "This is Lucy Gerber. She's the president of this chapter."

"Hi, Amelia," Lucy says. She has gray hair that hangs just above her shoulders and a large mole on her right cheek. "You're in high school?"

"A junior."

"There *are* more people your age here," Lucy says. "I think they grabbed donuts and took off. Check upstairs."

"Okay."

"I hope you find it helpful." She smiles, then turns to leave. "Excuse me. I need to talk to someone. We'll get started in a few minutes."

"Thanks," my mom says.

My dad inhales another donut.

My mom squeezes my shoulder. "I love you, Amelia. Thank you for coming."

I head upstairs and down the hallway. As I look at all the kids' paintings taped up on long bulletin boards, I feel a wave of nostalgia. Mrs. Dulac's kindergarten class has drawn zoo animals; second graders have made heart collages. At the end of the hallway I hear laughter. I stand outside and listen.

"And he was like catatonic at that point," a girl says. "I said to the cop, if you can get him to talk, be my guest."

There's more laughter. I do not want to go in. I so don't want to talk to these people.

A guy who looks like a tall Harry Potter sticks his head out. "Hey! Are you here for the session?"

"Uh, yeah. I guess."

"Come on in," he says. "Make yourself . . . not at home.

But, you know what I mean. As 'at home' as you can be in . . ."
He looks at the name on the door. "Mrs. McKittrick's room."

I walk in feeling very new-girl.

"You talk too much, Jack," a very pretty African American girl with dreadlocks says.

"I'm Jack," Harry Potter says. "I talk too much." He's dressed in all black except for red sneakers. He looks cool, like someone who would've been at the New Year's party I ran away from. I push the thought away.

"I'm Amelia." I feel self-conscious as I walk to a small blue table in the back. The room smells like markers and cleaner. There are eight people altogether: two sitting on the windowsills, three at another table. Two girls are chatting in the back corner near a large stuffed bear.

"Want a donut?" Jack points to a stack on the teacher's desk.

"No, thanks." I feel a little like I might throw up and don't want to risk it on a crummy donut.

"Last month they had bagels," the black girl says. "What happened to the bagels?"

"Bring it up with Lucy," a guy with hand tattoos says.

A youngish adult guy with short dark hair and a button-down Oxford tucked into jeans walks in and looks at Jack. "Should we get started?"

Jack looks at his phone. "Oh shit, yeah. It's almost ten."

What I thought would happen is that some adult, maybe some parent or even a doctor or someone like that, would come in and tell us something about schizophrenia and bi-polar disorder, how we should love our siblings, blah blah

blah. But what actually happens is that everyone puts their chairs in a circle and faces one another. The guy with the button-down says his name is Ethan and that he's a psychiatrist at some hospital and that he's here as an observer since these meetings are peer-led. Then he turns to Jack.

"Hey. Most of you know me. I'm Jack. My sister Rebecca is schizophrenic. She's been that way for . . ." Jack looks down. "Ten years now. She's twenty-eight."

Ten years. In ten years, I'll be twenty-seven, which seems like a very faraway time from where I am right now.

"What's going on, Jack?" the black girl asks.

Jack shrugs. "Rebecca's doing good. She got a work attendance award. She's been doing her blog and tweeting. We went out to dinner. It was fine. She has a boyfriend . . . He's bipolar, but things have been pretty mellow." He shrugs and looks at the fat boy next to him.

"I'm Scott and I'm an alcoholic," he says dryly.

Everyone but Dr. Ethan and me laughs.

"Seriously, I'm Scott. I have two brothers. One has severe bipolar disorder and the other one has schizo-affective disorder. I haven't been diagnosed yet." He laughs and a couple of other people do, but not everyone. "Boy, oh boy, what a month," he continues. "Mark ended up back in Bellevue." Scott shakes his head.

"What did he do?" a small girl with braids asks.

"The whole nine schizoid yards," Scott says. "Assaulted two nurses, an orderly. Got all the furniture taken out of his room. Again." Scott looks at his hands.

I wonder if my brother would do something like that. I can't imagine Toby violent.

"How's Caleb?" Jack asks.

"He's alright. Doing his painting thing."

I hear about two other siblings who have bipolar disorder and one who has something called BPD. The black girl, Celia, has a schizophrenic mother. Celia says her mom smoked marijuana and spent the weekend in the ER, which stunk since it was her mom's birthday and Celia had made plans for them to spend the day together. Lilly, the girl with the braids who looks barely thirteen, has a schizophrenic twin sister. "She's got reactions to her meds, but nothing out of the ordinary," Lilly tells us. "The part that bothers her the most is the vision thing. It's blurry and she has trouble going on the computer and texting."

"Is she on Clozapine?" Celia asks.

Lilly shakes her head. "No. Haldol."

"And she's getting blurred vision?"

"That's what she says."

Celia nods thoughtfully, but I feel like everyone is talking in a completely foreign language. People just go around talking about their brothers, sisters, or parents using words like "assisted outpatient treatment" and "cognitive rehab." I can't believe that the actual doctor hasn't said a word!

I'm so busy absorbing names like Celexa, Lexapro, and Risperdal that I don't realize it's my turn until Scott waves his hand in front of my face.

"I'm Amelia," I say.

Everyone nods or says, "Hey."

"My brother is, uh, you know, sick." I feel embarrassed and stupid.

Dr. Ethan gives me a little nod and Jack smiles, but I can't say anything more. Once again something blocks the path from the words in my brain to my mouth.

"Is it a new diagnosis?" Celia asks gently.

I nod.

Celia nods back. "That's the worst time. Trying to figure out what's wrong, then they gotta spend forever trying to figure out what meds to give."

"He just got diagnosed," I spit out. "It's been pretty shitty." I pretend I have a camera and I'm just filming. If Abdi was here, he'd definitely get all the posters in the class-room—especially the list of the classroom rules: *We are nice and respectful. We help each other. We are good listeners. We share. We stay safe.*

"Is he older or younger?" Jack asks.

These people don't know Toby at all, I realize. They know nothing of Toby's awesomeness. To them he's just an-other mentally ill patient who takes a lot of pills.

"He's older," I lamely say. More than anything I wish there was a way to show people what Toby used to be like. There he'd be doing a cartwheel, singing along to the Beatles, cracking jokes, and entertaining everyone around him. After I showed the group everything there is to know about Toby, I would ask them approximately 1.3 million questions: *What do they tell people? Do they keep the illness a secret? Is it wrong to keep it a secret? Do they worry about how much everything costs? Is it possible to go back and have just a regular, fun day? And did they ever get really wasted and hook up with the most totally wrong person because they just couldn't deal?* Questions buzz through my brain, but before I get even one out, Lucy pokes her head in and says everyone is back in the cafeteria.

And that's it. It's over. Everyone shuffles back through the hall and into the cafeteria where the adults are drinking coffee and, to Celia's delight, eating bagels. I walk over to my parents, who are talking to a short older couple.

"This is Angela and John," my mom says. "This is our daughter, Amelia."

Angela smiles.

"How was it?" my mom asks.

I shrug. "Okay."

"Our daughter used to find the peer groups really helpful. She made some good friends. She's all grown now."

"Angela and John's son is also schizophrenic," my mom informs me.

At first I'm embarrassed that my mom has just announced this to the whole room, but then I think, *Why not?* Everyone here is related to someone who's mentally ill. That's the whole reason we're here.

"Apparently Ted was just a little older than Toby when he was diagnosed," my mom says. "And now he's . . ."

"Thirty-four," Ellen says. "Ted lives in an apartment with a roommate. He's held a job for almost three years."

"That's great." It's the only thing that I can think to say. I'm relieved when I see Dr. Ethan signaling for me to come over.

"I'll be right back," I tell my mom and head over to Dr. Ethan.

"Hi, Amelia," he says. "I have to go to the hospital, but I wrote down a couple of websites for you. I know your time got cut short. There are some pretty good message boards. There can also be some scary ones. Avoid those." He hands me a piece of pink construction paper. "I had to steal this from the classroom. I put my email address on it."

"Thanks."

"Sorry you didn't get a chance to really talk to the group. Most of the peer group knows one another so it can be a lot of hanging out."

"That's okay. Thanks for the websites."

"No problem. Hopefully I'll see you next month." He turns and walks away.

My mother comes over and puts her arm around me. "Your father wants to get going. He's worried he's going to get a parking ticket." She looks at the paper I'm holding. "What's that?"

"Just some web stuff," I say, shoving the paper deep into my pocket. "We can go."

29

THE SAFE-AND-SOUND SIBLING SOCIETY

WHEN TOBY HAS BEEN IN MASSACHUSETTS FOR almost five weeks, my mom tells me that he's coming home.

"For good?"

"No, honey, not yet. Just for the weekend. He's getting a pass for good behavior. Did you know he gets to listen to music twice a week?"

I shake my head. I don't know anything about Toby, because I haven't bothered to talk to him since he left. And I still haven't written or sent him the email in my drafts folder.

"The staff thinks a visit home might be good since Family Weekend isn't till summer."

"Oh." I'm not sure how I feel about all of this. I guess I'm happy that he can visit, but I also feel like it's good that he's going back since it doesn't seem like he's been gone long enough to get better. Then I feel bad wanting my brother to live far away. "When's he coming?"

"Next Saturday."

"What about the twins' birthday?" It feels like Sam and David have been talking about turning eight for eight years now.

"Well, Sunday is their birthday, so we'll have a small family party. We don't want to overwhelm Toby."

For the next week, since she's been a total BFFF, I think

about telling Ray that Toby's coming home. After everything we've been through in the last few months, I feel like I owe her. So on Friday afternoon I tell her as we walk into Starbucks. We're planning on maybe doing some practice SATs before Ray has to go to work.

"So, uh, Toby's coming home," I say. We sit down in the fake leather chairs in the corner of the store.

"Really?"

"Yeah. Tomorrow. Just for the weekend. My dad takes him back Monday."

"Cool."

Cool. Toby Anderson used to be cool. His visiting from his rehabilitation center in Massachusetts is pretty much the opposite of cool. "Yeah, I guess. Yeah."

"How's he doing there?"

"Good. I think. Better. He gets to listen to music now or something. I don't know." *You'd know if you actually talked to him when he called.* "Anyway, do you want to come over for dinner on Sunday? It's the twins' birthday. We're just having a family party thing."

"Really?"

"Yeah. If you want. It's not a big deal. I thought you might want to see him."

"Yeah, that would be awesome. I have work, but I could be there by 6:30. It'll be so good to see Toby." She looks at me like she expects me to say something profound, but I don't know what to say. I look out the window at a stream of elementary school students in the playground across the street. It's a big blur of puffy hats and pom-pom hats and multicolored mittens. *It would be a good shot*, I think, wishing I had taken the camera. It would be a good opening shot to pan over the kids and their My Little Pony and Star Wars backpacks and then have a narrator say something like, "Will any of these children be diagnosed with schizophrenia in ten years?"

My dad must drive like a maniac because Toby is home by 3:00 on Saturday. He still looks like a hippie Jesus with his long, slightly matted hair and gross beard, but he gives me a hug. A real, open-armed Toby Anderson hug!

"Hi," he says.

I hug him back. It's weird, but in just the thirty seconds he's been here, I feel like my brother is more present than he has been in months. He hugs the twins and gives them each a funky birdhouse that he made in the Two Moons art studio.

Then, after playing video games with them, Toby helps me set the table for dinner. Not only does he talk while we eat, he even compliments my parents on the food.

"Pulled pork is one of the most amazing foods," he says. "The food at Two Moons is terrible. I was complaining about the potatoes yesterday and it was actually fish."

We all laugh. I look at my parents and see the relief in their eyes. *He's getting better. He's finally getting better*, I think.

But the next morning, the twins' long-awaited eighth birthday, Toby doesn't come down for breakfast, even though my mom skipped brunch to be home. By noon, she's more than a little concerned and calls my dad. He tells her to wake him up. I don't know exactly what happens, but a few minutes after my mom goes upstairs Toby starts screaming.

"I hate you!" he yells. "I'm not your prisoner!"

"Toby," my mom says. "I'm trying to help you. I want you to get well more than anything in the world, honey."

"Then let me go out! There's nothing wrong with me. How many times do I have to tell you?"

I stand at the bottom of the stairs listening to them go back and forth until my mom comes out and he slams the door behind her.

"I think maybe being home is too much for him," she tells me as I quietly walk up the stairs.

"But he seemed so much better yesterday. What happened?"

She shakes her head. "I think he was up all night, reading an old copy of *Lord of the Rings*, writing in his notebook. I hope he's taking his meds. At Two Moons they make sure he swallows. I have a check-in call with a staff person this afternoon, but I'm going to call now."

I don't know what to say. I feel furious that Toby was so much better yesterday. It was such a tease, like an amazing seventy-degree day in March with a blizzard the next day.

My phone buzzes.

Toast: hey! is Toby back in town?

Me: yeah? why?

Toast: he left a vm asking for pot

Shit. I remember how Celia at the peer group said pot landed her mom in the ER.

Me: don't sell/give him any. it's bad!!!

Toast: K

Me: promise?

Toast: Cross my heart. but he might ask someone else.

What am I supposed to do?

Toby comes out of his room, slamming his door. "Mom is a bitch," he says.

"She's worried about you."

"She treats me like a baby. Have you seen my keys?"

"No," I tell him, happy that it's true.

"I WANT MY FUCKING CAR KEYS!"

I feel a little frightened, but my mom opens her door and comes out. "We don't talk that way here, Toby." She sounds resigned and stern. "There are house rules. You follow rules at Two Moons, don't you?"

"Fuck your rules," he says. "I want my keys."

"Toby," I say. "It's not Mom's fault."

"Not her fault? Who said I can't live here? Who makes me take pills?"

"Where do you want to go?" my mom asks.

"Out."

"I'll take you somewhere."

"I want to go alone."

"I don't know," she says, meekly. "Let me call Dad."

I can't believe my mom might let Toby go out by himself! I can't let her do that. The old Amelia would have ignored it or covered for Toby, but this Amelia will do everything in her power to stop her brother from getting drugs or going out on his own. I walk into my parents' room. My mom is sitting on her bed, rubbing her eyes.

"Mom?"

"Yeah, sweets?"

My heart races but I'm going to get the words out. "Toby wants pot. He's been trying to get some. He texted Toast." I'm surprised that a wave of relief floods over me. "We can't let him leave. He'll get in trouble."

"Thanks, Meals. I know it's not easy—"

"I covered for him," I blurt out. "I covered for him a lot. He didn't go snowboarding that time. And I lent him money . . . and . . ."

"I know," my mom says. "I mean I didn't *know*-know, but you've always been so close, incredibly loyal. I'm not surprised."

"You're not mad?" Tears stream down my face.

"Oh, Meals." She shakes her head and hugs me. "I'm not mad at you. I know you don't want Toby to be hurt or sick. I know you covered for him out of love."

"Yeah. It *was* out of love." *But I'm also telling on him out of love, too.* I'll always love Toby but I'm not going to lie for him. The Secret Sibling Society isn't about covering up and lying. Not anymore, anyway. It's going to be about protecting one another and making sure we're safe and sound. The Safe and Sound Sibling Society. That could work.

When my dad gets home, he and my mom have another call with the staff at Two Moons. After that, when Toby refuses to open the door or turn down the music, my dad says he's taking Toby's door off.

"Lou?" my mom calls, but my dad is already halfway down the stairs and doesn't respond. We hear the back door close and then open. He must be getting his tools out of his truck.

"If you drive a car, I'll tax the street. If you try to sit, I'll tax your seat," George Harrison sings. *Toby would be so proud that I know it's George singing.*

We hear my dad run back up the stairs. Less than five minutes later, the whole house gets intensely quiet.

"There are rules, Meg," my dad says, walking back into the bedroom. He puts Toby's speaker on their bureau. My mom and I are lying next to each other on their bed.

"Are you sure that was the right thing to do?" my mom asks.

"It's *our* house. He has to be a cooperative member of the family. That's what the doctors say."

My mom exhales loudly. "I need to nap for a minute. Is that okay?"

My dad turns to me. "Want to help me get ready for the party, Meals?"

Crap. With Sam and David out with our grandma all morning, I totally forgot about their birthday. I really don't feel like celebrating.

"Sure, Dad." I follow him out of his bedroom, past Toby's quiet open room, and downstairs, where I hang up a very used "Happy Birthday" banner across the dining room wall.

"You really are a good egg," my dad says as I tack up the last Y.

The good egg. I don't know if I want to be a good egg anymore. I don't want to be bad, but *The Good Egg* sounds like the name of a movie Abdi would recommend. Would it be about me? *Maybe chickens*, I think, actually laughing out loud.

I force myself to seem extra cheerful when the twins come home with their newly purchased video games and Legos.

"Where's Toby?" David asks. "I want to show him my new game."

"Sleeping," my dad tells him. "Show him later."

My grandmother looks at me quizzically. I look at my dad, and he gives me a what-do-you-want-me-to-say look back.

Three hours later, when Toby still hasn't made an appearance, but the six-cheese macaroni and cheese and the slow cooker full of hot dogs and baked beans are well past done, my mom says we should eat.

I feel my body tense as my dad walks up the stairs. I'm sure that he and Toby are going to start screaming, but it remains quiet and my dad comes down two minutes later. "He's made a choice to stay in his room. Sorry." We look at him, but he just sits down. "Let's eat," he orders.

Just as I sit, the doorbell rings. In the chaos of trying to not get too upset about Toby, I totally forgot about Ray. When I open the door, she's holding four "Happy Birthday" balloons, which she hands to me while she slides off her coat. "These are lame, but I had no idea what to get for boys with every Lego set in the universe."

"It was nice of you to buy them anything."

"I traded CinnaYum! sticks for them." Ray grins. "I can't believe it's taken me so long to figure out bartering. How's Toby? I can't wait to see him."

"Um, yeah. Sorry, I should have texted. You're probably not going to. See him."

"What happened? He's home, right?"

I take a deep breath. "Yeah, he's home, but he's really pissed off. My parents wouldn't let him go out alone. My dad took his door off so he won't come downstairs. Sorry."

"It's fine," Ray says, even though I can see she's disappointed. "No biggie."

"He was great yesterday. Like the old Toby. I wish I had filmed him so I could show you. But today . . . Today is really sucky. My mom thinks he was up all night. He really wants pot, but it's bad for him. I told my mom about it." I shrug to make it seem like it's not a big deal, but my heart races. "I basically told her not to let him out."

"Well, that stinks. Sorry, Amelia. You must be bummed."

"Yeah."

"But I might as well party while I'm here," she says, walking into the dining room. "Happy happy Thing 1 and Thing 2!"

Ray sounds so cheerful that I love her more than ever.

"Are those balloons for me?" Sam asks.

"Sure are." Ray hands him two.

"I love Minions," he says.

"Balloons are lame," David says sullenly.

"David!" My mother looks at him. "That's rude. Apologize to Ray!"

"Sorry," David mumbles to Ray. "How come Amelia gets a friend over? It's my birthday!"

"I know, honey. That's why we're taking you and your friends to celebrate at Legoland Discovery. Next weekend, when Toby's back in Massachusetts. This is just your family party."

"Ray isn't family and next weekend isn't my birthday. It's not fair!" David stands up. "This is the worst birthday ever. Amelia gets a friend over and stupid Toby ruined my birthday!" His face turns purple.

"Oh, honey." My mom walks over to David. "I know you're upset." She tries to put her arms around him but he ducks under her.

"Davey," my grandmother says.

"Don't call me 'Davey'!" he shrieks. "I'm not upset. I just hate you. I hate everyone!" With that he runs upstairs.

I look at my mom, who looks at my dad, who looks at me. A door slams above us.

"What should we do?" my mom asks.

"He's spoiled," my dad says. "Let him stew."

"He's *not* spoiled, Lou. He's *upset*," my mom says. "Can't you see that?"

"I'm hungry," my father says like he hasn't heard my mother. My mom looks like she might cry or throw up, but my dad doesn't look at her.

"I'll talk to David," I volunteer, surprising myself.

Everyone looks at me.

"It's okay, Amelia," my mom says. "It's not your responsibility."

"I don't mind." I stand up. "I want to. I'll be right back," I tell Ray.

"It's cool," she says. "Did you hear the one about the chicken who tried to get a tattoo?" she asks Sam.

I run upstairs, avoid looking in Toby's room, and knock on David's door.

"Don't. Come. In," he says.

I open the door a crack. "I'll give you a million dollars."

"You don't have a million dollars."

"Sure I do," I say, widening the crack.

"A million real, minted USA dollars?"

"Shoot. How'd you know to ask that?"

David doesn't say anything.

"Toby got you on that, didn't he?" I open the door halfway. "He used to do the same thing to me." I step inside his room. "But I ended up with tons of Monopoly money. I was so mad."

"I *didn't* say you could come in. You're not going to give me real money."

"If I had money, I'd give you some. I have like ten bucks to my name."

"You'd spend a million dollars on clothes and makeup and other stupid girly stuff."

"I wouldn't spend it all on stupid girly stuff. Just half of it." *If I had a million dollars maybe I'd buy a camera like Abdi's.* "But listen. If I, Amelia Jane Anderson, ever have a million dollars, I will give my brother, David Logan Anderson, a minimum of twenty thousand dollars. How's that?"

"I don't care anyway. You're never going to have a million dollars."

"You never know."

"I know everyone in this family is stupid. And I hate everyone."

"Hey! I have an eighty-three average. That's a B. That's not stupid." I lie down on the bottom bunk. "The only reason I have a B and not a B+ is because I didn't do so hot in French or math last semester. But a B is not stupid. It's been a hard year, you know." I pause for a second. "Sam isn't stupid, either."

He snorts.

"He's not. Did you know I used to pretend Toby was my twin?"

"Being a twin sucks. You *always* have to share. I wish Ryan was my twin. Or Zachary. Anybody would be better than stupid Sam."

"Sam *is* a little weird."

"A lot weird!"

"But you're weird, too."

"Am not."

"Are too. You're so into baseball. You know more about the Mets than everyone in our family, and the word on the street is that you're amazing at karate."

"I'm just a green belt," David says. "But Sam's still yellow."

"But you're the most weird because you don't like ketchup. Everyone likes ketchup. Especially seven—I mean, eight-year-olds. French fries were invented solely as a means to eat ketchup."

"Ketchup is tomatoes," David says. "Tomatoes are gross."

"Tomatoes are in pizza sauce, which is on pizza. I've seen you eat pizza. Like a million slices."

"I close my eyes when I eat pizza," he says, like it's totally logical.

"Oh. Maybe I'll try that. You know, David, people who aren't weird aren't interesting." I can't help but think about Epstein. He was weird, and definitely interesting. And very thoughtful. He thought I was interesting too. I push the thought away and focus on David. "I'm weird because I love movies and always want to think about them. Sometimes when I don't want to pay attention to what someone is saying, like a teacher, I come up with random lists like Kid Movies That Don't Suck or Movies About Twins with Actual Twins."

"Why would you do that?"

"I don't know. It's kind of a game I play with myself. Like right now all I can think of are all the Olsen twin movies. *New York Minute* and the one where they go to Rome. And there's a movie called *House of Yes* with Parker Posey and she has a twin in real life even though he's not in it."

David stares at me. "You're *really* weird, Meals."

I nod. "You're right. I might be the weirdest one in the family. Do you think Toby is stupid?"

He doesn't say anything.

"Toby is definitely not stupid," I tell him. "He's one of the smartest people I know."

David swings his body over the bunk to look down at me, and I wish I were filming him. "Then why did he ruin my birthday? Why won't he come downstairs?" He flips himself back up. "What happened to his door? Why did he get sent away?"

I swallow.

"Mommy says he's getting help to get well, but I don't understand what's wrong with him. Why does he not want to hang out with me?"

My heart breaks for David. It's been horrible for me, but at least I've been told what's wrong with my brother and taken to meetings and given books. If I wanted, I could spend the next eighteen hours reading blogs and websites and podcasts all about mental illness. I could email Dr. Ethan. But poor David just thinks his brother doesn't want to hang out. "He does want to hang out with you, David. But his brain just isn't acting right. And he didn't get sent away."

"He doesn't live here anymore."

"No, but he's going to come back. He didn't do anything bad. He's just. Well, you know when someone is sick they're tired and grumpy and don't act like themselves. It's not their fault. They just got unlucky and got a cold or the flu."

"Toby isn't sick like that."

"Yeah, I know he's not sick like that, but his brain got sick. His brain makes him act weird. The healthy Toby wants to be downstairs more than anything, David." Why did I think I could play parent? Why am I pretending that I know anything about schizophrenia? "Remember the awesome snow village you guys made last Christmas?"

My brother nods.

"I like thinking about that Toby."

David hangs his face down again. "Meals?"

"Yeah?"

"I miss Toby."

"Me too, buddy."

"The *old* Toby. The one who made the snow village and played video games and played Star Wars with me."

"Me too. I miss him all the time. But you know where he lives, in Massachusetts, they're trying to help him get back to being the old Toby."

"Do you think it'll work?"

"I really, really hope so."

David pulls his face back up to his bunk. *Wow!* I think this might be the longest, least annoying conversation I've ever had with David. It also might be the longest—and, in some ways, the most honest—conversation I've had about Toby. Maybe it's sad that it was with an eight-year-old, but who cares?

"Meals?"

"Yeah?"

"I'm going to get cake now." He swings himself off the bunk like a monkey. "Will Mom and Dad be mad?"

I shake my head.

"Are you coming? Grandma bought two ice cream cakes. So we don't have to share."

"In a second."

"I wouldn't spend too long on Sam's bed," he warns me as he walks into the hallway. "It smells like butt farts."

"I won't." I look at the sheep on Sam's pillowcase. I should go downstairs. I have to be there when they sing "Happy Birthday." I wonder what Toby's doing in his room.

He'd hate me if he knew I'd told my mom about him wanting pot and said not to let him go out. But I don't feel bad about it. It feels really good not to feel bad, too.

"Amelia?" Ray whispers from the hallway.

"In here."

She opens the door. "Your parents think you're amazing. What did you say to David?" She walks in and sits on the bunk near my feet.

"Nothing, really. Sorry I left you downstairs with my stressed-out family. I should have told you not to come over since Toby won't come down."

"I'm glad to come over. I like your family. They've always been super nice to me. It's not your fault that Toby is in his room." She smiles. "Plus, Sam laughs at all my jokes."

"I still suck."

"You don't suck. You're having a shitty year."

"Yeah . . ." I pick up Sam's stuffed panda. "I went to this mental illness support group meeting with my parents a few weeks ago. There were people our age with a family member who has some kind of mental illness. It was weird. A doctor was there, but he barely said a word. The kids did all the talking."

"Huh."

"I don't know. If I go again maybe I would have something to say to Sam and David. They're kind of getting the short end of things. At least my parents have told me the truth—the twins are always being told to go play or watch TV."

After a few minutes, Ray says, "At least the twins like TV."

I laugh. "Yeah, who knows what my parents would do with them if they didn't." I think about the twins watching TV and wonder what would happen if I borrowed a tripod from film club and filmed myself talking to David. *Or made something that David and Sam could watch. I wouldn't have to show it to anyone else.* I could make them something about Toby. I wonder how I could do that and if they'd watch something that wasn't cartoony or about a superhero. I wonder if I could use one of their superhero figures in the movie. Yoda might be good. Of course if it were terrible, I wouldn't have to show them. But for now, I just get off my brother's farty bed and go downstairs with Ray for birthday cake.

30

THE GIRL WITH THE BROTHER WHO . . .

TWO WEEKS AFTER TOBY'S DISASTROUS HOME VISIT, I take the SATs. I think I did okay, considering I stayed up late logging footage Abdi had of his great-uncles. The uncles are in their eighties and live on a farm in Somalia. I said he could have the title *The Good Egg*, but he said it didn't fit because they don't have chickens. I know I helped Abdi a lot because I made really detailed notes on the Excel spreadsheet he sent me. I didn't think watching old farmers in Africa would be that exciting, but logging the footage turned out to be way more interesting than taking another practice exam. I still think I did okay on the test, though.

After the SATs, Abdi and I hang out trying to edit Sam in his Batman costume, but the kid talks so much, so quickly that it's kind of impossible, so Abdi starts playing some of the footage he has of Toast. I still can't look at Toast without remembering the night at Ray's, so I ask if there's anything else he could edit.

"Sure. I have tons." He fast-forwards the footage so Toast is moving in hyperspeed around Smoker's Gate.

"It'd be so great if you could fast-forward life like that," I say as Toast zips around the screen. "Like a Mr. Rubinstein class."

Abdi nods. "Those triangulation lectures are the worst."

"I'd like to speed up traffic jams and bathroom lines."

"I wouldn't mind fast-forwarding a day or two or eleven of Ramadan."

"That's when you fast for a whole month?"

"You fast between sunrise and sunset. Depending on when it falls, we eat at like three or four in the morning and then again around eight or nine at night."

"That's a long time to go between meals."

"You're telling me. It's bad when it falls in the summer. There's so much daylight." He speeds up another section and I point to a blur behind Toast.

"Stop! Is that Toby?"

Abdi pushes play.

It is Toby. My brother smiles at the camera. He looks like the old Toby. No beard, good hair, nice clothes.

"*Bonjour*, Abdi," Toby says in an exaggerated French accent. "Is it *cinema verité* day at Washington Lincoln?"

I hear Abdi laugh from behind the camera.

"What's cinema verité?" I ask.

"Observational filmmaking. A style of documentary."

"How did my brother know that?"

"He's smart."

Yeah, I think. *He is.*

"Do you want to keep watching?"

I nod, sort of in a trance as I watch Toby talk about the ridiculousness of high school French, do two cartwheels, sing "*Michelle, ma belle, sont les mots qui vont très bien ensemble*" before saying, "*Au revoir, mon frère.*" The camera follows him out of Smoker's Gate and I watch him get smaller and smaller. I wonder if he's going to class. Or to get stoned in Prudence? How did he feel that day? What is he doing right now in Massachusetts? Is he thinking about me? If I actually emailed him would he email me back?

"Amelia?" Abdi looks at me. "Are you okay?"

I take a deep breath. "Yeah. I'm okay."

"I have more footage of Toby on a different card if you want to watch it."

I shake my head.

"Sorry," Abdi says. "I forgot all about filming that."

"That's okay," I say. "I'm glad I saw it. Maybe I'll watch some more, some other time."

When I get home, my mom is waiting to see how the test went.

"So?" she asks.

"It was okay. I think I did okay."

"That's great, honey."

"I'll take them again in the fall, but I'm not going to Harvard or anything. Don't get excited."

"I don't expect you to go to Harvard. Although you'd be fine there. You'll go somewhere that's right for you. Who dropped you off? Ray didn't get a new car, did she?"

I shake my head. "Ray went to work. Abdi Osman brought me home."

"The boy from the film club?"

"One of them. There are two. Abdi makes documentaries."

"Do you like him?"

"No!" I say loudly. "He's just a friend. He's really smart

about movies and knows all about editing . . . but I wouldn't go out with him. Besides, I'm not Muslim. He's pretty strict about that." It dawns on me that Abdi could make an interesting documentary about himself. Moving from Africa to a random, mostly white town in upstate New York is a pretty good storyline.

"Just asking," my mom says.

"I think I still like Epstein." I swallow hard. "But I'm not sure what to do about that."

She nods, and I know she's trying very hard not to ask me a billion-million questions.

"I just have to figure some stuff out," I say.

"You'll figure it out. Now all you need to do is schedule your road test and you'll be test-free." She smiles. "Until finals, of course."

"Mom . . ."

"You *passed* Driver's Ed, Amelia."

"Everyone passes Driver's Ed."

"I'm kind of joking."

"I know."

"*Kind of.*"

"*I know.*"

She gives me a kiss on the head. After she's gone I realize that we just had an entire conversation that wasn't about Toby. *It was fun, almost jokey*, I think with a thud. I'm not sure when it happened but somehow the pause button of my life that got paused when my brother got sick has gotten slightly unpaused.

» » · « «

A few hours later, when I'm settling down to watch *Toy Story 3* with David and Kepler, Ray and Muppet knock on the door.

"Hey," I say. "What are you guys doing here?"

"We're taking you out," Ray says. "Mrs. Anderson?" she calls.

My mom comes out from the kitchen. "Hi, Ray. Hi, Emily. Long time no see. How are you girls doing?"

"We're great, Mrs. A," Ray says. "We thought we'd celebrate taking the SATs by going over to a friend's house."

My mom looks at me.

I give her a look that says: "I have no idea why they're here."

"Can Amelia come?" Muppet asks.

"Of course she can," my mom says. "Generally she's free to come and go as she pleases. As long as someone drives her, of course." My mom smiles.

"I'm driving," Muppet says sincerely. "When are you going to take your road test, Amelia?"

"Soon," I say.

"Is there going to be drinking?" My mom sounds concerned. "Is this a party?"

Ray shakes her head. "Just a few people hanging out."

"Drive carefully," my mom says. "Don't drink and drive."

"Never," Muppet says sincerely. "I would never do that, Mrs. Anderson."

"But David, Kepler, and I are having a *Toy Story* marathon tonight. We're starting with the third one and working our way backwards. How cool is that?"

"Pretty cool," Ray says sarcastically. "So, no offense to you, David, because you're a great guy with a wicked sense of humor. But it's Saturday night, and your sister is seventeen and has already seen about seventeen million movies in her young life."

"Sixteen million," I say.

"And Kepler's a dog," Muppet says.

"No, you're not," I tell Kepler's ear.

"I thought you weren't going to watch so many movies," Ray says.

"It's not so much watching movies as schooling the next generation," I say. "It's important that they know there's more to life than Minions and Star Wars and Legos."

"I love Star Wars," David says. "Let's watch *Toy Story* tomorrow, Meals."

"You're the best, David," Ray says.

"They have a point," my mom says. "It's not healthy to watch movies every night."

"Whose side are you on?" I say.

My mom shrugs.

"You guys are annoying," I say, but I get up and go out with my friends.

Things start off okay even though Ray totally lied to my mom that it wasn't a party. Because I still can't go near alcohol without thinking of Toast and the night I trashed Ray's house, I discover that Skittles and Sprite taste delicious together and have a long but fun conversation with Ray and two other girls about words we don't like, like "moist," "ointment," and "nostril." I'm just starting to feel kind of good about being out on a Saturday when Ari Kaufman, who's home for the weekend, shows up with her boyfriend, who is really cute, well dressed, and without an ounce of facial hair. I hate him so much that I kind of sort of slam into him on my way to the kitchen.

"What's wrong?" Muppet asks.

"PMS," I tell her. "I'm going to go bum a smoke off Ray."

"She quit, remember?"

I do remember, but I don't want to be in the house anymore because Ari is there, along with a bunch of other people Toby used to hang out with.

"You want a beer?" Muppet asks me cheerfully.

I shake my head because beer makes me think of getting drunk at Ray's, which makes me think about kissing Toast, which makes me feel horrible because sweet Muppet is being so nice, and I hate that the last person I kissed was Toast when it should have been Epstein. *If only I hadn't told Epstein to go*, I think for the millionth time. If only I'd said, "This is a really rough day for me."

"You okay, Meals?" Muppet looks at me.

I hear a bunch of people in the next room laugh at something Ari says, and I feel almost sick to my stomach.

"Yeah. I'm just going to get some air."

"It is kind of hot in here."

As I'm walking outside, my phone buzzes with a number I don't know. Without thinking too much about it, I answer.

"Hi, Amelia," Toby says.

"Toby?" I haven't spoken to my brother since my dad brought him back to Two Moons.

"That's me."

"Hey! You seriously could not have called at a better time!"

"Yeah, well, you're not calling me lately. I got another phone privilege so I thought I'd use it to catch you."

"Sorry," I say lamely.

"I get it," he says. "I was an asshole when I was home. I smoked a secret joint. Shit got bad. But I'm taking all my meds now. Well, they give me no choice—but, you know, I'm taking them. That make ya happy, Annie?" He laughs. "That's my house mom. She's listening to everything I say."

I try to imagine Annie. When I think about where Toby is, part of me can't help but remember movies like *It's Kind of a Funny Story* and *Girl, Interrupted* and imagine doctors and nurses trying to control a bunch of kooky characters and emotional teens. I never imagined a house mom.

"It's alright," he says. "She's cool. I just can't tell you about my murder plans. Joke," he says quickly.

"Ha, ha." I walk off the porch and around to the side of the driveway. There's a couple cuddling on a plastic lawn chair but I'm too far for them to hear me.

"Anyway, my new pills make me a zombie. The headaches aren't as bad, but I'm getting fat."

"I can't imagine you fat."

"It's not pretty."

"Ahhhhhhhh!" Owen Stevens comes running out of the

house. Jake Sweeney and Craig Farley come bounding out after him with a stick that's on fire. Camera in hand, Abdi trots after them and gives me a wave.

"You at a party?" Toby asks.

"Kind of."

"Weird."

"It is kind of weird," I say. *Weird that I'm here without you.* Weird that even though I didn't talk to him for the last eight years, it's now perfectly normal that Abdi and I would wave at a party and I'll probably watch this Owen and Jake scene on Wednesday afternoon.

"Everyone thinks I'm totally nuts, right?"

"No. Not really."

"Yeah, right. Anyway, when are you coming to visit?"

"Me?"

"Yeah, you."

"I guess Family Weekend."

"That's not till the end of June."

The end of June does seem very far away. "Maybe I could come sooner," I say without really thinking.

"That would be cool. I can probably get a pass approved for you and everything."

"Okay," I say slowly. I still can't imagine hanging out with Toby in his treatment center.

"It's not that bad. You can come for the day. I'll show you around. They'll let *you* leave."

"Yeah. No, I know. I'm going to visit you soon. Actually, I watched some footage of you today."

"Of me?"

"Yeah. At Smoker's Gate. I've been hanging out with the film club. You know Abdi Osman?"

"The Somali kid, yeah."

For a second I think it's weird that my brother thinks of Abdi as just "the Somali kid," but then I remember that's exactly what I thought of him just a few months ago. "He showed me a scene of you at Smoker's Gate. Probably back in the fall. I didn't know you knew about cinema verité."

"Huh?"

"You just said something like, 'I didn't know it was cinema verité day.' Then you went off about learning French and you sang 'Michelle.' When you left you said 'au revoir.'"

"I sound like a dork."

"Actually it was kind of perfect," I say and realize at the same time. I'm happy that there's footage of my brother from the Before part of our lives. The Before part is real, too. It's okay to want to remember it and talk about it, even if we're definitely in the After part.

"We have movie night here, once a month," my brother says.

"That's great."

"The movies always suck, but it's one of the more exciting evening programs."

"I'm trying to get Sam to watch better movies. He has terrible taste. I feel like a bad older sister. He really likes *Space Dogs*."

"Oh. Okay. I gotta go. Someone needs the phone."

"Uh . . . okay." I feel like our conversation has ended

abruptly. "I'll visit you," I say, but Toby has already hung up. Still, I talked to my brother on the phone! I look at the screen. For seven whole minutes!

Of course it figures that I bump right into Ari as I walk back in, and my happiness bubble bursts like a balloon on a stake.

"Amelia Anderson," she says like Parker Posey in *Dazed and Confused*. "How the fuck are you?"

"Fine," I say, looking for someone I know. I'd even consider talking to Toast, but no one I know is in sight.

"How's it going?" Ari runs a perfectly manicured hand through her perfectly highlighted blond hair.

"Okay. How's college?"

"Awesome. I totally love it. I pledged Alpha Delta Pi. I never thought I'd be in a sorority but it's amazing. My sisters are amazing. My classes are amazing."

What's amazing is that Ari didn't know she'd be in a sorority. She was born to be in one.

"Things at Washington Lincoln good?"

"Same old. Same old."

"And Toby? How's your brother?" From her tone I know that she knows.

"He's good. I just talked to him."

"Cool." She doesn't sound like she thinks it's cool.

"I'm going to visit him." *Or at least email him.* And make sure I'm not always walking the dog when he calls on Sundays.

Ari's boyfriend slides over and puts his arms around her. "Hey, Ar," he says. Together they look like they could be on the cover of *Hot College Couples* magazine. "We should roll if we want to make it to that bar, hon."

"Okay, babe," Ari says. "I'm ready. Um, James—this is Amelia. Amelia is, uh, *Toby's* sister."

"Oh," James says in a way that must mean *he* knows about my brother, too. "Nice to meet you, Amelia."

Knowing that Ari has told all her college friends about my brother gives me that same feeling I had when I realized Epstein had told his parents and Holden about him. But people are going to know. People do know. Ray and Abdi and Toast and Jessie and Tony and all the teachers at Washington Lincoln and Ari and her boyfriend and all their friends. All these people know, so why try to hide it?

It hits me with a thud why I don't want to talk about my brother's illness. Toby, to all the people that don't know him or love him the way I do, has become just the guy in the story— like the girl from fifth grade whose mom dropped dead, the boy who cut his wrists last year, the girl whose dad drove drunk and ended up in jail. Not that long ago I thought of Jessie as the Hello Kitty freak, but there's so much more to her than that. And there's so much more to me than being the sister of the guy who had a rant in the high school cafeteria.

"We're going to Shooters, if you want to come," Ari says.

"Thanks, but I'm good."

She turns to leave but then looks back at me. "Hey, Amelia?"

"Yeah?"

"Tell Toby I say hi. When you see him tell him Ari says

hello, okay?" She sounds like she means it and for a second I think maybe I was wrong. Maybe I misjudged her. But then I look at her with her perfect hair, manicured nails, and perfect James attached to her side. She's got the perfect life.

"Sure," I say a little too loudly. "I'll tell him you say hi." I imagine seeing my brother and saying, "Arianna Kaufman says hi." After everything we've been through it seems like the most random thing in the world. What would he say? Would he find it funny? *It is kind of funny,* I think. It could be a movie called *Arianna Kaufman Says Hi.* You wouldn't have any idea of what it was about from the title, but it would be about this. All this. The good, the bad, and all the parts in between that led me to this random party on a Saturday night talking to my brother's ex-girlfriend. I wonder if it's legal to use someone's name in the title of a movie and I wonder if I could actually do it.

31

ANOTHER MEETING, ANOTHER DANCE PARTY

THE NEXT NAMI MEETING I GO TO IS AT A MIDDLE school on the Upper East Side. When we get there, Jack isn't there, but Scott—the fat kid with two mentally ill brothers— and Celia and Lilly are there, in addition to a few others.

When I walk in, Celia smiles at me, Scott offers me a Twizzler, and Lilly points to the chair next to her. It's weird how I met these people once for an hour a month ago and now we're all best friends. In real life, we'd never be friends this quickly. *But this is real life*, I tell myself. It's all real and happening.

"Uh," Scott says in his deep monotone voice. "I think I'm, like, supposed to get people talking. I thought Dr. Ethan was going to hold my hand, but as you can see, he's a no-show."

"He's on call," Lilly says. "He told us last time he might not be here. He told you to do it."

"Do you want to be leader?" Scott looks at Lilly. "You're a natural, Lil."

"No," Lilly says. "I'm tired." She yawns.

"Okay. Get talking, people. Make me look good."

We laugh.

"*You* have to start," Lilly tells him.

"Right. Okay. Most of you guys know I'm Scott. I'm a

Virgo. I know it's going to come as a huge surprise, but I'm single. So if any of you ladies . . ."

Everyone laughs.

"Seriously," Scott continues. "My two bros suffer from severe mental illness. And uh, the last month . . . well, it sucked. For me. For them it was okay, actually. No one violated any privileges or got anything revoked—but, like, I don't know. It was just another blah month in the life of Scott."

Wow, I think. *Scott is being so open. I guess there's more to him than jokes.*

"Because of your brothers?" a girl with curly brown hair asks.

Scott shrugs. "Yeah. I guess. I don't know. They've always been ill. But school sucks. I don't have a girlfriend. I'm fat."

"But you can change those things," Lilly tells him. "You can work out. You can get a girlfriend."

"Yeah. I know. Of course, my brothers bum me out. Last weekend, I saw these three brothers, they all looked alike—and I got mad thinking that I'll never be able to go to the mall and joke around with my brothers the way those guys were. I mean, we can go to the mall, but the whole time I'll be wondering if something is going to happen, did someone skip his meds, you know, all that bullshit. You guys know what I mean. But my school friends don't get it."

"We're the only people who get it," Lilly says seriously. "When mental illness is in your family, you get it. Well, you hope you *don't* get it . . ." Lilly laughs nervously, but no one else does.

"So, okay," Scott says. "I've shared my shit. Who's next?"

Celia says that her mom didn't come to her dance performance, which bummed her out, and a girl named May says her brother is moving into a halfway house soon. Lilly talks about some boy she's been chatting with until Scott asks about her sister. Then Lilly says she's fine and goes back to talking about the boy again. Then Scott looks at me. "Amelia? Wanna share?"

I take a deep breath. "Yeah," I say. "My brother, Toby, was diagnosed with schizophrenia four months ago. It's been horrible. My dad eats all the time and I don't think he comforts my mom enough. She's actually started trying to do stuff, like she was the one who got us to come here, and she's been reading a lot about mental illness, but she's really sad. My little brothers think Toby's this scary, insane dude. He came home for a weekend and it was a total disaster. Plus, I never know what to tell people. I just spend all this time wishing I could bring back the guy my brother used to be."

Everyone nods.

"And my friends. It's just weird. And I think I broke up with my boyfriend because my brother is sick. And I feel really bad about that. For a lot of reasons." I take a deep breath. "But I talked to my brother on the phone for the first time. It was one of the longest conversations we've had since his diagnosis. He's in Massachusetts. He invited me to visit him at his rehab center."

Everyone talks about the beginning for them and, while no one says anything amazingly helpful, I do feel a little relieved. After I talk, a boy talks about seeing his dad, who's been homeless, for the first time in two years! I can't imagine not seeing my brother for that long.

As we walk down to the cafeteria for bagels, Scott walks next to me. "I think I know where your brother is," he says. "It's nice."

"My mom says it's not like a hospital."

Scott nods. "It's not, like, the fanciest one, but it's decent. Nothing like *One Flew Over the Cuckoo's Nest.*"

"I think I watched that movie once."

"It's the book that's amazing. The movie is good, but the book will blow your mind. But actually, you should read *Sometimes a Great Notion.* Like, right now. It's the greatest book of all time. *One Flew* is good, but you're probably too sensitive right now."

"I'm pretty sure I did see the movie. Maybe with my dad. He likes Jack Nicholson. Did you know that Jack Nicholson is the only actor to play a joker, a werewolf, and a devil?"

Scott smiles. "Cool. Personally, I'm all about the Beats, man. Ken Kesey is like the god of the Beats."

I like how easy it is to talk to him. Scott is heavy, but he's not bad-looking. We grab bagels and tubes of cream cheese and go sit at an empty table. "Lilly's going to say that I like you," he says.

I blush.

"It's cool. I know you have a boyfriend."

I shake my head. "It's complicated."

"I get it. Lilly will want to know everything about it, of course, but I'm cool with complicated."

"She's funny. You guys are funny."

"I've known Lil since she was ten."

"Wow." *That's not that much older than Sam and David.* It's hard to imagine the twins coming here, but I guess anything is possible. And it could really help David.

"Yeah. So," he says between chews, "I'm not going to say it gets easier. Having mental illness in your family is never easy, but . . ." He swallows and wipes the corner of his mouth with a napkin. Then he smiles. "Are there seeds in my teeth? You have to tell me even though we don't know each other that well. I don't know why people get embarrassed about that."

"You're fine. What were you going to say? It doesn't get easier. But."

"Oh, right." He smiles again. "I like that you're paying attention, Amelia. It's good for my ego. Anyway, I will share my infinite wisdom of many years living alongside the hell that is mental illness." He leans in closer. "It doesn't get easier," he whispers. "You just get more used to it."

This is the great advice I got up at six in the morning for?

"You don't look satisfied," Scott says.

I shrug.

"You want your money back?"

"Kind of." I give him a half smile.

"It's long gone," he says, standing up. "I spent it on bad jokes and cheap thrills. But here's my card. Email, text, Vine me if you want." He pushes a card at me.

I look down at it. It says "Scott J. Johnson" with a cartoon drawing of him. Underneath that it says "Lover. Dreamer.

Me." Under that it gives his email, phone number, and a website. "You have a business card?"

"I was bored."

"I can see my brother making these, too."

"Listen, I have to split, but my advice is this: It's okay to laugh. Actually, you need to laugh. You have a sense of humor, right?"

"I guess."

"Yeah, you do. I can smell it." He sniffs loudly. "My advice to you is: Don't lose it. Things can still be funny."

And with that, he takes off.

When we get back from the city, my mom says she's going to tackle the garden. My dad walks around the yard and then, totally randomly, says he'll go with her to Home Depot. I throw an old tennis ball to Kepler while trying to think of Movies Where People Get Stuff Stuck in Their Teeth, but I can only think of *Ace Ventura*. After the dog and I are back inside, I'm tempted to watch some Jack Nicholson movies or text Abdi to see if he can think of any stuff-in-teeth movies, but instead, I ask Sam and David, who are comatosely watching cartoons, if they want to have a dance party.

"A what?" Sam asks.

"A dance party."

"Dancing is for girls," David says.

"So. Not. True." I turn off the TV. "Dancing is not just for girls. Haven't you watched *Dancing with the Stars*? Haven't you heard of Mikhail Baryshnikov and Fred Astaire?"

"No," David says.

"I like *Happy Feet*," Sam says. "It's about a dancing penguin."

"I know *Happy Feet*," I say. "Go put on your suits."

David makes a vomit face. "My suit?"

I nod. "Yeah. I'm going to put on a dress and high heels."

"Can I wear my top hat?" Sam asks, heading toward the stairs. "And my Batman costume?"

"That would be awesome," I tell him. "What about you, David?"

He scowls. "I don't want to have another dance party."

"Another one? I don't think we've ever had one and that's criminal with our Astoundingly Amazing Anderson Dance Abilities!"

"You're really weird, Meals," David says, but he heads for the stairs.

I take a deep breath and try to think about getting more used to this. I know it's weird to have a dance party with your younger brothers, but in the best possible way, it's something Toby might have done and that makes me feel the tiniest bit better.

32

THE 1,001 JOKES MEMORIAL DAY
WEEKEND ROAD TRIP TO TOBY TOUR

"SO IT'S LIKE A ROAD TRIP?" MUPPET ASKS AT LUNCH.

"It *is* a road trip," Ray tells her. "And if you want to come you need to cough up some cash for gas. And food."

"And jokes," I remind her.

"Oh yes. And jokes. Everyone needs like a hundred and five jokes."

"I suck at jokes," Muppet says. "I never remember the punch lines."

"That can be funny in its own way, but I suggest you study up." Ray sounds stern.

"Why do we need the jokes?" Muppet looks at me. "What does this have to do with visiting Toby at his . . ." She looks at me.

"Adolescent rehabilitation treatment center," I say. "The jokes are just for the car. Not Toby. Unless he wants to hear some, but he probably won't." I can't really explain my idea to Muppet. I'm not sure even Ray totally gets it. But she texted "Yes" the second she got my "Do you want to go on a 1,001 Jokes Memorial Day Weekend Road Trip to Toby Tour" text. She took time off from work and stopped bidding on eBay to make sure she had enough money. It was her idea to invite Muppet, because Muppet just being Muppet would double the hilarity. It took weeks to get all the okays from my parents, the doctors, and the staff at Two Moons.

But waiting for all the okays gave me enough time to sign up for and pass my road test! On the first try! Not even Toby, Ray, Abdi, or Muppet did that. Despite my official State of New York license, my parents have been making me practice with one of them every day after school. After everything, it's pretty amazing that I feel totally fine behind the wheel.

And I rock at parallel parking.

Partially because they're super supportive about my road trip and partially because I'm totally broke, my parents are paying for food and gas and for Ray and me to share a motel room. The plan is for us to leave Saturday, visit Toby most of Sunday and Monday morning, and then drive home Monday afternoon. After explaining this to Muppet, she says she'll sleep on the floor of the motel.

"Thanks for inviting me," she says. "I actually prefer the floor to the bed."

"That's why you're a dingbat," I say, smiling. I'm pretty sure she'll never find out that I kissed Toast, but I still feel bad about it.

Everything is set until Friday when Ray comes up to me after third period. "I fucked up."

"What?" Part of me wants her to say she can't go, because then I wouldn't go. But another part of me wants to get it over with. Bad-joke-telling and all.

"I sort of invited Toast."

"You invited *Toast?*"

"I made him try out. He told me a legitimately funny joke about a nun and a screwdriver . . . I don't remember it, but it was funny."

"*Toast?*"

"Weird as it is, he's one of Toby's friends, Amelia. It's not like he doesn't know what happened. He was there. He helped."

"I don't even want to go," I snap. "I wish I'd never heard of Two Moons."

"I know," she says sympathetically.

I'm so miserable about Toast coming on the road trip that I blow off math and English and go see if anyone from film club is around, but the room is dark. I wander into the library, check my email, and scan Rotten Tomatoes for any potentially interesting movies, but then Scott from the NAMI group gchats me.

BeameupSCOTTY: hey, Amelia! u there? It's Scott . . . from
the group thing.

amelia.anderson: I know!

BeameupSCOTTY: so . . . what's up?

amelia.anderson: i'm supposed to go c my bro in 2 days. Road
trip with friends.

BeameupSCOTTY: Cool.

amelia.anderson: Cool?

BeameupSCOTTY: Road trips r fun!!!!!

amelia.anderson: I guess.

BeameupSCOTTY: Be +

amelia.anderson: I'm making my friends tell jokes. They need to have enough to tell the whole way there and it's like four hours away. I got the idea from u. keeping my sense of humor. ☺

I wait for him to respond for more than a minute and then write U still there?

BeameupSCOTTY: Yeah. Just emailed u some jokes. I love jokes! My jokes rock!!! They're dirty!!!!

amelia.anderson: I'm sure Toast (guy) will love them.

BeameupSCOTTY: You're taking a dude?

amelia.anderson: Unfortunately.

BeameupSCOTTY: Is he the "complicated" boyfriend?

amelia.anderson: No!!!!!!!!!!!! ☹☹☹

BeameupSCOTTY: Got it.

amelia.anderson: He's my friend Muppet's boyfriend. And he helped my brother one night. A bad night.

BeameupSCOTTY: Oh. Got it. Does everyone in your town have a weird name?

amelia.anderson: Yeah. Everyone calls me Meals.

BeameupSCOTTY: You can lead the next meeting, Meals. ☺ You'll have lots to share after seeing your bro.

amelia.anderson: Maybe.

BeameupSCOTTY: looking forward to hearing about your trip.

amelia.anderson: It's called the 1,001 Jokes Memorial Day Weekend Road Trip to Toby Tour.

BeameupSCOTTY: Awesome!!! Glad 2 contribute.

amelia.anderson: Thanks.

BeameupSCOTTY: Good luck. Don't be offended. The jokes are nasty!!! But remember I'm a sweetheart. Bye.

amelia.anderson: Bye.

I print the jokes, log off, pick up the five (!) pages of material Scott sent me from the printer, and book it to class just as the bell rings.

I get a late start on Saturday because my dad practically takes Prudence apart making sure she's safe.

"It's going to be fine," I tell them. "I'm a good, licensed driver. The car has new everything."

"It's a long trip," my mom says. "You've never driven that long by yourself."

"You're crossing state lines," my dad says. I can't tell if he's joking or not.

"I won't be alone," I remind them. "Ray and Emily and Toast are all good drivers."

"Toast?" My dad looks at me.

I shrug. "He's Emily's boyfriend. And, well . . . you know."

My dad nods. "Don't be scared of the highway." He hands me his Visa. "For gas. And emergencies. Only."

"Thanks, Dad." I remember Epstein's mom telling him to "take the Visa." I wonder what he'd think of my road trip. Epstein would be great on road trips. As long as he promised to keep the jam bands to a minimum. "I should get going," I tell my parents.

My mom nods. "I'm so proud of you. You're a brave, strong girl, Amelia Jane."

"I wanna go," Sam says. "I love Massachusetts."

"When school's over," my mom says. "This is Amelia's thing, sweetie."

"You're a wonderful egg," my dad says. "But do not

speed. Do not text. Do not play loud music." I swear he looks to see if my seat belt is buckled.

"I won't," I say. "I have to pick everyone up." It feels really good to be the one picking up for a change.

When I get to the bottom of the driveway, I look up at my parents, who are looking down at me. I know I'll start crying if I look at them for too long, so I beep and drive over to Ray's.

"I never thought I'd live to see the day," she croons when she comes down with way too many bags.

"Me neither. What can I say? People change."

"You look good behind the wheel, Amelia Jane."

"I do, don't I?" I fiddle with the rearview mirror again and drive to get Muppet and Toast.

As soon as I get on the highway, Toast says he has a terrible headache from not smoking pot all day. Then he says he didn't bring any, either.

"Are you going to be okay?" I ask. "Are you going to go into withdrawal or something?" I try to say it nicely so he knows that I no longer think he's horrendously horrible.

"Yeah, Toaster, should we alert the authorities?" Ray says.

"Jeez," he says. "What do you guys think? That I can't go like forty-eight hours without weed?"

"Yeah," Muppet, Ray, and I say at the same time, which cracks us up.

I'm not surprised that the funniest jokes come from Scott. They are *really* disgusting. Toast laughs so hard he says he peed his pants a little and he hopes he remembered underwear, which makes me and Ray laugh hysterically for about ten miles. Muppet is so atrocious at telling them that Ray and I practically stop breathing from laughing so much. She either screws it up or doesn't remember the punch line or uses the wrong punch line. It gets to the point where Ray and I are crying. I'm not crying *too* much, though—I wouldn't want to affect my vision. It feels good to laugh so hard. It's been a long time.

I drive for three hours before Ray takes over. I look out the window at the passing scenery and try to imagine filming it. For one second I thought about bringing the film club's camera, but I decided not to. I might bring it for Family Weekend, but I'm not sure.

I call my parents the minute I get to the motel. Even though my mom tries to sound chill, I know she's been waiting for me to call.

And even though he didn't bring any weed, Toast *did* bring a bottle of rum, which we mix into some cans of Coke from the vending machine. I have a few sips and then switch to water. I don't want to feel sick when I see my brother. We order pizza and hang out in Toast's room, but after we're done with dinner, Ray and I head back to our room since it seems like all Toast and Muppet want to do is be alone.

"I'm so glad we don't have to hear any sex noises." Ray plops down on one of the beds. "I would not be happy if we were right next to them."

"Or below them." I turn on the TV.

"Although they kind of make a good couple. Don't you think?"

"In this weird, totally unexplainable way, they do. I can't imagine either one of them with anyone else."

"Do you think he's trying to make a statement by not getting high?"

"Like, to honor Toby or something?"

Ray nods.

"Maybe. He's not the worst guy. I know he was good to Toby. I just have a hard time looking at him without thinking about . . . everything."

"I understand."

"Thanks." The air in the room feels really sad and serious. If I were filming it, I'd add a violin or quiet piano to really get the mood. But I'm not filming, and I'm tired of sad and serious, so without thinking too much about it, I grab one of the pillows from my bed and whack Ray with it.

"This is how you thank me," she says, flinging one at my head.

I throw another one and before I know it we're whacking each other with pillows and laughing hysterically all over again.

33

TWO MOONS IRL

I AM NOT EVEN CLOSE TO LAUGHING WHEN I WAKE UP
at 5:00 AM on Sunday. *You're going to see your brother,* I
think. I lie worrying about it for almost an hour before I drag
myself out of bed, get dressed, walk out of the motel, and get
in the car. *My car,* I think. *I have a car.* Technically it's still
Toby's, but for the next few months it's mine.

You can go anywhere. For basically the first time in my
life I have the freedom to drive. My plan is to find a beach,
because in the movie version, the sister contemplates the
meaning of life while looking at the waves, which gives her
the inner strength to visit her brother in his rehabilitation
center. In the Amelia Anderson real-life version, despite the
newly installed GPS, I end up driving away from the beach
and down a long road lined on both sides with big-box stores.

"I could be anywhere," I say out loud, looking at the
Home Depot and Best Buy and Target stores that line the sides
of the road. I actually think there might be something beautiful
about filming the stores so early in the morning. I like the look
of the endlessly empty parking lots. I wonder if Abdi would
think it was cheesy if I filmed in black and white. I wonder if I
could work it into *Arianna Kaufman Says Hi.*

When I get back to the motel, Toast, Muppet, and Ray are
in the lobby, eating the free breakfast.

"Where were you?" Ray asks. "I sent you like three texts."

"I went for a drive. It's illegal to text and drive, you know."

"We were wondering if you'd bailed," Toast says. "We were wondering if we had enough cash for a bus." He smiles at me so I know he's joking.

Ray shakes her head. "I knew you wouldn't bail."

I could bail. I could drive home without seeing Toby. I could swear my friends to secrecy. Then I remember Sky's party and am filled with regret for not staying, for not at least trying to tell Epstein the truth.

"I just went for a drive, that's all. I'm here."

"You can make your own waffle," Muppet tells me. "It's really cool."

"Doesn't take much to impress this one," Ray says.

After my waffle, I take a long shower. When I get out, Ray mutes the TV. "Hey, Meals?"

"Yeah?" I have a feeling I'm not going to like what she says next.

"So, uh, I was talking to Toast and Muppet and we kind of think you should go see Toby by yourself today. It might be a lot with all of us."

"He knows we're all coming. *You* invited Toast anyway."

"I know. But I think we should let you guys hang out alone today. Don't schizophrenics get overwhelmed by a lot of people?"

I kind of hate Ray. Mostly because she's totally right.

I get dressed in silence, wishing Ray would unmute the TV, but she doesn't. When I'm ready to go, she stands up.

"Don't be mad, Amelia. I don't especially want to spend the day with the lovebirds."

"I'm not mad." We walk down the hall together.

"Then can I drop you off? I'm sure Muppet and Toast will find a way to entertain themselves in their lovely motel room, but I can't sit here all day."

"You want Prudence?"

"There's a mall like twenty miles away. And yes, I know it's pathetic to go to a mall on my day off from the mall."

"Okay." It doesn't seem fair to make Ray sit around all alone in the motel when she did make a huge effort to come on the trip with me. "You'll pick me up the second I text?"

"I promise. Wanna hear a joke?"

"No." I slide into the driver's seat. I'm not in the mood for funny and don't even turn on the radio. We follow the GPS lady's directions and drive through a suburban-ish neighborhood and then up to a big, green Victorian-style house on top of a hill at the end of the block.

"Destination on your left," the GPS lady says.

Just because I can, I parallel park across the street. There's a small, nondescript cement building attached to the side of the house. I can't see the ocean, but I can smell it. There are a bunch of crooked wooden steps leading up to the house. I take a deep breath.

"Not what I imagined," Ray says.

I nod.

"Text when you're ready to go."

I open my eyes and think about Scott. What would he do? "If they let me out," I say. "You never know. They might make me stay." It doesn't come out as funny as I want, but Ray gives me a little smile.

As soon as I knock, a heavyset woman with shoulder-length, curly red hair opens the door. She's wearing a large wooden-beaded necklace and a thick wool sweater. She looks like she's a little older than my parents and kind.

"You must be Amelia," she says. "Come in, come in."

I follow her down a hallway and into a room that feels like a very big living room. There are a bunch of mismatched couches and a long coffee table with board games stacked on top.

"Welcome to Two Moons. I'm Anne Coughlin, but everyone here calls me Annie or Mom." She smiles. "I'm a house parent. I work a lot with Toby."

"Hi."

"We're so happy to have you. I thought some of Toby's friends were visiting, too."

"Yeah, well, um, we decided it would just be me today. They're going to come tomorrow."

Annie nods. "I think that's very good. Let's sit for a minute and chat. Toby is in group for another thirty minutes." She points to one of the recliners. "That's the ugliest but most comfortable chair here."

I sit in the ugly chair. Annie sits across from me and opens a folder.

"From what I understand, you and your brother were very close."

I nod and bite my bottom lip so I won't cry.

"He might seem a little nervous. You should remember that he's had this space all to himself, so he feels very safe. Not that you're dangerous, but it's a bit of a bubble here."

"Oh."

Annie smiles at me. "It's going to be fine. It's going to be good for Toby to have someone see what he does here and how he's doing. Especially because I understand his first home visit wasn't so successful."

I shake my head.

"It's normal to have bumps in the journey, but he's been doing well since he got back. He's had a good week." She looks at the paper in front of her. "He's socializing during meals and likes art class."

"He's good at drawing," I say lamely. "He's always had tons of friends."

"He struggles with free time."

What does Annie want me to say? Shouldn't she be telling this to my parents during Family Weekend?

"I'm only keeping you informed about your brother," she says, like she's read my mind. "I don't expect you to do anything." She smiles. "It's good for you to understand what he does here. You're going to learn a lot."

A tiny Asian girl with dyed pink hair comes in. "Can I have the lighter?"

Annie nods. "I'll get it. This is Toby's sister, Amelia."

"Hi!" the girl says. "I'm Piper."

"Hi," I say. I notice that Piper has many scars on her skinny arms.

Annie stands up. "Your brother should be out soon,

Amelia. Feel free to make yourself comfortable. The lounge is over there." She points down the hall to a room with a green door.

I walk down to the lounge, which is empty. It's not huge, but cozy, with a big, flat-screen TV mounted to the wall, an Oriental rug, three couches, and an oversized pillow on the floor. There's a pool table in the corner and taped on the wall is a big piece of cardboard that says in big letters "Rules of Pool." I'm surprised that there are twenty rules, but then I remember that this place is based on rules. The only art on the walls are cheesy posters: One says "GROWTH" with a picture of some enormous trees, and another one says "PERSISTENCE" with a picture of a wave crashing into a bluff. There are quotes under the pictures, but I don't bother to read them. There's a bookcase crammed with books. I recognize a few. *The Hunger Games*, and *Game of Thrones*, and a few of the *Pretty Little Liars* series, and one called *An Unquiet Mind*. Next to the bookcase is a desk with a bulletin board above it with sign-ups for a yoga class, a trip to the art museum in Boston, and a talent show for Family Weekend. Toby hasn't signed up for anything, which makes me sad.

About five minutes later, Toby walks into the lounge. "Amelia. Hey. You came." He sounds sort of deadpan, but I try not to take it personally.

I stand up and give him a hug. I'm relieved that he hugs me back.

He *has* gotten kind of heavy. He's not fat, but definitely more puffy-looking. His hair is still long, but it doesn't look

as greasy as it did before. He still has his beard, too. *It's real,*
I think. My brother is really here. This is where he lives for
now.

"Let's get out of here," he says.

I panic, thinking he wants me to help him run away,
but he just wants to go outside where there's a small fence,
a bench, and a few ashtrays. He tells Annie and she walks
outside with us and lights his cigarette.

When she goes back inside he says, "They don't let us
have lighters."

"When did you start smoking?"

"A few months ago. People up here are into their cigarettes." He bounces his knee up and down as he talks. "I
know cigarettes are bad, but they're better than pot. At least
for me."

"Oh," I say lamely.

"My shrink says mental illness and addiction often go
hand in hand. She'd like me to stop smoking, but it's pretty
much a lost cause while I'm here."

I'm interested that Toby has actually said "mental illness." It might be the closest he's come to ever acknowl-
edging his illness. I'm not sure what to say to him about it,
though, so I just look at part of the fence that's rotting away.
A skinny guy with bad acne and a sleeve of tattoos walks
out. Annie follows him and lights his cigarette, too.

"Does she do that all day?" I ask Toby.

"Nah. Usually there's more staff around. I think 'cause
it's a holiday weekend there's less staff." He shrugs.

"Hey, Toby," the guy in black asks. "That your girlfriend?"

"Hi, Drew. My sister." Toby bounces his knee some more. It makes me nervous, but I don't ask him to stop.

"Hi," I say to Drew.

"I had a girlfriend," Drew says to his cigarette.

"Ray quit smoking," I tell Toby.

"No shit."

"I know. It's insane." *Insane, Amelia? What's wrong with you?*

"That's great. That's really great. Where is she, anyway?" He spits on the ground and it feels like the old Toby being gross. "Mom said you were bringing an entourage."

"She and Muppet and Toast are going to come tomorrow. Hope it's okay. Toast wants to see you."

Toby chews his bottom lip for a minute. "It's cool, I guess. I think he'll make me want weed, but it's okay." He puts his hand around his head and cracks his neck.

"He doesn't have any."

"Yeah. It's okay even if he did. It's good he doesn't, though. I'm glad it's just you for right now."

Good call, Ray.

Drew looks at me and crushes his cigarette under his boot. "Is that your girlfriend?"

"Sister," Toby says as Drew walks back inside. "He's got memory problems," he explains. "Guy did tons of drugs before he got diagnosed."

I'm curious to know what exactly is wrong with Drew, but it's not something you can come out and ask.

After we go back inside, Toby shows me the room he shares with a sixteen-year-old named Lev, who tried to commit suicide. Lev is out on a day pass with his mom and stepdad. The room is on the third floor with low-hanging angled ceilings. There are two made beds, two small dressers, and a table that's piled with a neat stack of books and magazines. Toby sits on the chair next to the table and reties his shoelaces. In this light I see the bags under his eyes. But I don't think they're as bad as they were before. Or maybe I'm trying to be positive. He's shaking his leg up and down so fast that his knee might fall off.

"I can't believe you actually made your bed," I joke.

"It's a rule," he says seriously.

"Oh. Right." I feel stupid.

Since there's not a lot to do in his room, we go back to the lounge where three girls are looking at old copies of *People* and *Us Weekly*, and a boy wearing big headphones is sprawled on one of the couches. Toby says hi to them and they say hi back. It's weird. If I didn't know where I was, I could imagine we were all at someone's house, flipping channels and hanging out. You wouldn't know everyone here has a mental illness.

Toby has to see his psychiatrist before lunch so he says I should just hang out here and he'll come get me when he's done. The TV is on the Cartoon Network and even though no one seems to be watching it, I feel like I shouldn't change the channel. I look out the window and try to picture the ocean, which is less than a mile away. It's hard to believe I'm here. But I am. I'm doing it. I'm visiting my schizophrenic brother in his residential treatment center. *And I drove here myself.*

A short, toned woman with a lot of earrings and a streak of hot pink in her hair opens the door. "Alan," she says.

The boy on the couch doesn't respond.

She walks in and taps him on the shoulder. He sits up.

"Hand them over," she says.

He scowls, but hands the headphones to her.

"You lost this privilege, remember?"

"I hate you," he says.

"I'm going to pretend that my earwax is terrible and I didn't hear that. But you owe me, buddy. Not everyone would be this cool about this violation."

He nods.

"I need a pee test."

"Figures," he mumbles, walking out.

"*Vamanos*," she says. She turns to me. "I'm Natalie. I'm on staff here. You must be Toby's sister."

"Yeah," I say.

"I'll sit with you and your brother at lunch. Nice to meet you."

"You too." I'm buzzing with questions. Why did Alan get his headphones taken away? What does he have to do in order to get them back? If his brain is messed up, it seems unfair to make him act a certain way. Then again, I guess he should take his medicine even if his brain tells him not to.

When Toby comes back to get me twenty minutes later, he says it's time for lunch, so I follow him out of the lounge and down the hall, past the living room and a small office, and into a big dining room. There are five round, wooden tables with five or six chairs at each one.

"You okay sitting with some of my, uh, friends?"

"Of course."

He leads me over to a table by the window where there are two teenage-looking girls, a guy who looks like he's in his mid-twenties, and Natalie.

"Hey, Toby," says one of the girls with very long, dyed black hair.

"What's up, Jesus?" the guy asks. He has a lot of tattoos on his arm and a big scar on his chin.

Toby smiles. "This is my sister, Amelia. This is Gina, Angelique, and Frank."

"And I'm still Natalie, still on the staff. We just met in the lounge," she tells everyone else.

The people at the table nod at me and I sit down. If I try hard enough I can just pretend we're back in school and Toby has become friends with the emo kids.

A guy with a beard who looks like he's my dad's age stands up in the front of the dining hall and announces various afternoon programs and a trip to CVS if you're on the list.

After the guy is done with his announcements, Frank says, "Sorry your brother is making you eat this shit." He points to a plate of soggy wraps on our table. There's also a plate with sad-looking oranges and mass-produced chocolate chip cookies.

"Language," Natalie says, but she sounds like she doesn't really care that much if someone curses.

"Can't leave," Toby says quietly.

Frank takes out a bottle of hand sanitizer from his pocket and squirts some into his palms.

"You don't have outside privilege back yet?" Gina asks Toby.

Toby shakes his head and looks embarrassed. I wonder if this has anything to do with what happened on the twins' birthday.

"You'll get them back," Natalie says. "You're having a good week."

I remember how Annie told me the same thing. It's frightening and comforting that people know exactly how and what my brother is doing at any given time, but I like knowing that he's having a good week.

"Lev says his parents are taking him for steak," Frank says.

"Probably just at the Outback," Gina says. "Outback sucks."

"Did you hear about my roommate?" Angelique asks Natalie.

Natalie nods noncommittally.

"I heard she punched out a bunch of people," Frank says, chewing a big piece of his wrap.

"Yup. Vickie punched Dr. Cummings and Caitlin and tried to get Bryce, too."

"Vickie punched the doctor?" Gina asks.

Natalie shakes her head, but Angelique nods. "She really got messed up."

"Dr. Cummings is a psychiatrist," Gina tells me, flicking the top of the wrap onto her plate. "It's a good thing she wasn't seeing Dr. Yu or Dr. Malick. Dr. Yu is tiny."

"I love Dr. Yu," Angelique says.

"You always say that," Frank tells her. "You always love your new doctor. But then they can't cure you and you start to hate them and then they need to give you a new doctor."

"Shut up, Frank. You're an asshole."

"Language," Natalie says. "Let's direct this convo in a different direction. Vickie is getting the services she needs at this time. There's no need to discuss it further." She sounds way more serious than she did before and I get the feeling that she can do the "hang out and chill" thing to a point, but when it comes down to it, she's all about making sure everyone is okay.

"We'll be cool," Frank tells her.

"'You're so cool, you're so cool, you're so cool,'" Toby says quietly.

I look at him.

He looks at me.

"*True Romance*," I say. "Alabama Whitman."

He nods and then goes back to eating his cookies.

And just like that, I realize things are cool.

Well, things aren't *exactly* cool. That's the overstatement of the year. But I feel like I'm actually doing something by finally visiting my brother and seeing what his life is like here.

After lunch we go back outside with Gina, where they each smoke two cigarettes. Then we go back to the lounge and watch cartoons until Toby's next session. He says he wants to nap during free time at 3:00, which I take to mean I should go. I'm not sure if it went by fast or slow, but I'm surprised to see almost five hours have passed.

I message Ray and Toby gets permission to walk me to

the steps out front. I wonder what he'll think of us driving Prudence up here. I want to tell him the same way I want to hug him, but I still feel like there's an invisible wire fence around him, so I just tell him that I'll see him tomorrow.

"You want us to come, right? Me, Toast, Muppet, and Ray?"

He hesitates, but then he nods almost shyly and says, "Yeah. See ya tomorrow, Meals," before shuffling back inside.

When my friends come get me, I tell Ray to keep driving. Since Muppet is riding shotgun, I sit in the back next to Toast, who doesn't say anything, which I appreciate.

Eventually, because no one can think of anything to do, I tell Ray to just drop me off at the motel while they go try to find a movie.

It might be the first time ever that I have actually chosen not to watch a movie, but for some reason sitting in a dark room watching people play other people doesn't sound appealing.

Back at the motel I sit on the bed and try to cry. I just spent a day with my brother at a rehabilitation center. He shakes his leg all the time and his friends call him Jesus. But no matter how many sad thoughts or movie scenes I force myself to think about, the tears won't come. Eventually, mostly because I can't think of anything else better to do, I take a nap.

When I wake up, Ray is standing over me. "Rise and shine, Sleepyhead."

I yawn. "What time is it?"

"Dinnertime, yo. We're thinking Chinese."

"Really? You already saw a movie?"

She nods. "Don't feel bad, it sucked and not in a good-bad, Amelia Anderson way. When did James Franco get so lame?"

I look at my phone. I can't believe it's 6:30 PM. "Holy crap. I've been asleep for three hours!"

"You're tired," she says.

"Why? I slept fine last night."

"'Cause you're, like, dealing."

Dealing. She's right. I am dealing. Maybe this is what Scott was talking about. You get more used to it because you start dealing with it. "Man, dealing is exhausting."

"Yup," she says. It's not that I've never thought about it, but all of a sudden I remember how Ray has had to deal with a lot of crappy stuff, too. True, she doesn't have a schizophrenic brother, but her dad bailed when she was a baby, and her mom is not exactly normal, what with obsessive TV-watching, chain-smoking, and nutty diets. Even if she's kind of a shopaholic, it strikes me as amazing that Ray has turned out to be such a good, stable person.

"Why are you staring at me?" Ray asks.

"Sorry." I look down at my hands. "I was just thinking that you've had to deal with shit, too."

"Yeah, well . . ." She seems kind of embarrassed.

"Thanks. You're a really great friend, Ray."

"Best Fucking Friends Forever."

"It's more than that . . ."

"Please don't quote *Sisterhood of the Traveling Pants*."

"Please."

"Or *The Fault in Our Stars*."

I shake my head.

Ray smiles. "Or *Harold & Kumar* or *The Motorcycle Diaries* or *Stand by Me*."

"That's an impressive Traveling with Friends list. I'm so proud of you. And me. But I've got a good one."

"Alright. Let's get it over with."

"'You are my superior officer. You are also my friend. I have been and always shall be yours.'"

"You're a geek, Amelia Anderson. You know you're incredibly dorky?"

"I know. Do you know what movie that's from?"

"Yes. Unfortunately I do, because you always make me watch random *Star Trek* movies, which I actually like so that means I'm a geek, too!" And with that, Ray chucks a pillow right at my head.

34

PROMISES

VISITING TOBY WITH EVERYONE IS WEIRD. HE HAS
more free time because it's Memorial Day, so we spend most
of the time in the lounge, where Ray asks him a lot of how's-
the-food and are-you-allowed-to-go-on-the-computer kinds
of questions and Muppet comments on the size of the TV and
the color of the walls. Toast is very quiet, but perks up when
he learns that it's okay to smoke cigarettes. No one says anything when Don, one of the staff, comes out to light Toby's
and Toast's cigarettes.

"Amelia said you quit smoking," Toby says to Ray.
"That's really cool."

Ray smiles. "I guess you started. That's not so cool."

My brother nods. "It's better than other stuff."

"Do you miss the other stuff?" Muppet asks Toby. "Do
you miss like pot and beer and stuff?"

I feel kind of panicked that Muppet has asked such a
personal question but Toby just shrugs. "I miss not having to
go to eight therapy sessions a day and not waking up at like
six every morning. But the drugs and stuff kind of stopped
being fun."

"Why?" I ask.

"Drinking and smoking was something I did mostly to
get out of my head. To get the voices and all the noise in my
head to stop."

"That sucks, man," Toast says in an unusually low tone. We all get quiet.

"Can I have a cigarette?" I ask my brother after the silence has gotten awkward.

"*You* smoke?" Toby looks shocked.

"Not really. Don't tell Mom."

"I wouldn't tell. You're my sister." He hands me a cigarette and I light it off his.

Secret Sibling Society forever. Unless, of course, my brother wants to do something dangerous.

"She's not really a smoker," Ray tells him. "Don't worry. I won't let her start buying them or anything."

"I wouldn't buy them. Not that I have any money, but it's a stupid thing to spend money on." I look at Toast. "No offense. But I'm going to use my money on gas and car insurance and stuff."

"Did you even know Amelia drove here?" Muppet asks Toby. "Isn't that awesome?"

"Jeez. Amelia smoking and driving. Ray not smoking. Toast not stoned." Toby shakes his head. "Me up here . . ."

"But you'll come home?" Ray asks. "When you get out, you'll come back, right?"

"I might do a halfway house. That's what a lot of people do."

"Maybe you can graduate with us," Muppet says.

Toby shrugs and shakes his knee. "I might have to graduate after you guys."

"It's not a big deal," I tell him, even though I know it is.

"You might want to try to graduate before Sam and David, though."

Everyone laughs, even though it wasn't that funny.

"Your sister's taking good care of Prudence," Toast says.

"You're driving my car?" Toby asks.

"She was just sitting there." I look at him.

He sighs. "It's okay . . . just play her some Beatles. She likes the Beatles."

"I will," I promise. "I'll play her lots of Beatles."

35

ACT SEVEN, SCENE ONE

"HOW WAS IT?" MY MOM ASKS WHEN I GET BACK IN time for the family BBQ. Her voice sounds like she's bracing herself.

I think about the past forty-eight hours like it's a movie montage. There's me saying goodbye to my brother and crying when I drove away, even though I know Two Moons is good for him and that he needs to be there. I picture how he smokes and shakes his knees and his terrible beard. But then I picture Frank, Angelique, and Gina, and how great Natalie and Annie are. I think about pillow fights with Ray, rum and Cokes, jokes, movie quotes, and driving, driving, driving. Finally I say, "There were some good parts and some not so good parts, but most of the visiting part was okay."

My mom smiles weakly.

"Better than okay," I tell her.

"How was the driving?" my dad asks.

"Great. I really like driving." The best part of the drive was dropping Muppet and Toast off when we got back home and driving up to the top of Reservoir Park with Ray, blasting the Beatles and smoking the cigarette I mooched off Toast. The old Toby would have totally approved, and I might tell the new Toby when he calls on Sunday. Depending on how our conversation goes, I might ask him to email me a "Driving" Beatles playlist recommendation. Now that I've had a taste of driving, there's no way I'm going back. But that means I need a job. One day Toby is going to need Prudence back, so I better start saving for my own car. I could waitress this summer at Ginger's, or work with Ray at the mall, but I kind of want to do something different.

"I'm so happy you went, Meals."

"Me too," I say, surprising myself that I actually mean it.

I'm halfway up the stairs when my mom calls up to me. "Oh, Claudia Carter stopped by. She wants to know if you'd be interested in watching her girls in Montauk again this summer."

Wow. They want me to come back? Of course they do. I'm an awesome babysitter. My brother is ill, but that doesn't mean I can't have a summer job. The Carters will be thrilled to know I can actually drive, too. And when they have family time, I won't be trapped at the house watching movies. I'll be able to drive all over the island! I could drive to the lighthouse.

I'll have to see if Abdi thinks I can get away with borrowing the film club's camera all summer. If I do attempt to make *Arianna Kaufman Says Hi*, I need a shot of the lighthouse on Montauk. And Prudence, the twins, and the sunlit hallway in Washington Lincoln that Toby used to glide down.

The lighthouse is very close to Epstein's sailing camp. What would he say if I went to see him, really apologized, and maybe told him a little more about my brother? Maybe I could show him *Sherman's March* and *Bankrupt by Beanies*. Maybe he'd watch *Walk Away Renee*. I haven't watched it yet, but I'm curious. I don't even know where Epstein is going to college. Even if he doesn't want to get back together, I'd like to at least have a real, back-and-forth conversation with him. I want to tell him that I can drive now, that I visited my brother at Two Moons, and that I have an idea for a movie I'd like to try to make.

"Meals?" my mom calls. "Did you hear me?"

I return from my movie image of Montauk with Epstein and take a deep breath. "Yeah," I yell downstairs. "I heard you. I'll call tomorrow and let them know I'll do it. That's okay, right?"

"Sounds good," she says.

I walk into my bedroom, put my bag down, and close my door. Part of me feels like crying and another part feels like getting back in Prudence and blasting "Let It Be" as I drive all over town. Part of me wants to think of a better ending to all of this, a Hollywood ending. But I don't cry, and I don't get back in the car, and I don't go and see if the twins want to do something, and I stop myself from imagining how this would end in the movie version. I just sit on my bed, close my eyes, and think about what I'm going to do next.

ACKNOWLEDGMENTS

THIS BOOK WOULDN'T HAVE BEEN POSSIBLE WITHOUT Rachel Orr, a movie star of an agent, and Erica Finkel, a movie star of an editor. Their hard work made this book infinitely better. I'd also like to thank the entire Abrams team, including Susan Van Metre, Michael Clark, Alyssa Nassner, Caitlin Miller, and Elisa Gonzalez.

Thanks to Sara T. Hansen, MSW, Dr. Brenda Vale, and David Williams, PhD, for sharing your knowledge about adolescents and mental illness. The following books were valuable resources: Patrick Cockburn and Henry Cockburn's *Henry's Demons: A Father and Son's Journey Out of Madness*; *The Quiet Room: A Journey Out of the Torment of Madness* by Lori Schiller and Amanda Bennett; *Schizophrenia for Dummies* by Jerome Levine and Irene S. Levine; and *Surviving Schizophrenia: A Family Manual* by E. Fuller Torrey. Jonathan Caoette's documentary *Walk Away Renee* was also insightful.

Thank you to all the movie star babysitters who watched my kids while I wrote: Ellen Partain, Erica Doyle, Kelly Hewes Corbin, and Lynne Bazilchuk. Special thanks to Madi Alves for years of babysitting and for answering my random "teen questions." I am also grateful to Becky Denning, for watching my kids while I worked out and for all our YA book talks.

Thanks to Claudia Palmer for the daily laughs and checking in on the book's progress whenever I took off from work-work to write-work.

Thanks to Michael P. Hidalgo for screenplay-formatting and Snapchat advice. I'm still terrible at both, but you really tried.

Thanks to Karla Greenleaf-MacEwan for early edits and confidence that the early draft could be a book.

My deep gratitude to filmmaker Cheryl Furjanic, who explained film editing and equipment and even gave me handouts.

Sarah Wunsch and Chris Ernst generously gave me a Vermont house of my own whenever I asked.

Tremendous love and gratitude to my mom, the writer Karen Wunsch. You really helped me with Amelia's inner life and her relationship with her brother. Thanks to my dad, Jim, and my brother, Jacob, for your love and support.

Much love to my daughters, Georgia and Dahlia, whose enthusiasm and (most of the time) patience for my writing makes me feel like a movie star of a mom.

This book would not have been possible without the tremendous amount of love and support from my husband, Nicholas Gaffney. Nick read draft after draft and generously picked up the slack whenever I took off to write. These acknowledgments would be way too long if I were to accurately describe his championing, so instead, I'll be the Katharine Hepburn to his Henry Fonda and say, "Listen to me, mister. You're my knight in shining armor. Don't forget it."